THE MAGEYE

PARIS KAUFMAN

Second Edition: December 2025

Cover Art Copyright: GetCovers

Edited by: Michaela Bush

Formatted by: Paris Kaufman

Library of Congress Control Number: 2025923325

ISBN: 979-8-9916725-2-8

To Mom & Arie,
I would travel to
The End for
you.

Also by Author

The Mageye Trilogy
The Mageye
Illusion of Fear
Beldestine

Unbound: A Mageye Novel

The Return of the Mageye Trilogy
The Kidnapped Queen

Theater of Memories
Paris Kaufman & McKenna Rowell

Middle Grade
The Empty Manger

PRONUNCIATION GUIDE

Ackley Elephants: Ack-lee Elephants

Alveraada: Al-ver-ah-duh

Mageye: Magi

Volcaniacs: Vol-can-ee-acks

Wolvien Guard: Wool-vin Guard

Author's Note

At the end of 2021, my family moved from New Hampshire to Ohio due to extenuating circumstances and while I struggled with this, I ultimately made myself a promise with God as my witness. In 2022, I promised I was going to take my life back, and I did. On August 26th 2022, I published my debut novel, *The Mageye*, on my nineteenth birthday. And I didn't stop there. My goal was to publish the entirety of my debut trilogy while I was nineteen, and I published the conclusion to the trilogy, *Beldestine*, the day before my twentieth birthday.

This was a decision that changed my life. Since then, I have met amazing people in the writing community, published four more novels (one of which was co-authored), hit Amazon bestselling status on three books, had the honor of attending several book signings, and continued publishing more books in the world of the Mageye.

Throughout this process I have grown as a person, a sister, a daughter, a writer, and a Christian. And as I have grown, I have looked back on *The Mageye Trilogy* with infinite love, and yet with the slow-growing knowledge that I could do it better. Now that I have a prequel to the trilogy *Unbound*, and a sequel trilogy, *The Return of The Mageye*, already partially released, I have what will one day be a seven-book world. And if I am going to have readers entering that seven-book world, I want them to have the best version possible.

So here we are. *The Mageye* is returning to shelves in the form of a second edition. New scenes. New formatting. New bonus content. Same. Mageye.

Whether this is your first time reading the trilogy, or you are returning to see what is new, thank you for trusting me with your heart. And remember to always expect the unexpected to be unexpected.

~Paris

Chapter 1

"Three men found dead after a witch hunt," Ren read aloud as he leaned over Ryder's shoulder. I looked up from pouring a glass of water in time to see him try to steal the newspaper from Ryder. "Wait, that sounds interesting. Why are you drawing on it?"

Ryder yanked the newspaper out of reach. "Don't touch it! It will smudge." The words of the newspaper filled the iris of the intricately detailed eye he'd been drawing with charcoal. "Besides," he continued, "this is from five years ago; there's nothing relevant in here."

I put the pitcher down and leaned closer to admire his drawing. "I don't know if I consider dead bodies interesting... but the eye is beautiful."

"Thank you, Rose," Ryder said, angling the paper so I could get a better look. "Glad there is someone here who won't ruin my artwork."

"Out of all the paper in the house, you chose a newspaper?" Ren asked. His sleeves were bunched to his elbows, and it was clear he had yet to brush his hair as his brown locks appeared flattened on one side.

"An old one," Ryder said, turning back to the drawing. "And I am trying a new art medium." Like Ren, his sleeves were bunched, but to ensure he didn't stain the white linen, and he continually wiped his blackened fingers off on an old rag.

"I remember when that witch hunt happened," Mom said,

looking up from drying dishes. "They were looking for a girl they claimed was using black magic." She frowned. "Poor child."

"What happened to the girl?" I asked.

She shrugged. "She disappeared."

"As in she escaped?" I questioned. "Or..."

Mom shook her head, her full lips downturned with the same look of worry she gave us when we were sad. "I don't know."

"Maybe she did escape and that was what her *power* was," Ren said, blue eyes wide. "She could turn invisible."

Our eldest brother, Raymond, leaned over my shoulder to grab a muffin. "Sure, Ren. She can turn invisible and we are all going to sprout wings and fly." He smirked. "That will come in handy for patrols once I join the guard, don't you think?"

Mom tsked. "I highly doubt a group of magical people are hiding right under our noses. And you shouldn't tease. What would you do if your sister was framed for magic?"

"I'd make Rose do my chores in exchange for secrecy," Ren said, nudging me.

I pushed his elbow away. "You already make me do your chores. Remember when you promised if I did your chores for two weeks, you would build me a new bookshelf? I still have books piled on my floor."

Raymond split his muffin and passed me half. "Bookshelves don't appear overnight, Rose."

I turned to face him. "You mean Ren is building it?" His eyes widened and from how his dark brows creased, I knew I had my answer.

"Raymond," Ren scolded, leaning over his seat to swat at him. "If you had magic powers, I'd turn you straight in."

"Gosh, what would your dad think of that?" Mom said in pretend disappointment. "He once told me he loved the idea of magic. He felt it must have a good side, because nothing but the devil is pure evil."

"That sounds like Dad." Ryder looked up with a smile. "I remember Ren and I were in a huge fight once and he made us sit and share ten nice things we liked about the other. He said no matter how angry we get, we need to remember we are brothers, and brothers don't say cruel things to each other."

Mom smiled, her blue eyes twinkling. "Yes, but if I remember correctly, you two were sitting in the living room for a quarter of an hour before you actually started sharing nice things."

"Had to filter out the cruel things," Ren joked.

"Well, I'm happy you two have memories of your dad like that," Mom said. "He was always positive."

I finished my half of the muffin, closing my eyes and trying to picture Dad's face. He had died when I was very young, so I didn't have quite as many memories as everyone else. But Mom talked about him all the time, and it seemed to help the few memories I had stick. "We always shared positive things about our day when he tucked me into bed."

Raymond nodded. "He did that with me, too. And the twins, though I think they were always rowdy, so he spent half the time wrestling them until they were too tired to climb out of bed."

Mom laughed. "Yes, he would come to me with his shirt half untucked and hair all a mess, and announce he defeated his terrific twins once again."

"Terrific twins," I echoed, looking between Ren and Ryder. The two seventeen-year-olds were practically inseparable and shared everything, including looks. And while they often bickered, the vast majority of the time, they were a duo that only our family could tell apart.

Ryder was a couple of minutes older, but Ren had about an inch height on him, and his hair was usually a little longer and messier—accentuated this morning, seeing as he had clearly rolled out of bed and come straight down for breakfast.

"I called them the terrible twins once," Raymond whispered. "Dad was so mad, he made me take over both their chores for a week."

Mom wiped her hands off with an old rag and walked to the kitchen counter. Picking up a wicker basket, she placed it on the table in front of me. "Magic and night routines aside, do you remember Dad's favorite dessert?"

"Strawberry pie," I said. "Are you making one tonight?"

"As long as you don't mind strawberry-picking for me."

I grabbed the basket and held it high. "How many?"

"Fill the whole thing!"

"And don't eat too many," Ren teased. "Otherwise, we'll catch you red-handed."

Raymond rolled his eyes and gave me a knowing look. "Very funny, Ren."

"I could eat the entire patch and you'd never know, so long as the basket is full."

"I think we would know when you are too sick to eat any pie tonight," Ren stated solemnly.

"Or when rumors start spreading through town about who stole all the strawberries," Ryder said, setting his charcoal down.

"That's true." I stood, taking the basket with me. "I am going to leave now so I can help make the pie this afternoon."

"Bye, Rose," Mom called, "be careful."

"I will."

"Wait up," Ryder said as he carefully picked up his drawing and slid it onto the top shelf of the cabinet. That shelf was dedicated to his art, and there was a shelf in the living room dedicated to the wooden trinkets Ren carved. "I'll walk out with you."

I waited by the front door and he snagged Ren's bag from its hook, slinging it over his shoulder.

"Where are you going?" I asked as he opened the door for me.

"To the market. Mom wants me to see if they have any chicks for sale."

I grinned. I had been secretly hoping for new chicks for my birthday a few weeks ago. With the start of summer came an increase of traveling merchants, meaning when school let out, most of my friends were busy. That left me with plenty of time to raise chicks, go strawberry-picking, and offer to help Mrs. Bentley, a neighboring widow, with her booth at the market. "How many are you getting?"

"Good question... we will see how many I can find," he said as he bent to adjust his boot buckle.

"Well, make sure you get cute ones. I've been wanting new chicks for ages."

"Late birthday present?" He winked. "I may have let it slip you have chick-fever to Mom. And as for cute ones, is there such a thing as an ugly one to you? I swear, I think your *magically* colored eyes don't let you see any animal as ugly."

I laughed, shaking my head. "Maybe."

Mom's sky-blue eyes had been inherited by all of my brothers, but my eyes were unique. While Dad's eyes had been gray like storm clouds, my eyes were green like peridot—a gem many women wore as jewelry.

Ryder turned to walk around the back of the house to the stables. "I'm going to take Lucy, since she won't jolt the chicks like the other horses."

Lucy was a beautiful gray mare, and our favorite horse. She was Esmeralda's daughter, Dad's horse, and had inherited her mother's gentle demeanor. "Give her some extra pats for me."

"I haven't forgotten since you threw a fistful of mud in my face," he teased, walking backwards.

I rolled my eyes. A few years ago, he had tripped and accidentally smacked Lucy. Despite tending to be the less-mischievous twin, he had promptly told Lucy the slap was thanks to me.

My aim had never been truer than that day when I hurled mud in his face. And Raymond had found it so hilarious, he hadn't even tried to get between us. "Lesson learned," I sassed.

"Drilled into me." He shuddered, turning back to the barn. "See you later."

I relaxed my stance and smiled. "Good luck at the market." With him gone, I turned down the cobblestone path and opened the white picket fence surrounding our small cottage. Shutting it behind me, I turned left onto the packed dirt streets of Sunset Hollow.

Sunset Hollow got its name thanks to the beautiful sunsets over Cherry Ridge. The village was small, but the center was always busy, particularly during market days in the summer. Merchants and traders from across the country of Alveraada gathered to sell and trade their goods there.

Our guard, the Sunset Guard, were amongst the most respected in the country, and Queen Cynthia had connections to call them to the capital city in times of crisis. That hadn't happened in my lifetime, for which I was thankful, because Raymond planned to join the guard this autumn.

The cool shade of the woods welcomed me as I walked down a well-worn traveling path. Our favorite strawberry patch wasn't exactly hidden, but it was a little bit of a walk. The path led right through the middle of the patch, and sunlight streamed through the leaves, the sweet scent of fresh strawberries filling the air.

I knelt, carefully tucking my dress under my knees, and began picking. It didn't take long for my fingers to be stained red. After picking the bushes by the path bare, I strayed farther into the patch, carefully stepping over the small plants as I went.

From time to time, someone would walk past on their way into or out of Sunset Hollow. But other than that, it was me, the woods, and strawberries. It usually took about an hour to fill the basket, and following my tradition, I didn't eat a single one until it was full.

When the strawberries were level with the top, it meant it was time to go home and wait on the front step until Ryder arrived with the chicks.

I plucked the top off a small strawberry and popped it in my mouth as I stepped over a thorny bush. My foot slipped, and I yelped as I lost my balance, twisting my ankle as I fell.

The thorns pricked my hands and legs as I landed in the midst of them. "Ouch!" The basket of strawberries rolled onto the path before settling upright, and I grimaced at the throbbing in my ankle.

My dress had caught in the thorns and I sat up, sucking air through my teeth as I jostled my ankle. It pulsed like a sprain, and I cautiously pulled my dress back to examine it.

Traces of blood etched down my leg from the thorns, dripping towards my stockings. I untied my apron and patted my leg to clean it before all of my clothing got stained.

When I pulled it back, the blood was gone from my leg, and I tossed the apron aside with the strawberries.

My problem now was my ankle. It throbbed and I hesitated with my hands on the laces of my boots. Taking my boot off would certainly hurt, but unless I wanted to crawl home, I had to at least try to take a look. I shut my eyes while I slid my boot off, breathing a sigh of relief when my foot didn't come off with it. Next was my stocking, and rolling it over my foot wasn't nearly as scary.

My fingers probed my ankle carefully and when nothing seemed bruised, I stretched my leg and rolled it in a slow circle. My tendons ached as they stretched, but the ache soon became a relieving strain. I pointed my toe out as the last of the strain left, then rolled it some more. The pain was gone.

"Thank you, God," I whispered, holding my hands to the sky above me. "I can still walk!"

I put my stocking and boot back on and stood, slowly putting pressure onto my twisted ankle until I was certain it wasn't actually injured.

Besides some dirt on my dress, the only evidence of my fall was a stinging on my leg. I pulled my skirt back again, glaring at the long thorn sticking out from the side of my calf. A droplet of blood bloomed when I tugged it out, and I awkwardly held my dress away from my calf as I grabbed my apron to blot the blood. But my hand froze as the droplet rolled back up my leg and disappeared without a trace.

I poked the spot where the cut was, but there was no pain. I looked at my dirty palms and frowned. They were covered in dirt and my apron was stained red—that was, except for the fact that there were no stains other than dirt on my apron. I unfolded it and held it at arm's length, scanning it for blood, but there was none.

All right... the sun and shadows were playing tricks on me. I tied my apron around my waist and snagged the basket of strawberries, wincing when my finger got pricked by a long splinter from the handle.

"Ouch," I whimpered, pulling my hand back. In seconds, the stinging was gone and I paused, examining my finger closely.

The skin was smooth with no sign of torn skin from the splinter. I pinched the sides of my finger, watching the color fade from it and rush back when I released it. Nothing, not a drop of blood from the prick.

I returned to the thorn bush and carefully pricked the tip of my finger on one of the thorns. The pain was sharp, and a droplet of blood began to blossom, but before it could spill out, it disappeared.

Never had I witnessed a wound healing in *seconds* before. I sucked the tip of my finger, still half expecting the metallic taste of blood, but instead, I spat out the taste of dirt.

Three men found dead after a witch hunt. Magic. Is that what was happening to me? My wounds were healing by magic? But I wasn't a witch.

One more prick with a thorn had the blood reversing itself, and I grabbed the basket to begin the march home. Mom would know how to fix this.

The strawberry patch was still in sight when I stopped walking. What would I tell her? That my wounds magically healed? She would likely assume I was continuing the jokes from this morning. I could show her, but she'd never let me actually hurt myself. And even if she did let me demonstrate, her reaction might be even more negative if my wounds *didn't* heal.

I pulled my skirts up to again examine my leg. If I didn't tell

Mom and this was some speedy healing... and someone else witnessed a scratch heal itself... Well, they would likely accuse me of black magic, which I wasn't using. Right?

Witches and warlocks used magic intentionally, and the healing I just witnessed had been anything but intentional. Yet, magical healing seemed pretty witchy to me.

I twisted the bottom of my braid between my fingers. Maybe half a muffin for breakfast wasn't enough and I was hallucinating? Or maybe I was coming down with an illness that caused hallucinations?

I sat down with a huff and munched on some strawberries. I certainly didn't feel sick, and what disease presented hallucinations as a starting symptom?

Once there was a small pile of stems beside me, I searched for something to prick myself with. Another thorn caught my eye and I plucked it, pricking the tip of my finger. Crimson shone on my finger, and I nearly cheered, before the droplet disappeared back into my skin and the wound sealed shut.

Hallucinating on a full stomach with no other symptoms seemed as witchy as a potion. Yet, what was the point of magic if you didn't know how to use it? If you didn't believe in it? Because, I *didn't* believe in magic, nor did anyone else I knew.

Except, maybe my dad... but he couldn't help me today.

Mom was already out of the question, because her concern would prevent me from any kind of demonstration. The twins would likely tease me, unless they truly believed the story, in which case they would go straight to Mom to get me help. Raymond would either react identically to Mom, or at least seek her out if I presented such a concerning story to him.

And while there were other friends and neighbors to consider, every last one of them would either go to my mom or let the secret slip.

Leaving me with... no one, and nothing but an undeniable truth. Something was seriously wrong with me.

Chapter 2

"I imagined it. I imagined it," I whispered over and over on my way home. The strawberry basket bumped against my thigh every few steps and I found myself wishing I would have a bruise by the time I made it out of the woods. "I imagined it..."

A crackling sound startled me, and I yelped, breaking into a run and not daring to look back.

I burst out of the trees like a spooked hare and back into Sunset Hollow. A few neighbors called out, but I didn't stop to reply.

I flew up the cobblestone path leading to our cottage and flung the door open, running straight into Raymond.

"Ow!" He stumbled back, grabbing onto my shoulders. "Goodness, Rose, be careful."

"S-sorry." I turned, slamming the door shut and taking shaky breaths to calm myself.

"Are you all right?" Raymond's brow furrowed. "You look terrified."

"I-um... I'm fine. Sorry, I'll be more careful next time." I avoided his gaze and adjusted my grip on the strawberry basket. By raising Raymond's nerves, I was at the risk of concerned questions. Questions I couldn't afford to answer. At least, not until I figured out what had happened in the strawberry patch.

He caught my chin with a finger and tilted my head back so he could study my face. "Did something happen while you were out?"

"No." I swatted his hand away. "I was trying to see how fast I could get back."

Typical of Raymond, he didn't buy it for a second. "You were racing *yourself?*"

"When you say it like that, it sounds weird." I forced a smile, hoping he would brush it off.

His eyes now scanned my body for any sort of injury; an injury I *wished* still existed. Because then I wouldn't be a witch and I wouldn't be under the scrutiny of Raymond. He was the least likely of my brothers to let me get away with my lie that quickly. "Sibling secrecy?" he finally asked, crossing his arms. "I won't tell Mom unless the secret risks imminent death."

"There's no secret," I insisted. "I've just maybe been roughhousing with Ren too much, and ran into the house without watching where I was going."

He rolled his eyes. "You almost bounced off of the couch when he tossed you last night."

"That was my idea," I said with a shrug, turning to walk past. "Sorry for almost knocking you over."

He caught my arm. "I have to visit with General Jacobs, or else you would be getting more of an interrogation. Come talk to me when I get back. If you're hiding something."

"I'm not hiding anything," I lied. "But thank you."

He hesitated for a moment longer before walking out the door and closing it gently behind himself. I leaned against the flowered wallpaper when he was gone, the strawberry basket hanging by my side. When I finally caught my breath, I examined my hands, devoid of any cuts.

"I imagined it," I whispered to my fingers, before turning to face Mom in the kitchen.

A wispy strand of brown hair hung from her bun as she kneaded bread at the back counter. "How did the strawberry picking go?" she asked when she noticed me.

I had never lied to her face before. "It went well."

She wiped her hands on her flour-covered apron and looked at the basket I had set on the table. "You didn't quite fill it. I thought you wanted a pie," she teased.

While the basket had been full to the brim before my fall, it now bore an empty inch. "I tripped and lost some. But you still have enough, right?" I picked up a strawberry, waving it in the air with a smile. "I can't have gone all that way for nothing!"

She laughed, moving the basket to another counter. "I should be able to make things work. Did you get hurt when you tripped?"

I bit the strawberry I held to avoid my voice pitching. "No... not really. A little dirty though, so I'm going to clean up."

"All right, but you might want to hurry. Ryder should be back soon, and I asked him to get some chicks. We need more egg-laying hens, and I know you like raising the babies."

I forced a smile. "He told me earlier."

"He mentioned something about them being a late birthday gift. Does that mean you'll take care of them and claim them as your own?"

I perked up, temporarily forgetting my newfound magic. "Yes, I can take care of them."

"Well, then you are the proud owner of a dozen baby chicks."

"Thanks, Mom." I grinned. "I have to think of names."

She hummed, turning back to her dough. "If I think of any good ones, I'll let you know."

I left her to finish the bread, my smile falling as soon as she was out of sight. My boots clicked against the hardwood floors as I hurried up the stairs. Once my bedroom door was safely shut, I held my palms up, staring at the soft pink skin.

Not a cut, scrape, blister, or bruise in sight. With no wounds on my body, could anyone really claim me as a witch? Maybe... probably... definitely...

Magic or not, I had a dozen chicks that would soon be depending on me, and they provided a perfect distraction. Both from my personal worries, and as an excuse for my emotions to be all over the place—with excitement.

I tossed my dirty clothes into the hamper and once dressed, I carefully fixed my braid. Tonight, I would get to the bottom of whatever happened at the strawberry patch. But until then, I was a normal girl living with her mom and three older brothers. Nothing witch-like about that.

When Ryder called out that he was back, I hurried to leave my room, but paused with my hand on the door. A few sewing needles scattered about on my dresser, taunting me. Maybe I *should* prick my finger now to reassure myself that nothing was wrong...

But, if the prick magically healed itself like my cuts had in the woods, there would be no way I could fake anything. The test would have to wait. "Later," I whispered to the needles as I left.

The house was full of the sound of peeping, and I took the stairs two at a time. Ryder waited in the living room, flourishing his hand at a small, wooden, and very loud crate. "Do they meet your cuteness expectations?"

I opened the lid and was met with golden fluff. A few looked to be speckled and I gently stroked one with a finger. "Yes, they do. You were right that they are partially for my birthday. Mom said I can keep them."

"Oh, good," Ren said as he joined us. "That means I won't need to deal with them."

I rolled my eyes. "You have to admit they're cute."

"I never said they weren't." He leaned over my shoulder. "Just that I don't want to be responsible for them." He pointed at one. "She has an angry eyebrow."

Ryder peered over my other shoulder and laughed. "That's the only one I picked by hand. Her legs are black too, looks like pants."

I giggled and scooped up the chick, its legs kicking my hand until she settled. "I'm going to name all of them."

"You don't need to tell us that," Ren teased, resting his elbow on my shoulder. "In what world would you let them exist nameless?"

"Not many," I agreed, shrugging him off and putting the chick back in the box.

"I set up a pen in the stables," Mom called from the kitchen. "How about you help get them settled, Rose?"

I gently placed the lid back on the crate and lifted them. "I'm going now."

"Good luck," Ryder said, going down the hall to kick off his boots. "Maybe I should practice my portraits on the eyebrow chick."

"You can practice on all of them," I sang. "Family portrait."

"Yellow balls of fluff," he sang back with the same teasing tone. "I'll try my best to get the egg-shaped bodies accurate."

"You're not egg-shaped," I whispered to the chicks as I stepped outside. They peeped loudly and I giggled. "Well, maybe a little. But that's because you were in an egg hardly a day ago."

I hugged the box to myself with one arm while shoving open the barn door, sliding it shut again behind myself. Several of our horses poked their heads out of their stalls to see what I was doing.

The chicks' pen was next to Lucy's stall, the warm smell of fresh hay radiating from it. Her soft brown eyes silently begged me, and I patted her nose, promising to get her a treat. I picked the chicks up one at a time, carefully dipping each of their beaks into their water dish to teach them where it was. They ran around, pecking at everything they could find, including each other. After they settled, I went about my other chores in the stable, not forgetting to give Lucy her promised treat, and the rest of the horses to keep things fair.

When I finished, I checked on the chicks again. They had formed a cozy ball of fluff, sound asleep. A good distraction from the woods, indeed.

Once outside, I eyed the sky, judging the time. The chicks

had eaten up a little over an hour, but there were still hours until I could escape to my room.

I clenched my fists, plastered on a smile, and went back inside, offering to help Mom. Apparently, my act worked as she didn't ask me any questions, besides whether I had named any chicks.

The front door swung open as I was setting the table and Raymond stopped in the kitchen doorway. He raised an eyebrow, but I shook my head. I couldn't have him asking about me in front of Mom. In fact, I couldn't have him questioning me at all. He was much too good at seeing through lies. Even Ren couldn't get much past him.

I turned to Mom with a smile. "Since I helped you bake it, can I have the biggest slice of pie?"

Raymond relaxed and shook his head. "Not if I get it first."

"You don't like pie," I said with a frown.

He laughed and left the kitchen, calling over his shoulder, "Maybe I changed."

Mom shook her head and brushed a strand of hair from her face with the back of her hand. "Sometimes I forget that Raymond isn't a triplet. Some days he acts like a father, other days, he acts like the twins."

I grinned mischievously. "You don't get me mixed up. I'm just *so* mature."

"No, you're not!" Raymond shouted from down the hall.

As I turned back to setting the table, I breathed a sigh of relief. My act really was working.

After dinner, I ran out to check on the chicks before it got too dark. Each received a mandatory kiss goodnight, and once they were safely tucked together, I gave Lucy a final pet and stepped back outside.

Our back door was currently hidden behind a pile of wood

planks, evidence of Ren's latest project, and I spent a minute examining it. It did kind of look like a bookshelf and I smiled, going around the house to the front door. Before I stepped inside, Ren called me. "Rose, can you give us a hand?"

A trader's horse-drawn cart had stopped in front of our house. The canvas top was dyed with fire-like swirls of red and orange. In the setting sunlight, the painted flames almost appeared real. Some of the goods had fallen from the cart and Ren helped the trader gather them.

He had a crooked look about him, his dark eyes almost seeming to carry a hardness to them. He watched as I grabbed a fallen basket and didn't look away when I looked up. Instead, he raised a brow, not making any effort to appear less obvious.

Ren stiffened, gently nudging me aside before bending to pick up a heavy box. I went around his other side to put the basket in the cart and the man gave me a crooked smile. "You have such beautiful eyes. I've never seen such clear green eyes in all of Alveraada."

I forced an awkward smile. "Thank you."

Ren put the crate into the back of the cart with a thud and the man frowned. "Rose, how about you head inside?" Ren said. "I can finish up here, and I'll meet you."

"All right." I walked past him, and as I pushed open the front gate, I heard the trader chuckle.

"You're a protective one, huh?" he said to Ren. "Don't worry. I didn't mean anything by it."

"Then leave her alone next time," Ren challenged.

I hurried inside before I heard the trader's reply. Ren wouldn't want me sticking around if he was going to snap at someone.

I waited in the living room and when Ren came inside, he joined me, a subtle look of concern on his face. "Are you all right?"

"Yeah, I'm fine. Are you?"

He shrugged. "Stay away from that man if you see him again.

There's something about him that made me uncomfortable."

"He was only commenting on my eyes, and you told him off," I said, glancing at the shut curtains. "He seemed ill-mannered."

"I think it was more than being ill-mannered," he said, frowning. "So, if you see him again, stay away and let me know. Or Ryder, or Raymond."

"I doubt I'll see him again. I'm sure he's heading to the market tomorrow, or maybe even just passing through."

"You're probably right, but I still don't like him."

I knocked his shin with the toe of my boot. "You're a protective one, huh?" I teased, imitating the man's voice.

Ren scooped me up, tossing me over his shoulder. "You're right. Let me escort you to your room so you don't get kidnapped on the way."

I laughed, bracing my hands on his shoulders and half-raising myself. "Put me down," I protested.

He tightened his grip and brought me upstairs, pushing my door open with one hand. He tossed me onto the bed and I bounced. He flourished his hand and bowed. "Goodnight, m'lady."

I tossed a pillow at him and he caught it, snickering as he stole it from the room. I gave chase to the doorway, and he dove into his and Ryder's room. My chest heaved from laughing and I shut my door, leaning against it while my smile slowly slipped from my face. With the door closed, and my room quiet, except for the twins having a pillow fight down the hall, my gaze went to my dresser and the needles waiting on it.

After double-checking my door was locked, I lit an oil-lamp and took a needle over to my desk.

"All right," I whispered aloud as I held the needle in front of my face. The flames from the oil lamp flickered behind it, making it appear to glow. I slowly lifted my left hand, fighting back the woozy feeling that came with purposefully pricking myself. "*Please let me be normal, God.*"

The needle pricked my skin and a small droplet of blood

bloomed from it, and slowly trickled down my fingertip. My shoulders slumped with my relief. It was normal. *I* was normal.

My brief moment of relief was shattered when the droplet disappeared.

I sucked in my breath, frantically pricking myself again. This time, I tore through my skin and caused a larger puncture. The cut stung, and a drop of blood dripped onto my desk.

Then, as if by magic, the wound sealed without a trace. The droplet of blood on my desk, nowhere to be found.

I dropped the needle and stood quickly, nearly knocking over my chair. The shadows of the trees hadn't been playing tricks on me after all.

Tears filled my eyes, and I lifted my hands, watching them tremble. There had to be an explanation for this. One that didn't involve me being a witch. In Alveraada, the use of black magic was punishable by death. From time to time, news would reach Sunset Hollow about a hunt to destroy someone using black magic. Exactly like the one we had discussed over breakfast.

The men had died, and the girl had *disappeared.* What if something like that happened to me?

Keeping this a secret was an obvious next step... but how? If I cut myself in front of someone, what would they say if the wound disappeared? A small scrape I could play off, but what about something more severe? A broken bone or larger gash?

"Ouch!" Ryder said, snickering in the hall. "That was rude, Raymond." A door shut, quickly followed by another, and then the house was quiet save for me and my coming tears.

My hands continued to tremble as I lowered the flame on the oil lamp to extinguish the light from its wick.

"Everything will be okay in the morning," I whispered into the dark. "Things are always better in the morning."

And that promise included magic powers, right?

Chapter 3

When I got out of bed the next morning, I went straight to my desk and grabbed the needle from the night before. In a matter of seconds, the prick I gave myself was gone.

There really was no denying it at this point. When I tripped in the strawberry patch, I somehow gained the ability to heal my wounds... in seconds.

Surely, *surely*, there was an explanation for this, a *non*-magical explanation. After all, wasn't the point of black magic to brew potions and whisper incantations and whatnot?

When I was little, Raymond learned a coin trick. He would dramatically reach behind me and pull a coin from my ear. Magic trick. But not actual magic, it was sleight of hand, a game, an *illusion*. So, maybe my magic wasn't actually magic, but some kind of illusion. Something *not* real.

Maybe a traveling merchant could have dropped one of those new antidotes that they claimed healed any wound. When I fell, what if I had put my hand on the spilt curative, and this "magical" healing power would fade away if given enough time?

I put the needle away, sighing in relief. If a spilt curative was the cause, then I could go back to the strawberry patch and find the source.

After checking on my chicks, I grabbed a scone in one hand and a small basket with the other. Mom was in the parlor, working on a quilt.

"I'm going strawberry-picking again since I didn't fill the

basket yesterday."

She looked up. "You don't need to do that. You got plenty."

My hand tightened around the basket handle. "Well, I don't have many chores today, so I thought it would be a nice thing to do."

"All right." She turned back to her quilt. "Stay safe. I love you."

"I love you, too." I hesitated at the parlor door, taking her in. She carried a calmness about her, a loving welcomeness that seemed to glow from her heart and light up her features. Pale skin, tanned from working in the garden, soft hands, even after raising four kids alone, and a gentle demeanor that took every fiber of my being to turn away from.

I could tell Mom everything, but my magical healing would have to wait until I found the curative that was the culprit.

"Bye, Mom," I called, hurrying out of the house before my will to continue this hunt myself could fade.

I took a moment to steady myself on the front step, pausing to savor a bite from my scone. General Jacobs's wife dreamed of owning her own bakery, and if she ever did, the scones she loved to gift us would certainly be a hit.

The door opened, and Ren and Ryder stepped out. "Oh good, you're still here," Ren said.

"I'm going strawberry-picking," I said as I turned down the front path.

"I know, we're coming with you."

My scone suddenly felt like a rock in my stomach. "You are... why? Didn't you tell Mrs. Bentley you would help fix her fence today?"

Ryder shrugged. "We can stop by her house to let her know we'll be there later than expected. If that trader you and Ren helped is still around, we don't want to risk you being alone with him."

Ren nodded. "We'll stick with you while you pick the strawberries. Then we will drop you off at the house before we head out to Mrs. Bentley's farm to help rebuild her back fence."

I shook my head. "You don't need to come. I'll be fine on my own."

They shared an identical worried look. "What if someone attacks you and you are all alone?" Ryder asked.

"No one is going to attack me." I rolled my eyes, stepping off the front stoop. "I can take care of myself. Besides, it's a Saturday. I'm sure the trader will be in the town square."

Ren frowned, exchanging a look with Ryder. "Fine, but take this." He tossed me his folded jackknife. "Stay safe, and don't stay out too long. We'll wait at the house until you get back, so make sure you're home by noon, or we'll come looking."

"I'll be careful. I promise." I made a show of putting the jackknife in my pocket, admiring it as I did so. It had an intricate *R* burnt into the handle. Ryder had given this knife to Ren on their birthday this past March, and it was his most prized possession. Being trusted with it was an honor.

Ryder crossed his arms. "And if you do see that guy..."

"Run the opposite way screaming?"

He pointed a finger at me. "You better!"

I slowed my pace as I neared the strawberry patch, looking for any signs of spilt medicine, or other curatives. Many of the strawberries glistened with morning dew where the sun had yet to shine, but none shone with anything that suggested a spill.

When I found the spot where I had fallen, I knelt and crawled on all fours, scrutinizing the ground for anything out of place.

Nothing.

Maybe I had put my hand in some spilt potion that had since dried up? I rubbed my palms over the ground. If it was a potion used for black magic and I touched it again, the effects should wear off.

My palms were soon covered in dirt, and I rubbed them together as if I was washing them. Then, I took out Ren's jackknife and cut the tip of my finger, wincing at the sting.

A small droplet of blood rose from my skin and unlike yesterday, the blood continued dripping. That meant that... The droplets of blood slowly reversed, and disappeared back into my skin.

I cut my finger again, and again, and again. It kept healing, but was definitely slowing down, until finally, one didn't heal. I squeezed both sides of the cut. It burned, and I screwed my nose up as a drop of blood dripped out and fell to the ground. Neither that drop nor any of the fresh ones disappeared.

"Yes!" I exclaimed as I jumped up, hurriedly putting the knife away and admiring my bleeding finger. No more wounds healing unnaturally fast... dangerously fast. Whatever antidote I had fallen in was gone, and I didn't need to worry about black magic anymore.

Before I left, I hurriedly picked enough strawberries to fill the basket with my good hand. A white dove flew past the path in front of me, its breast feathers almost seeming to glint in the sunlight. A beautiful dove to celebrate wonderful news with.

As I stepped out of the woods and back into Sunset Hollow, I slowed, unease starting filling me. Normally, the streets were bustling this time of day, but now they were empty.

The hairs on the back of my neck stood on end, and I looked behind myself. A low hanging branch swayed, but besides that, all was quiet.

I sighed with relief and headed back into town, entirely alone. My boots crunched over gravel; the usual welcoming call of my neighbors eerily missing.

A light breeze brought a smell that made me stop, strawberry basket hanging by my side. Smoke. I lifted my gaze above the rooftops and my breath caught. A plume of dark smoke rose into the sky, coming from the direction of my house.

"Mom..." I whispered, breaking into a run.

The smell of smoke grew thicker as I turned onto my street and was finally able to lay eyes on my cottage.

"No!" I screamed, dropping the strawberry basket and dashing towards the crowd, pushing neighbors aside until I stood in front of the white picket fence I had left through hardly two hours prior.

Where my family's home had been standing this morning, was a smoldering pile of broken belongings. Not one pillar stood, replaced with ash and indistinguishable soot and cinder.

The house and stable behind it were gone, leaving nothing but the fence surrounding our ashy lot. Lucy galloped past the crowd in panic. A few men tried to block her, but quickly jumped out of the way when she reared, bolting after the rest of our horses.

"Mom?" I called, frantically scanning the faces in the crowd. "Raymond? Ren, Ryder!"

Mrs. Bentley was the first to recognize me. "Rose." She hurried to me. "Are you all right?"

I shook my head, turning back to the house. The Sunset Guard had already begun digging through the rubble. It seemed like the entirety of Sunset Hollow surrounded me. Everyone but the four people that mattered the most.

Mrs. Bentley pulled me into her arms. "Where were you? Were any of your brothers with you?"

"I was... I was strawberry-picking. Ren and Ryder..." I pulled away. "They said they would wait at the house for me to come back. What... what happened? Where's my family?"

She shook her head, tears welling in her eyes as a man approached us. I recognized him by his blonde hair. General Jacobs. The head of the Sunset Guard who had promised to train Raymond beginning in the autumn.

"Rose, you're here. We thought..." He hesitated. "I'm so sorry, Rose. Your family..." He motioned to the men digging through the rubble.

Tears blurred my vision and I shook my head. "No, they can't be dead! They have to be there." I tried pushing past him. Maybe they hadn't seen them yet. I would take a look, and *I* would be able to find them.

General Jacobs held an arm out to block me. "Rose. They aren't there. None of them are there."

"Let me look," I insisted, attempting again to push past.

This time, he caught me. "They aren't there," he repeated.

"Yes, they are," I argued, but my voice died in my throat, staring at the ashy remains. Mom should be in the kitchen. Raymond should be cleaning the stables...

General Jacobs's voice grew gentle. "They're not dead, Rose. We have reason to believe they were kidnapped."

"Kidnapped? By who?" I took a shaky step back, my gaze flicking between him and the ashes. "The fire wasn't an accident?" I choked on the last word, loathing the sound of it.

"We don't know, Rose. The fire was vicious, but a few men were able to get inside before it fell, and no one was inside. They've disappeared, and we think they were taken. We think... we think whoever took them is trying to get to *you*. It looks like they took your family as bait."

"No," I whispered. Only a few hours ago, I had been talking to Ren and Ryder. They had told me that they would wait for me to get home safely. They had promised that they would be here.

General Jacobs pulled a folded paper from his pocket and handed it to me. "This was stuck to your fence."

I took it.

To the girl with the magical, green eyes,

If you wish to see your family again, come to The End.

X

The ground seemed to sway beneath me, and my hands

shook as I looked back at General Jacobs.

"Who...?" I stopped when orange fire caught my eye. A light breeze sifted ash from the ruins of my house, and carried a scrap of fabric with it. The scrap was dyed an orange that eerily resembled flames, and a set of brown eyes and a crooked smile came to mind.

The trader. With his flame-dyed canvas and unsettling interest about my eyes, he might just be the only person in Sunset Hollow with enough stacked against him to bear the blame.

But why? Why me? Why *them?*

General Jacobs pointed at the letter I still held. "Do you have any idea who could have written that, or why they would have done this?"

If I told him the truth. If I told him everything I knew. If I told him the real reason I had left the house this morning, he might suspect *me.*

So, I slowly shook my head, blinking back fresh tears. "No, sir."

He nodded grimly. "All right, we don't know what they want with you or even who 'they' are, but someone is obviously trying to lure you in. And whoever it is, they're dangerous. I have never seen nor heard of a fire reducing a house to ash so quickly. I have no idea how they did it."

Magic.

It was the only reasonable explanation. Oh, the irony of magic flipping from unfathomable to reasonable so quickly, yet it was obvious, wasn't it? The trader wouldn't have used the phrase "magical green eyes" without reason, yet my eyes weren't magical and neither was I.

But what other explanation was there for my house and family disappearing so quickly?

"I have to find them," I whispered.

"No, *we* have to find them," General Jacobs corrected. "The Sunset Guard. Rose, I need you to promise me that you won't go looking for your family. We will protect you and find them ourselves."

Words alone couldn't describe the amount of grief and terror that flooded my veins, yet I managed to respond calmly. "You're right. Even if I wanted to, where would I start looking?"

He nodded grimly. "That's for us to figure out. Now, let's get you out of here. We don't know if the perpetrator who took your family is still around."

I turned my gaze back to the men searching through the ashes. Faint murmurs passed between them, the smell of smoke burning my nostrils. "I haven't seen a fire burn this quickly before, either."

General Jacobs also turned back to the house, and I stuffed the letter in my apron pocket, praying he would forget to ask for it back.

"That's part of the reason why I want to get you out of here," he admitted. "All we have are suspicions, none of which offer a good solution." His expression darkened. "I fear we are dealing with something beyond our natural world. But that won't stop us from pursuing your family."

A chill went through me. He had come to the same conclusion I had. Magic. *Black* magic.

I hid my pricked finger, pushing the thought out of my head before I accidentally confessed my "magical" healing. Instead, I let myself be escorted to the center of town, leaving the Sunset Guard to look for clues. Clues I myself would be examining tonight.

Plans were set for me to stay with Pastor Wilson and his wife until my own family was found.

They didn't pester with questions, only offered to pray with me and vowed to keep me safe. Being in the center of town meant many eyes to ensure I wasn't kidnapped. Which was exactly why General Jacobs had decided that I would stay here and not with Mrs. Bentley, who had kindly offered.

Regardless of the well-meaning intentions of my neighbors, something was up. And the more I considered the phrase "magical green eyes," the more my pricked finger seemed to pulse, taunting me. Healing. Magical healing. What else could the trader possibly want me for?

Yet, I was the only person in the entirety of Alveraada with knowledge of what had happened in the strawberry patch. Unless I had unknowingly injured myself while Ren and I had helped clean up the trader's spilt goods.

It didn't matter what he wanted, I had to follow the instructions on the note. Go to The End, wherever that was.

Mrs. Wilson draped a quilt over my shoulders, but I hardly reacted, instead watching the flames in the stove. One thing was for certain, if the trader could kidnap four people and destroy a home without a trace of evidence against himself, he must be strategic enough to set up a game only his target could play. *Me.*

Not only that, but I had a reason to find them that the Sunset Guard didn't have and would never understand. My family was missing, and I would stop at nothing to find them.

Chapter 4

Mrs. Wilson was known for making some of the best cheese-stuffed buns in Sunset Hollow, but I couldn't stomach more than a bite. Every tick of the clock standing behind Pastor Wilson had me checking the time to estimate when I could begin my mission to save my family.

"Would you like to be excused, Rose?" Pastor Wilson asked, the wrinkles around his eyes softening.

I stared at my full plate, nodding. "Yes, please."

"Leave your plate," Mrs. Wilson said. "I'll clean up for you."

"Thank you," I whispered, standing shakily. "I'm... going to bed."

"Come get us if you need us," she said gently. "For any reason."

I paused with my hand against the doorframe, staring at their locked front door. "I will," I murmured, slipping down the hall and up three flights of stairs.

Their guest room was on the top floor of the house, and fully furnished. A dresser with stunning flowers engraved on the drawers, a small cot against the back wall, and a window that overlooked the town square.

The door clicked shut after me, and I took a few steadying breaths. The note crinkled as I pulled it from my pocket, reading its contents again.

Come to The End.

I traced my finger over the words, before striding to the

window, peering at the streets below. The moon was the only source of light down in the town square and I watched as a group of young girls hurried across the street, ducking under the canopy of the bakery. When I pushed open the window, I could hear their laughter, and I quickly shut the window again.

With the letter safely returned to my pocket, I found the satchel Mrs. Wilson had loaned me, filled with basic necessities. While I had no real need for a satchel as a guest in their home, I had thanked God the second it entered my hands, as it was perfect for my mission.

She had also loaned me a few of her daughter's old dresses, and I slipped into a pale blue one. It had additional pockets on top of my own apron, which I tied around my waist again. The letter safely stored in one pocket, and Ren's jackknife in the other.

Once I was packed, all that was left to do was wait, and I resisted the urge to pace in case the Wilsons heard my footsteps. Muffled voices made their way upstairs and I went to the door, sitting against it and listening for any other sounds.

When the silence became deafening, I stood and lit a small candle, carrying it with me as I cracked the door. The house was quiet, so I slipped onto a small loft and tiptoed down the stairs.

The stairs creaked as I passed the Wilsons' room. I went rigid, not daring to move for fear of the step creaking again. Pastor Wilson continued snoring and I started lifting my foot, wincing at the loud creak that came with my movement.

Thankfully, the Wilsons were deep sleepers.

I scurried down the rest of the stairs, holding a hand over my mouth to muffle my heavy breaths. To my left was Pastor Wilson's office, and to my right, around the rail of the staircase, was the kitchen.

The light from the moon cast eerie shadows across the dark room, and I hesitated in the doorway. What I was about to do was wrong, but I didn't have much of a choice. My family needed me and that came above the moral dilemma of whether stealing with the intention of replacing it later was actually stealing, or if it was simply prolonged borrowing... without permission.

I placed my bag on the table and quietly went through the cabinets, grabbing a couple of rolls and some dried fruits and meat. Mrs. Wilson had a vegetable bowl on the counter and I took a carrot for Lucy. She was our best trained and fastest horse; I could take her and stand a chance at catching up tonight. After all, the trader had only had two horses pulling his cart and he now traveled with four prisoners. That must be a heavy load.

With Lucy's carrot secured, I crouched by a large hutch, hoping to find supplies I could use.

"Phew," I whispered. There were a couple of waterskins inside. I would have to fill one before I left, but for now, I tied it to my waist and quietly shut the hutch doors.

As I stood, something moved outside the window. I jerked my head towards it and peered into the back garden.

Mrs. Wilson's flowers danced hauntingly in the night breeze, alone under the moonlight.

My racing heart slowed, and I turned back to face the kitchen. I now had food, a way to carry water, Ren's jackknife, and a boatload of prayer, which left me needing only one thing. Money. Where would they keep extra money?

Pastor Wilson's office.

The door to his office was shut and I paused. Had it been shut when I first came down? Surely, I would have heard him walking down the stairs, or he would have noticed the light of the candle in the kitchen. Though one could never be too careful.

I waited by the door, attempting to think of an excuse for being out of bed with a bag of stolen supplies. Pressing my ear to the door, I held my breath, listening for any sounds inside. It was quiet, just like the rest of the house.

My fingers trembled as I twisted the handle and opened the door an inch. The room was empty. I slipped in, leaving the door cracked so I could hear anyone coming from upstairs.

The back wall of the room had been turned into a bookshelf, and a desk faced the door.

Two couches sat on opposite sides of me, facing one another, and a large rug spread between them. The color was masked by the dark, but if it was the same one from the last time I was here, it was an ugly shade of maroon both Ren and I had despised. We had vowed to never own anything so horrid in our lives.

The candle flickered as I placed it on Pastor Wilson's desk. A fountain pen and ink bottle stood on one side, and a Bible sat in the middle. I touched it gently, and my heart spoke a prayer I dared not say aloud, *"Please help me find them in time."*

A spark of fierce determination surged through my body and I turned away from the Bible. It was time to find my family.

The top drawer opened with a quiet hush and I diligently scanned the contents. It contained nothing but papers. The next drawer was a lot messier. I sifted through the contents, pricking my finger on a pin. I drew back and waved my hand in the air as the pain quickly faded. Just before I shut the drawer, a small, dark pouch caught my eye. It was a suspiciously similar shade to the rug.

My fingers seemed to grasp it of their own accord and upon feeling the weight of coins, pulled it out. This must be the offerings from Sunday's service, which meant I was stealing from those in need. But then again, *I* was in need.

"I'm sorry, God," I whispered. "I'll return it when I find my family. I promise. And everything else, too."

I blew on the candle to extinguish the flame and left it on the desk. I had all that I needed. The front door was just to the left of Pastor Wilson's office, and I wasted no time leaving, shutting the door gently behind myself. Cool night air greeted me and I hesitated, eyeing the shadows suspiciously.

The town square appeared deserted, except for a stray cat. Its yellow eyes studied me haughtily before it sauntered off into the night. Closed market booths lined the edge of the square, and distant laughter from an inn echoed through the night.

The shadows of the street welcomed me, and I broke into a run towards where my house had once stood.

My chest heaved as I reached the picket fence. A slight breeze caused the ash to stir, and a soft sifting sound made me shudder, the smell of smoke suffocating.

All of our horses were missing. The Sunset Guard must have caught them and taken them to the community stables until we had a new place for them. My heart sank and I glanced back the way I had come.

Of course, the horses would be brought to the community stables. It wouldn't have been safe or fair to tie them to our fence out in the ashy open.

I pulled out the carrot I had stolen for Lucy before reluctantly putting it away. Sneaking into the stables and breaking her out was too big of a risk, and too time consuming anyway.

The note had suggested the trader *wanted* me to follow, after all. That meant he must have left some clue for me. As long as I had a direction to go in, I could walk.

I scavenged through the rubble for any clues, but there was nothing left except for ashes and a few unidentifiable broken objects. It looked like the horses were the only survivors that had been left behind... I hadn't even gotten to name my chicks.

Each step I took made me wince at how loud they seemed, though I did my best to step over any burnt chunks of wood or lose boards.

I turned back when I reached the gate, kneeling down, and then laying on my stomach. I sneezed as I breathed in ash, narrowing my gaze as I examined every inch of the ruins. Nothing. Not a single clue, only the letter.

A cloud of ash rose in the air as I sat upright and I wiped my hands on my apron before fumbling for the note. This, I held up to the moon, but nothing displayed itself except the same message I had read a dozen times.

"Where are you?" I whispered to the night, standing again and putting the note away. Surely, there was *something* here for me to find. It was practically impossible to vanish with four prisoners, after all... right?

A dog barked somewhere across the street and I winced, turning to go. If there weren't clues left here, then where would they be?

The light of the moon sparkled against the gate as I opened it, and I did a double-take. A ragged X had been carved into the fence over the fresh paint job Ryder and I had done just two weeks prior.

I slammed the gate shut, ignoring how the metal clasp echoed through the night. My hands trembled as I pulled the letter out and held it up next to the fence. Both X's were identical to each other.

"X marks the spot," I breathed, jumping to my feet and looking around again. "There has to be more."

After almost an hour of searching, I found another across the dirt street. One of the branches on our neighbor's apple tree had been bent so that it pointed towards the woods, and an X was carved into the tip of it. Whoever had carved it had put some sort of substance on it that created a glow, similar to the one on the fence.

I had been right. The trader *wanted* me to find them.

I stopped at the outskirts of the dark woods, having followed the exact path the branch had pointed in... Which was no path.

The trees were thick in front of me. If the trader had been the one who took my family like I suspected, he had a cart. And there was no way that cart could fit between the trees, yet this was the direction the branch had been pointing. North.

I was supposed to head north, but why?

The closest trail that could fit a cart was over half-a-mile away, and it curved to the east, not north. Yet, here I was, staring at woods so thick, even Lucy wouldn't have been able to navigate them, and I didn't have a cart.

I fidgeted with my satchel; if I was supposed to go another way, there would have been more X's... Unless I missed one.

But with how closely I had been looking for another, it was doubtful that was the case. And every second of doubt was another second the trader had to drag my family farther away.

"I'm coming," I whispered as I ducked under a low-hanging branch. The letter had said to find them, and it wouldn't have said that if the hunt was impossible.

Another hour passed, and there was still no sign of any more X's, glowing or otherwise. Yet something in my gut told me I was heading in the right direction. An almost imperceptible pull kept me going forward, assuring me that I was on the right track.

Something crackled, and purple flashed out the corner of my eye. I whipped towards it, my heart racing.

Silence.

My breathing shallowed and I slid my hand into my apron pocket, grasping Ren's jackknife. The weight of it in my palm was a comfort, and I ran my thumb over the R on the handle.

The woods were silent, not even a breeze rustled the leaves overhead. And no other purple lights followed the first.

I shifted my feet. Could the trader be attempting to attract me?

No. The flash had been so quick I had hardly registered it before it was gone, so it couldn't have been a signal. If I had been facing the other way, I never would have seen it.

Besides, the X on the branch had been pointing north, so continuing north was my best bet. It was my *only* bet.

Chapter 5

One of my schoolteachers had once taken our class on a hike, quizzing us on directions until everyone was dizzy. But, five years later, that lesson now ensured I remained in a northern direction, using the moon as a guide. And, as the first streaks of dawn lit up the sky, I was rewarded with another X.

I practically threw myself down in front of it. It was made of two branches and leaned against a large boulder. This X, too, appeared to have been coated in a glowing substance.

The sun had begun to rise on my right-hand side, which meant lifting my gaze past the boulder the X leaned against was *north*.

A branch snapped behind me, and I spun around, taking the jackknife out of my pocket and flicking it open.

Was this The End that was referenced in the letter? I stood slowly, my gaze darting between the trees. All appeared still, but the woods were thick, and someone could easily be hiding in the shadows.

"Hello?" I called hesitantly, tightening my grip on the jackknife.

An electric crackle snapped behind me, followed by a calm voice. "Are you sure you want someone to answer that call?"

My heart practically exploded and I spun back again. A teenage boy leaned against the boulder I had been staring at. He was tall, easily taller than my brothers, even Raymond, who was a little over six feet. His brown hair contrasted nicely with lightly tanned skin and dark eyes. He wore brown leather breeches and a blue-gray vest over a cream-colored shirt, spotless despite being in the middle of the woods.

I looked behind him for anyone else, but he appeared to be alone. Almost like he had stepped out of thin air to stand behind me.

"Who are you?" I asked, fighting to keep my voice steady.

He watched me with an intensity that felt like he was staring through my soul. When his gaze darted to my jackknife, instead of looking intimidated, he looked as if he were trying not to smile. "Do you really think that knife can beat me?"

My knuckles were white around the handle, and I glanced at the dagger he had strapped to his belt. He made no effort to grab it, even as I continued to hold Ren's jackknife in front of me.

But this boy was a lot taller and stronger-looking than me. Even if he didn't have a weapon of his own, I wouldn't stand a chance. I had never been in a fight before, but he didn't need to know that.

"You've never seen me wield one." I adjusted my grip. "Are you sure I *can't* beat you?"

He grinned. "Maybe not, but I think we both know you're lying. You're holding it like a hammer; if you want to fight someone, you need a saber grip with your thumb along the top of the handle." He held up his hands. "And I'm not here to attack you."

Uh, no, correction, *I* knew that I was lying. He most certainly did *not*. And if I wanted to stab him with it as a hammer, I could do just that.

He had no rifle with him, so he obviously wasn't hunting. But why else would he be out here? He may claim to not have the intention to harm me, yet he had appeared in the middle of the woods, moments after I found the third X.

I glared, but took an involuntary step back as he stepped

closer.

"What do you want?" I asked with what I hoped was a carefree tone.

He offered his hand. "I'm Myles. Sorry for scaring you."

I hesitatingly switched my knife to my left hand, before cautiously shaking hands with him. If he was dangerous, he wouldn't approach me so calmly without his weapon drawn. "I'm Rose."

His grasp was firm, his hand calloused from hard work. When our gazes met, he smiled. "What are you doing out here all alone?"

"Oh, um..." I looked back at the X, and gasped. "No!"

I pushed past him and rushed to where the X had been. Myles had knocked it over, and the two branches now lay on the ground without an essence of their glow.

"The X!" I propped the branches back up, but it didn't appear exact, and the glow didn't return. "How could you do that?" My voice pitched with my frustration, and I fought against angry tears.

"Do what?" he asked, brows furrowed in confusion.

I pointed accusingly at the branches. "You knocked over the X!"

His eyes widened. "Is that what you were looking at, those sticks?"

I turned away from him, touching the misshapen X with the tips of my fingers and once again looking to the north. I had thought the trader kidnapping four people alone was a challenging feat, but maybe he hadn't done it alone. Maybe he had *help*. Help in the form of the boy who had been guarding this X. "I get it now," I said softly, standing again. The anger and fire were gone from my voice, replaced by a calm acceptance.

"Get what?" he asked, still looking at the misshapen X.

I folded my jackknife and dropped it into my pocket. "You know where my family is," I declared. "You were waiting for me to come to this spot, weren't you? I'm not going to fight you. Just please, let them go, and I'll come without a fight."

Now Myles looked genuinely confused. "Who do you think I am?"

"You work for that trader, don't you? The one with the flames painted on his cart." I removed the letter from my pocket, holding it out to him. "Please, let my family go. I don't know what you want with me, but please don't hurt them."

He paled as he read the letter. "Gosh, this is worse than I thought." He handed the letter back. "I didn't kidnap your family. When you left the pastor's house, I figured you were upset and acting irrationally." He frowned at the X I had rebuilt. "I assumed you picked a random direction, not that you were following a trail. Is the X some kind of marker?"

I frowned, suddenly unsure of myself. It sounded like he knew who had kidnapped my family but wasn't working for them? But if that were the case, why had he been stalking me, unless he was a spy?

"Do you know who wrote this letter?" I asked hesitantly.

He nodded. "That's why I'm here. I need to protect you."

"*Protect* me? Are you working with the guard?"

"Not the guard you're thinking of." He fell silent, an unreadable expression on his face. "All right, Rose. I think we need to start over. My name is Myles, and I'm a Mageye. Like you."

"A magi? Like a wizard?"

He shook his head. "No, a mag-*eye*. It literally means magic eye."

I stared. "I'm not a magic eye or anything. I don't know why you think I am."

"Have you ever seen anyone with your eye color before?" he asked.

I crossed my arms. "Well, no. But why does that matter?"

"The only physical way to identify a Mageye is through their eyes."

What was this boy going on about? Yeah, my eyes were unique, but so? His eyes were dark, but that was... My lips parted when I got a closer look. Myles's eyes were *purple*.

He smiled. "I'm a Mageye."

My heart began to race again and I took a small step back. "Our eyes looking different doesn't make us magical. Magic doesn't exist."

Now he looked confused and even a little annoyed. Like I wasn't catching onto something obvious.

"We get the *mag* in Mageye because of our magic. We have powers. I can tell you have one because of your eyes, and they're green, so I'm guessing your power has something to do with nature?"

I shook my head, but a sickening feeling had entered my stomach. *Magic healing.*

But the healing had stopped working, so he must be wrong, and I could prove it.

I held out my hand, showing him the cut from the strawberry patch that had never healed. "No, I don't have a power. See? I cut my finger, and it didn't heal."

"Huh?" He stared at my finger. "What do you mean? There's nothing there."

"What?" I looked at my finger, but where a cut had been yesterday was now perfectly healed skin. "How? How is that possible? This one *didn't* heal... so why?"

"So, you do have a power then? You heal quickly?"

"I... yeah. Well, no. The last one didn't heal, but it wasn't that bad, so—"

He cut me off. "Were your wounds healing before that?"

I hesitated. If I answered truthfully, I would be admitting to using some form of black magic. What if Myles *was* a spy and had been sent to trip me up? Maybe the Sunset Guard had caught wind of my healing powers and set up the kidnapping and fake trail to lure me away so they could capture me!

Myles's purple eyes bore into me, and I realized how stupid my thoughts were. Thank goodness mind reading wasn't a thing.

And I wasn't the one talking about magical eyeballs, after all. "Fine. They were healing, I guess. I tripped and fell in a thorn bush, but all the cuts disappeared and my ankle stopped hurting immediately after it was sprained. I thought I was crazy, so I kept hurting myself, and… well, it stopped. So, I must have tripped on some medicine, and it wore off."

Myles made a sound like a stifled laugh. "Have you ever heard of medicine that heals a sprained ankle in seconds? Much less one that works with only a touch? No, you hit your cool-down. All Mageye have one. If you use your power a lot, say by wounding yourself repeatedly, it will eventually stop because it needs time to replenish."

His words hit me like a storm of lightning. "So, you're saying that I *do* have some sort of freakish power?"

"That's why I've been following you. It's time for you to come home."

Chapter 6

Come home? My home was gone! If Myles had really been following me since yesterday, he should know that.

"What do you mean, *come home?*"

"Mageye City," he clarified. "I am a member of the city's Elite Guard and my job is to find Mageye and bring them to Mageye City, where they are meant to be. I am here to help you."

I stepped back, nearly tripping over a root. "No... there has to be a mistake. This *power* I have only started two days ago. And if it is supposed to be connected to my eyes, I should have been born with it. Maybe I dreamed the healing part."

He shook his head. "You didn't dream it. Your power is in your genes, and for the most part, it is genetically passed down. Sometimes, though, people are born the first Mageye in their family in a way only God properly understands. Either way, our powers can emerge at different times; you are no less a Mageye just because your power is new."

I studied his expression closely. One of my friends liked to say the eyes are windows into the soul. If that was the case, Myles's eyes were windows into sincerity and truth. That made me frown. "So, you're telling me I'm a witch?"

He stiffened, and I could have sworn his purple irises flashed with light. "No, not a witch, a Mageye. There's a difference; our powers aren't black magic."

"Then what are they?"

"There is good and bad magic. Our powers are a form of

good magic. Similar to how some people are born with more empathy than others, Mageye are born with magic. *Black magic* isn't a part of your being. It is something you call upon to cause harm to others. It doesn't exist, not truly. Mageye are often mistaken for witches, but that is not what we are."

"So, my power is a part of me, like my arms and legs?"

"Yes, exactly like that."

"Well, that still doesn't explain why my power only just started. I broke my leg when I was five; where was my power then?" I challenged.

He tapped his fingers against his thigh. "I don't know. As I said, they emerge at different times. Sometimes you have it from the day you're born. Other times, it slowly emerges over years, or maybe you did something to trigger it. The power is in your genes, but sometimes it takes time to mature into what it truly is."

I threw my arms, unsure why I was even continuing this conversation. "I didn't do anything out of the ordinary, though. I was picking strawberries, and I tripped."

"Was it a new strawberry patch?"

"No, it was the same one I always go to."

"Has your mom or dad ever gone there?"

"Since before my eldest brother was born."

"Well then, I think we have our answer. One of them probably did or touched something that caused you to become a Mageye. And your power didn't reveal itself until you did something similar to whatever they did. But these are all just guesses. All that really matters is that you *are* a Mageye. And *not* a witch."

I frowned. "I guess... What is this magical city you want to take me to?"

He smiled again. "Mageye City. Like I said, I am a member of the Elite Guard. I help find Mageye and bring them home."

"What if I don't want to go?"

"You don't have to, but it's safer for you there. Normal people are good. They really aren't any different from us. But our powers don't belong in Alveraada, *particularly* when it's something like yours. What would you do if you cut yourself and someone saw? You can't hide that. And just like how you thought it was black magic, they will think it is, too. And your circumstance right now is even worse. I was easily able to follow you all night. You're going to walk into a trap, and if I'm right about who I think took your family, then we need to go. Now."

Myles had officially offered confirmation to all of my worst fears, but I held my ground despite the terror. "What about my family?"

He stared over my shoulder. "I'm sorry, but there's nothing we can do. Following the trail that you found is suicide. If it's really a trail left by them, that is."

"So, we let my family die?"

"Maybe we can work something out when we get to Mageye City. But there is nothing that the two of us can do ourselves."

I looked back at the makeshift X, haphazardly propped against the boulder. "How long does it take to get to the city?"

"Depends on how we travel." His gaze flitted to the rising sun and then in a north-ish direction. "Three weeks, give or take."

"Three weeks?" I repeated incredulously. "You expect me to wait *three weeks* for a maybe we can figure something out?"

Myles held his hands out in a calming gesture. "Rose, I know you're upset. But..." His gaze flicked to the north and he shook his head. "There really isn't anything we can do."

His brow furrowed, and the sunlight hit his eyes in a way that made them flash. As if his emotions were being expressed through his irises.

I stilled. "You think they're dead, don't you?"

He hesitated, avoiding eye contact. "Yeah," he finally admitted. "I do."

Tears rose behind my eyes even before he finished speaking.

"But... the letter said..."

"I'm sorry," he whispered, meeting my gaze. "Those people are evil, and we're not just talking about the... the trader who took your family. The note mentioned The End, and that is somewhere you simply can't go. Not alone, anyway."

I blinked rapidly to stop my tears. "What if I'm not alone?"

Myles shifted his stance. "Listen, either way, it is a dangerous mission. The citizens of Mageye City are very kind, and they will be willing to help you. But not the kind of help I think you want. I'm sorry, but if your family isn't gone yet, by the time we arrange a force large enough to even stand a chance..." He cleared his throat. "We should go back to Sunset Hollow," he decided softly. "And we will make sure you're safe and then you can decide what you want to do. I'll help you figure this out."

I hardly registered the last part because I was too focused on the word *chance*. He had changed his suspicions from my family already being dead to not gone yet, which meant even Myles admitted the fight wasn't entirely over. "I don't want to go back to Sunset Hollow. We need to go to The End."

Myles blinked. "We?"

"Yes, *we*. You said that your job is to help Mageye find their way home. If you help me..." My thoughts raced, frantically thinking of a deal he couldn't refuse. "I'll let you bring me to Mageye City," I decided. "You are obviously good at what you do, and I can't get hurt. Well, I can, but it heals! I don't know what your power is, but it must be something impressive if you are allowed to look for Mageye by yourself."

"No, I can't. I'm sorry, but it's a suicide mission." He gripped the strap of his satchel, shifting his stance. "This isn't... your average kidnapping."

"Maybe not, but what if my family *is* alive? I'm not saying we start a war, only investigate enough to know for certain."

He stepped closer and I didn't flinch this time, as his expression had softened. "Let's focus on one thing at a time." Before I could argue that we didn't have time to focus on only one thing, he continued, "I am not saying no yet, Rose. But I want to ask you if you're okay?"

I blinked. "What?"

"Are you okay?" He held my gaze. "You haven't slept, lost your home and family, and pushed yourself to cool-down yesterday. So, are you okay?"

How could I possibly be okay when my entire family was missing and it seemed that the Sunset Guard had no clues, leaving this all to me? "It doesn't matter if I'm okay." My voice quavered. "My family needs me."

"Of course it matters," he responded. "Are you okay?"

"I'll be okay when I save my family," I decided, lifting my chin. "The note said to find them and I am going to do exactly that. And... you said you were following me as part of your job." I waved my hand at the trees to the north. "Maybe someone else in my family is a secret Mageye, too. We'll all visit Mageye City with you."

Myles's expression fell. "I really am sorry, but my job is to take you home. If you don't want to come with me, I won't force you. But I can't go with you to The End; King Duncan wouldn't allow it."

"But..."

"I can't help you with this," he said. "I'm telling you, what you're getting into is dangerous, and I don't believe it will be successful."

"Then it's not successful." I gripped Ren's jackknife. "If my family is already dead, they are already dead, but if they aren't? If there is any chance that they are alive, no matter how slim, I need to try."

"You're really not going to give up, are you?"

"No, and you don't need to come, but if you go... You obviously know more about these people than I do. Can you tell me about them?"

He sighed. "The people who live in The End are called Volcaniacs, and they live in a volcano. That volcano is where your family would be held *if* they are alive." He tapped his fingers against his thigh again, his gaze traveling past me and to the north. "From what we know, there are both Mageye and normal people living there, but their main weapon is their Wolvien Guard. A pack of magical wolves that can hunt better than anything else in all of Alveraada."

He broke off, his purple eyes meeting mine. "The volcano has a magical barrier around it. We suspect that the Wolvien Guard is somehow controlling it. Just like how a Mageye's eye color reflects their magic, the wolves have flames in their irises."

I shuddered. This was a lot more dangerous than I had originally believed it to be.

He pointed in the direction I had been going. "The End is up north, but... King Duncan has yet to have a successful scout make it there. And when the Wolvien Guard first made its appearance a few years ago, he deemed it too dangerous to send anything besides the full army. Not to mention that so-called bad auras can taint you. It isn't just the Volcaniacs living there, but the very auras surrounding them."

I looked back towards The End. All Myles knew was that it was dangerous, and seemingly much more perilous than I had originally thought, but that only gave me more of a reason to continue my pursuit.

"Thank you for the help, Myles," I said, turning back to him and lifting my chin. "When I get there, I'm sure that information will help. I'll be careful with the... auras."

He still looked conflicted. "You're not going to let me convince you otherwise, are you?"

"No. My family needs me. I'm the only chance they have."

His purple eyes seemed to drill through me before he hung his head in defeat. "All right... Be careful, and good luck. If you change your mind, look for someone with magical eyes. There are more of us around than you might think."

"I will." I turned north. "Thank you for the advice."

"It's what I do. It's my job."

I glanced back; he stood in the same spot, a pained expression on his face.

"Bye," he said.

"Bye," I echoed softly.

I sat on the bank of a wide stream, tugging my boots and stockings off. After parting ways with Myles, I had eaten the carrot I took for Lucy and continued to use the rising sun as a guide. It was still early in the morning, and I stood and splashed through the stream, holding my skirts above the water.

If I could keep going without any stops for rest, maybe I stood a chance at catching up before my family was brought to The End. The trader would have to rest his horses, after all. And as remarkable as it was to think he could somehow ride his cart between the trees... surely he was doing exactly that, since he wanted me to follow him.

I shoved my feet back into my boots and left the stream, a sudden electric crackle making me jump.

Myles stood behind me. His lips were pressed in a thin line, and his eyes again seemed to reflect the light in a way that expressed his emotions.

"I can't believe I'm actually doing this," he said in exasperation. "If my dad finds out, he'll kill me."

Chapter 7

Myles continued north and I stared after him in shock. "What do you mean? Are you coming with me?" I stumbled forward, jogging to keep up.

He walked briskly. "My job is to escort Mageye home safely. Letting you run into a trap by yourself would be going directly against that. This is part of my work assignment."

For every stride he took, I had to take two, and I grabbed his arm. "Thank you." My heart raced and I repeated it, trembling with my sudden relief. "Thank you, Myles."

That seemed to snap him out of his serious mood, and he offered a cocky half-smile. "Remember, you said that if I help you, you'll let me bring you to Mageye City."

I nodded enthusiastically, releasing his arm. "You have my word. I'll do anything to get them back."

"That's a good outlook," he agreed. "Since we have a lot of ground to cover."

"How much, exactly?"

He shrugged, his smile fading. "The End is on the northernmost tip of Alveraada, and since it is part of a magical biome, it will take us weeks to get there... Unless we can catch up."

My heart sank. "*Unless* we can catch up? I know they disappeared without a trace, but I left Pastor Wilson's house as soon as I could. They can't have too big of a head start... and my family doesn't have weeks for us to get there."

53

"You didn't let me finish. The Wolvien Guard can travel hundreds of miles in days. I've seen them run; they are fast, but not that fast, which leads me to believe they have secrets." He ducked under a branch. "If we can find their secrets, we can cover ground much faster."

"Secrets? What do you mean by secrets?"

"Magical secrets. Things that only Mageye can see, like that X you showed me."

"The X was magic?"

He gave me a look that suggested he was wondering how I could be so stupid. "Yes, there are some things that you can only see because you are a Mageye. We call it having your eyes opened, because we can use our auras to help non-Mageye see into our world."

No wonder the Sunset Guard had missed the X scratched into our fence. "How can I tell if something is magic or not?"

"Usually their aura, but it takes practice to be able to tell."

I frowned. "I thought it was the moon making them glow."

"No, it wasn't the moon. Everything has an aura, but magical things in particular glow. For Mageye, our glow is seen from our eye color, but other things shine like lights," he explained.

Wait a second... "Myles?"

"Yeah?" He stepped over small fallen tree, pausing on the other side as I stepped after him.

"Your eyes are purple. What power matches that color?" I studied the woods behind us contemplatively. "I saw a purple flash last night. Was that you?"

He grimaced. "I wasn't sure if you saw that. Yeah, that was me."

"What were you doing? You can create lights?"

He laughed. "I like to think what I can do is more exciting than purple lights; I can teleport. When I do it, I form a purple orb made of lightning. My eyes are purple because of the orb."

"Teleporting," I mused. "So, you can disappear from one place and reappear in another?"

He nodded. "Yes."

I stopped walking. "Wait, can you teleport us to my family? The trader had a cart." I waved at the thick woods ahead of us. "It should be impossible for him to travel through these woods, yet this is where the trail is. Why are we going to The End when we can catch up?"

His purple eyes seemed to flash as he surveyed the woods before us. "You think he drove his cart through this?"

"He had to have." I shook my head helplessly. "There are no roads leading directly north from Sunset Hollow."

Myles studied the ground at our feet and made an expression like he was concentrating closely on something. "I don't know if I believe we are following in their exact footsteps," he finally said. "But we are heading north." He looked up. "The note said to meet them there. Our best bet is to continue north regardless of if he wove his cart through these trees or not."

"Then maybe we should teleport?" I suggested quietly.

He grimaced, shaking his head. "That's too risky. We don't know if he had other Volcaniacs assisting him or not. I saw your house yesterday; it was burned by magic. You were the only Mageye in Sunset Hollow, so he's not a Mageye, but we have no way of knowing what other magic he may wield. Jumping ahead without knowing the extent of his strength is too risky."

Every fiber of my being wanted to argue, but I couldn't *force* Myles to teleport, and who knew where we would pop out? My shoulders slumped. "Can't you at least try to take us partway? And how do you know he isn't a Mageye?"

"What if they are out of my reach? Just like how your wounds stopped healing when you overused your power, I have a cool-down period. If I brought us to them, I might not be able to teleport again if I needed to. Besides, traveling that far wouldn't just affect my power, but me. I would probably pass out, if not worse. And the reason I know he isn't a Mageye is because I would have sensed his aura if he was. I could sense other forms of magic, but I assumed they were yours, which is why I was confused when you knew nothing about Mageye. I must have felt the presence of his cart."

I clutched Ren's jackknife in my pocket. "So, he has magical weapons, but isn't a Mageye. Doesn't that mean he won't hit cool-down?"

Myles nodded, holding a low-hanging branch out of my path. "That's exactly right, and it makes him even more dangerous. Depending on how many magical objects he has, he could last in a fight longer than us."

I bit my lip. "What happens if we overuse our power? Could it kill us?"

"If you push too far, there comes a point where you can no longer take from your power alone and have to take from your physical core. But don't worry, using up your power is nearly impossible, particularly when it is a power like yours. One that knows its own limits and stops when over-pushed."

"That is still scary, though... Is there a way to get rid of your power?"

Myles jerked to a halt. "Get rid of it? Why would you want to get rid of it?"

"Well, so far, it's caused nothing but problems. Sure, healing quickly is nice, but what about my family? They would still be here if it weren't for my power. If my eyes didn't look the way they do, that trader would have left without causing any problems."

Myles ran a hand through his hair, nodding. "I understand why you're upset; I really do. To some degree, you're right. Your family was taken because you're a Mageye, but that doesn't necessarily make your power bad. Think of all the good it can do."

"I don't know about that yet. I can only heal myself, so I'm kind of useless. If I could heal other people, maybe things would be different."

"How do you know you can only heal yourself?"

"Well," I paused; he had a good point. "I don't even know

how I heal myself. It just happens, so how would heal someone else?"

"Just because your power works automatically doesn't mean you can't control it."

"How do I control it, then?"

His expression lit up. "You need to trust it and do it. Think of it this way, could you explain to someone how you walk? You might think it means putting one foot in front of the other, but it's not. *How* are you putting one foot in front of the other?" He didn't wait for an answer. "By telling your muscles to move. If you want to heal others, then you need to tell your power to heal."

"So, you're saying I need to instruct my power to heal someone else, and that's it?"

He shook his head. "It isn't just telling your power what to do and letting it happen. You need to not only instruct it, but *guide* it."

I held my hands in front of myself. The skin was perfectly smooth, no sign of any of the cuts I had given myself.

Myles waited patiently, and I looked up. "If I put my hand on or over the wound, maybe I can instruct whatever magic is inside of me to heal the wound I am touching."

He grinned. "Let's test."

"Right now?" I lowered my hands. "Are you hurt?"

He shook his head, pulling the dagger he carried from his belt. I watched as he cut the tip of his finger, and held his hand out.

"Give it a try."

I hesitated, staring at the drop of blood forming on his fingertip. Like any normal wound, the crimson droplet rolled from his finger, dripping to the grass at his feet.

He waited and I hesitantly grabbed his finger, thinking about it healing. When I pulled back, nothing had happened. His blood smudged across my palm and I frowned. "Maybe I need to focus more? I'm just thinking about it, but I need to directly tell it, don't I?"

He nodded. "Yes. As you get stronger, your thoughts might be enough. But, for now, you will probably need to internally tell it."

I grabbed his finger again, and this time, I not only thought about healing but ordered my magic to heal the wound. I shut my eyes, and imagined the wound sealing itself.

When I opened my eyes, I released his finger. A droplet of blood dripped from his fingertip, and my shoulders slumped. "I really can't heal other people. I'm sorry."

Myles shrugged, his tone gentle. "Who knows, maybe that will be something you can do later. Sometimes your power grows over time as you get stronger. As I got older, I could teleport farther distances."

"Maybe. Either way, I can't right now, so you *better* not get hurt."

He pulled out a kerchief and wiped the blood from his finger. "I'll be fine. I might not be able to heal right away, but I will eventually."

"I know, but it's still preferable that you don't get hurt. It would slow us down." I froze as the rudeness of my words hit me. "I'm sorry," I said, my cheeks flushing with embarrassment.

He paused in wiping his hands, but quickly blinked away any offense. "I'll do my best not to get hurt."

With the awkwardness fading, we continued our journey, and a few hours passed before Myles pointed ahead. "There's an X."

I followed his finger and gasped. A small glowing X had been carved into the trunk of an oak tree. "We're on the right track," I whispered, hurrying to the tree and tracing the mark with my finger.

"Yeah." Myles followed, a concerned expression on his face.

My smile faded. "Is something wrong?"

His gaze wasn't locked on the X like I had thought, but at something on the ground. I followed his gaze and saw nothing but sticks and dirt.

"What are you looking at?"

"He did take his cart through the trees," Myles whispered.

My breath caught. "How do you know?" I looked around for any tracks, but there were none.

He shook his head. "We're walking into a trap."

"What do you mean?" I asked, attempting to justify a reason to ignore the signs of this being a trap. "I know we are following the trail he left, but what other choice do we have? Besides, if you think they *did* pass through here with the horses and cart, then we have a chance of catching up."

"No..." he said slowly, "No, I think they're already there."

I froze. "What?"

He pointed to the spot he had been staring at. "There is a magical aura, and... he used a teleportation crystal. They are some of the rarest forms of magic; the only form of magic that can truly take you anywhere, no matter how far that place might be. The trader used one, which means he took your family to The End already."

"What... what does that mean? It's not over, is it?" Tears rushed to my eyes. "Do you think our chance of saving them is gone completely?"

Myles's gaze hardened, a look of determination forming as he stared at me, stared *through* me. "No, it's not over."

A sigh of relief escaped me and I wiped my eyes. It wasn't over... It wasn't too late... We still had a chance, and I would cling to that chance with both hands from now on.

Myles reached a hand towards the X, but froze before his fingers grazed the tree. "They want us here. We're playing their game." He licked his lips, nodding to himself. "I want to play our own cards."

"What do you mean?" My voice shook. "If they are already at the volcano..."

"We are going to meet them there. Rose, you said that you're going to fight to save your family no matter how slim the odds are. Our odds of making it to The End by following the trail of X's left by the trader is zero. There is no chance. But if we stray off the path, if we forge our own..." His eyes seemed to spark. "*Then* we'll stand a chance."

Chapter 8

Stray off the path? If my family had already been magically taken to The End, we couldn't afford to leave the trail of X's.

"Rose, listen." Myles straightened, taking on a gently commanding air. "We don't know what the Volcaniacs have planned, but right now, they know what *you* have planned. If we follow this path any further, we run the risk of getting ambushed. And if that happens, how will we ever be able to save your family? If we go our own way, yes, it might take longer, but at least we will get there in one piece. We can't keep following these X's. That's going to get us killed."

I bit my lip, turning my gaze back to the X carved into the tree. It seemed to pulse as if it was listening in on our conversation. "This trail is a guarantee we will get there."

"It is a guarantee we will get there on *their* terms," Myles corrected.

The woods were thick, with no sign of danger or ambush or defeat, yet, I was being lured to The End for a reason. This wasn't a game of hide and seek where the trader would let my family go as a prize at the end of the trail of X's. No, he wanted me to follow this trail for a much more sinister reason, and if my family was already at The End, this trail no longer offered a way to catch up.

I looked back at Myles. "What if we went west for a few days instead of north? Then once we are far enough to be unpredictable, we go north again?"

Relief flit across Myles's face. "I like that idea." He took a step closer and turned again to the pulsing X. "Besides, I doubt a portal will be anywhere near this trail. Portals are the 'magical secret' I told you about, and the Volcaniacs wouldn't want you jumping ahead an unpredictable distance. We stand a higher chance of finding a portal off of this trail than we do on it."

A flame of hope kindled in my chest at the thought. "We're going to make it."

Myles met my gaze. "Yes. We are."

Noon had come and gone, and the sleepless night was taking its toll on me. My feet dragged as I walked, and I kept tripping on roots and fallen branches.

Myles caught my arm. "Do you want to rest?"

I shook my head. "We have to keep going. Every passing moment counts."

He laughed as he released my arm. "Never been on the receiving end of that outlook. I'll tell you what my dad always says. *Taking a break won't end the world.*" He smiled. "He usually forces me to sit, but I won't wrestle you down."

I glanced around for an excuse to keep going, then sighed. "You're right. I really do need a break." We sat across from each other. "What about you? If you followed me all night, aren't you exhausted?"

He shrugged. "I'm used to it. Tracking down Mageye can be hard, because you never know where you'll find them, or what situation they'll be in when you do."

I leaned against a tree, the rough bark snagging the fabric of my dress. "And you do it alone? Can I ask how old you are?"

"I'm eighteen. And yes, alone, but I've been doing this solo since I was twelve."

"You've been traveling across the country by yourself since you were *twelve?*"

He smirked. "I've even gone outside of Alveraada. It's not

that big of a deal, though. I had proper training for years before I started, and for the first two years, I worked solo with King Duncan."

"You were a king's apprentice?"

"Yes," he said cautiously. "I have trained under King Duncan since I was eight. He saw potential in me and I met his expectations. No two Mageye have the same power, and teleportation is exactly what he needed for my position."

"So, he trained you himself until you were old enough to work on your own?"

"Until I was strong enough to work on my own," he corrected. "In Mageye City, our power and experience go above age."

"You must be really strong, if you started working by yourself when you were twelve." My brow furrowed. He was well-muscled and despite the fact that he was functioning without sleep, he was alert.

He shrugged, giving me a slightly questioning look, but it passed before I could ask what it meant.

"Is Queen Cynthia aware of Mageye City and King Duncan?" I asked instead.

"She doesn't know because we are a separate country."

"What do you mean?"

Myles rested his elbows on his knees and clasped his hands. "Think of it this way. Alveraada is a large island country, and on top of that country, kind of like fog, is the magic layer. Our magic layer is a different 'world.' Only Mageye, and people whose eyes have been opened, can see into and live in this magic layer. When we are outside of Mageye City, we follow the laws of Alveraada. Not because we are Alveraadan citizens, but because we are acting the part of a member of the non-magical world. Mageye City is so large that it is a country of its own and is entirely independent of Alveraada. When we are in the city, it is as if Alveraada doesn't exist."

"So, it is like a country inside of a country?"

"Exactly. I'm from Mageye City, not Alveraada. Kind of like how you would say you are from Sunset Hollow. We are both from a sub-part of the country. Minus the fact that the magic layer has its own laws and leader."

And to think two days ago I was joking about how magic *didn't* exist. "If someone approached you and asked where in Alveraada you were from, what would you say?"

"I would probably pick a town near Mageye City. But, I am not an Alveraadan, I am a Mageye. I couldn't tell them that, of course, so if they pried, I would make something up." He shrugged. "It would depend on how much they pry, I guess."

"But you can tell me where you are actually from," I said slowly. "Mageye City."

He nodded, and watched as I split a small loaf of bread and offered him half.

"Thanks."

"I took what I could," I explained. "Bread can last us a couple days..."

Myles smiled and set his satchel on his lap, pulling a second, smaller bag from it. Inside, wrapped carefully, was what looked to be cooked meat. "I'm good at hunting," he said, offering a piece. "And I know what wild berries and such we can eat, so we will be fine."

The meat was cold but good, and I pressed it into my roll, eating them together. We lapsed into silence, contemplating what all of this magic could mean. The magic layer of the world was all new to me, but to Myles, it was his life.

A life he was now risking for someone he had never met.

When we finished eating, Myles stood. "It's probably better to move during the day and rest at night if at all possible. It will keep us on a normal schedule."

I stood beside him. "That makes sense."

After nearly an hour of walking in slightly awkward silence, Myles said, "You've been quiet."

I shrugged. "So have you."

He started to reply but froze with his gaze locked on a nearby cluster of bushes.

I turned to the bushes as well and was suddenly hit with the feeling that we were being watched. Something was wrong. Very wrong.

Fear seeped into my veins in a way it only had once before—yesterday—when I found my family missing and my house turned to ash.

Myles slowly reached forward and grabbed my hand, pulling me away from the bushes. "Don't panic," he whispered. "It's going to be okay."

We slowly backed away, and as we got farther from the bushes, my panic began to decrease, but the presence of imminent danger remained.

A golden light flashed behind the bushes and the leaves rustled before parting to reveal a huge mountain lion. Its intelligent yellow eyes filled with malice as its gaze locked on us.

I trembled, and adrenaline coursed through my veins, but Myles maintained a firm grip on my hand, preventing me from fleeing.

The lion's hackles rose, and it crouched, growling as it prepared to pounce.

My heart froze as I saw a black X on its left shoulder.

"Stay calm," Myles breathed. "Don't run." His gaze was locked on the lion, eyes narrowed.

The lion lashed out its paw, and pain erupted in my right arm, even though it hadn't touched me. I screamed and leapt back, Myles's tight grip the only thing stopping me from falling to the ground.

The lion growled as it tensed, then launched itself into the air.

Myles twisted, pulling me to the ground as a large purple shield erupted from him. The lion hit it and let out a blood-chilling scream as bolts of purple lightning sparked from the shield. It hit the ground hard, and scrambled backward as it fled, still screaming, in the opposite direction.

The shield disappeared, and Myles released my hand. "Are you all right?"

His eyes were flashing, almost like the lightning from the shield was still in the reflection of his irises. I shook uncontrollably as I clutched my bleeding arm.

"It didn't touch me," I whispered, looking at him in horror. "It had an X on it; do you think it was a trap?"

Myles frowned, scanning the woods behind us. "I saw the X, but I don't think it was a trap, or I don't know how that could have been set up." He examined my bleeding arm, leaning back on his heels as he watched it heal before his eyes. "Wow..."

He looked up, and our eyes met. "Are you okay now? Is the pain gone, too?"

I poked the skin with my finger. "Yeah, but how...?"

"Magic. That's how it hurt you without touching you. I didn't realize it could do that, otherwise I would have blocked you."

"No, it's better if I get hurt instead of you, since I can heal right away." My tense muscles slackened, though my heart still raced. "Did you get that bad feeling too?"

"Yeah, I felt it right before it appeared." He scrunched his nose. "It used a portal. And that aura was a warning that something bad was coming. Non-Mageye get it too, but fainter, because they can't always see the evil. I think our immediate fear as well as the lion's immediate urge to harm us explains the X; it must belong to the Volcaniacs."

"But you said you don't think it was a trap."

"I don't know. We are already far from the trail you were following, too far away for a trap. But it fled north, so when it gets back... they'll know."

I stiffened. What would the Volcaniacs do to my family if they realized I was no longer on their trail? "Do you think they will get upset? What if they—"

"Don't," Myles interrupted. "Don't think about that. There's nothing we can do about it. We just need to avoid X's at all costs."

"But we left the trail to avoid their trap. Now they know it will never be sprung."

Myles rested his hands on my shoulders, meeting my gaze. "Good. That means they know outsmarting you won't be easy."

"You also shocked the lion," I whispered. "Maybe it's hurt."

He nodded. "I'm sure it is. The orbs I create allow me to teleport, but I can also create forcefields that shock anyone they touch."

"So, that's why it kind of bounced off of the lightning?"

He nodded and released his grip on my shoulders. I traced my fingers along my healed arm, probing the skin for any lingering pain, but there was none.

The fear-induced anxiety from the mountain lion had all but faded, and I looked at the bush it had appeared from behind. A portal... "You said it used a portal, right?" I asked, bracing myself to stand. "Isn't that what you said we were looking for? We can use it."

Myles shook his head. "No, it disappeared. It must have formed specifically to let the lion out. Portals have minds of their own, and they usually only stick around for one or maybe two uses if you're lucky. But I wouldn't use that one anyway; it's tainted."

"What do you mean?"

"Different creatures leave different magical remnants. That lion was evil. It isn't usually in their nature to blindly attack. Using a portal, or anything else for that matter, that has been used by something so evil is dangerous. It could get you killed."

I parted the bushes with my hands, frowning at the grass on the other side. This whole magic thing was turning out to be a very unmagical experience. "Then what should we do?" I asked.

"We continue with the original plan. I doubt there are others nearby, but I don't want to risk it. Are you ready to keep going?"

"Very much so." I looked nervously after the lion. "I hope we don't run into anything else like that lion."

Myles sighed. "Me too."

Chapter 9

"Tell me about your family," Myles said as he tucked his arms behind his head. "You said that you have three older brothers, right?"

I nodded, looking back the way we had come. Crickets chirped around us, and the leaves rustled faintly in a refreshing night breeze. Since leaving behind the bushes where the mountain lion had sprung, we hadn't seen anymore X's or other signs of the Volcaniacs, as Myles called them. "Yes, Raymond's the oldest, and Ren and Ryder are twins."

He half-lifted his head. "You all have R names?"

Everyone we ever met commented on that, and I laughed. "My mom wanted us to match."

"Does her name begin with an R?"

"No. Her name is Cecilia, and my dad's name was John."

"What are they like?"

"My dad died when I was young, so Mom pretty much raised us herself. She is kind and has always been a good role model on how to love your family. And my brothers are protective. Raymond wants to join the Sunset Guard to help keep Alveraada safe, and it pays well too. And the twins can be mischievous, especially Ren. Ryder's a bit more laid back; he wants to be an artist, and Ren wants to be a carpenter."

"Ren and Ryder wanted to come with me when I went out yesterday," I continued, blinking back tears. "When I came back, they were gone."

"It's not your fault," Myles said.

"If I had been there, or if I had let them come with me..."

"Then what? Your mom and Raymond would have still been kidnapped. Or you would have been kidnapped alongside them."

"I guess you're right," I admitted.

"If Raymond was the one not kidnapped... Would you want him to wish he had been there and kidnapped too?" he asked.

"Of course not." I wiped my eyes. "But I know he would, just like I do."

"That's fair. Though, you are out in the middle of the woods right now because you are on your way to saving them. If you weren't a Mageye, you never would have found the trail of X's."

"If I weren't a Mageye, they wouldn't have been kidnapped," I countered.

His expression fell. "I know, but..." He ran his hand through his hair as he sat up. "Did you have any sort of conversation with this trader before he kidnapped your family?"

I reflected on the events that led to my final night in my home. "No. He complimented my eyes in a somewhat uncomfortable manner, and Ren told him off."

Myles raised his brows. "Did *he* have any conversation with him?"

"Yes." I pulled out Ren's jackknife, running my thumb over it. "I didn't hear it though, because Ren told me to go inside."

"All right." Myles stared at the jackknife. "Non-Mageye can identify us simply through our eyes, and the note leaves no room for doubt that he is targeting you because of your power. But you're not from Mageye City, so that seems counterintuitive."

"What do you mean?"

"Well, it seems like a hassle for him to go through the trouble of kidnapping your family and destroying your home instead of simply following you to the strawberry patch. That is, unless he wants something more than the presence of your power.

Something like information. Information you and your family don't have because you aren't from Mageye City."

"Maybe they don't want information." My voice came out as a whisper, and he gave me a quizzical look.

"What do you mean?"

"Well, he was interested in my eyes and we seem to agree the note makes it sound like he wants my power. And since I'm not from Mageye City, no Mageye will ever come looking for me..."

"I don't like the sound of that," he murmured, staring into the dark woods.

I fidgeted with the hem of my gown. "And maybe the reason he took my family instead of following me is because he doesn't know my power. Maybe... maybe the trail was to lure me into a controlled environment where he wasn't at risk of being harmed if my power turned out to be something like yours."

Lightning flickered in his irises and Myles nodded slowly. "That might be the best answer we can get until we make it to The End."

Myles fell asleep before me, and I lay on my back, listening to the night sounds. Crickets chirped, and there was an occasional rustling as an animal skittered through the bushes.

I sat up slowly, careful not to bump Myles. Using my pointer finger, I traced around the outline of my left hand, flexing my fingers and examining my palm. Not a scratch.

Leaves rustled as Myles rolled over and I waited for him to still before pulling Ren's jackknife from my pocket.

The tip of the blade put pressure on my finger and I pushed down, wincing at the sting. A dark spot of blood welled and I rubbed my thumb and pointer finger together, smearing my fingers in red.

The blood on my thumb disappeared first, then the rest rolled back into my wound with the stinging fading alongside it.

Not even a scar remained.

I was a *Mageye*, a status that had apparently, within the last two days, doomed my family.

A frog began croaking and I smiled softly, the sound comforting. Raymond, Ren, Ryder, and I had captured more frogs than I could count over the years, keeping them until Mom made us release them.

It continued croaking and I tilted my head. The comfort seemed to come from more than the familiar sound. I touched my hand to my heart, feeling its calm beat and lifting my gaze to the dark woods.

The comfort was definitely more than familiarity, it coincided with the presence of peace and safety.

Just like with the mountain lion, it was as if I could *feel* the fact that we were safe, that the woods carried no danger. A magical aura that surrounded me and laced over the entire world, exactly as Myles described it.

I looked at my finger again.

Maybe being a Mageye wasn't all bad, after all.

Chapter 10

Our camp felt alarmingly empty when I woke up in it alone. "Myles?" His satchel lay beside me, and I stood, turning in a slow circle. "Myles?" My voice raised and I spun in a circle again.

He was gone. Myles was *gone*. Just like my family. Just like my home.

The trader.

I tugged out Ren's jackknife, flicking it open and holding it before myself. Surely, if the trader had found us and kidnapped Myles, he would have taken me too. "Myles?" I called shakily, tears starting to roll down my cheeks.

Birds chirped and animals rustled through the leaves, but I stood completely *alone*.

Electricity crackled and I spun around, raising my arm with a shout. "Give them back!"

Myles dropped the apples he carried, stepping back in surprise. "It's me! It's Myles."

I lowered my arm. "I thought... I thought..."

He stepped forward as I fell to my knees, tears rolling down my cheeks. "Where were you?" I sobbed.

"I went to find something to eat." He hurried to kneel in front of me. "Did something happen while I was gone?"

I put a hand over my mouth, shaking my head as tears rolled down my cheeks. Slowly, I lowered my hand, whispering, "I thought the trader had come, and... and taken you."

Myles shook his head. "He didn't." He reached for his satchel, tugging out a kerchief and offering it to me. "Nothing bad happened. I'm right here."

The tears kept coming and I wiped my eyes to no avail, my chest heaving. Myles sat cross-legged now, offering me a waterskin. "Take a few sips of this," he directed.

"S-sorry..." I choked out, shakily grabbing the waterskin. "We need to... go..." I looked north, sniffling. "We n-need to save them."

"And we will," he assured me. "Take your time calming down and then we will eat breakfast while we walk."

"N-no." I started, handing the water back. "We can't wait."

He shook his head. "Tell you what. You focus on calming down, and I'll tell you a travel plan for today."

I sniffed, my gaze locking on his face until he began with his plan. "I know we wanted to head west to get away from the northern trail, but I think we covered decent ground yesterday. So, this morning I think we should travel northwest and tomorrow go fully north."

I swallowed some water, my tears beginning to slow. "You mean... we will get closer to them today?"

"Yes." He smiled. "We'll get closer."

My voice wavered but I smiled a little. "Good."

"They need us to get there in one piece," he added. "Better a day of traveling off the path than never getting there at all."

"We'll get there," I whispered, wiping away the last of my tears. "And we won't get kidnapped in the process."

"Exactly," he agreed. "I won't disappear on you again, I promise."

We waited a little while longer for me to fully calm down, then, like Myles suggested, we ate breakfast as we began our walk north. The morning was uneventful; no X's and no bad auras. Myles seemed to be listening to our surroundings, a concentrated look flickering across his expression as his gaze followed the sun.

"Is something wrong?" I asked.

He shook his head. "No... I feel a magical pull."

"A pull?" I followed his gaze, trying to listen like he had done. Instead of a sound, a faint feeling stirred in my gut. Not a pull, so much as the physical knowledge that something was ahead. An invisible hand waving us towards it, similar to how I had felt certain about heading north before meeting Myles.

"I feel it, too," I observed. "It doesn't feel bad... or good. But it's there."

He nodded, raising his brows. "It's a portal."

My eyes widened. "Really? Should we find it, then?" Before he could answer, my shoulders slumped. "We can't go north yet, can we?"

"It's far away, probably too far for us to reach until tomorrow." Myles tapped his fingers against his thigh before nodding slowly. "We are nowhere near the trail of X's anymore, and while heading north is predictable, a powerful portal could take us hundreds of miles. That's something we can't afford to pass up. Plus, that would put us far out of any radius they may try to find us in."

If Myles thought it was safe, I wasn't going to argue. "I want to find the portal."

He smiled. "Then we'll follow the pull."

To me, the pull still seemed more like a presence, and while it didn't get any weaker, it didn't get stronger either. Myles didn't seem phased, but after hours with no difference, I couldn't hold my worries in any longer. "Why isn't the pull getting stronger?"

Myles switched his satchel to his other shoulder, shrugging. "We're still far off. Usually, portals as powerful as this one will have radii around it. An outer one where it is like a presence telling you it is there, and an inner one where the pull is suddenly much stronger. We won't notice it until we cross whatever the barrier between the two radii is."

"So, it will suddenly feel stronger?"

"If we can feel it from this far away, then it must be a very powerful portal. You'll get what I mean when we enter the inner circle."

I shook my head. "Magic doesn't make very much sense."

He laughed. "You have a lot to learn about magic, but don't worry, I'll help you." He put on a fake formal tone. "Your first lesson is that magic never works the way you expect it to. There is no logic to it, and it breaks all of the normal world's laws, so learn to expect the unexpected."

"So, whatever you expect, it does the opposite?"

He shook his head, returning to his normal tone. "No, because that's what you'd expect it to do."

"But it's the *opposite* of what I expect."

"No, you're predicting that it will be the opposite, so it'll be somewhere in between."

"Every time?" I asked incredulously.

Laughter trickled into his voice. "Nope. Sometimes, it does exactly what you expect it to do, which makes it even more unpredictable, because you never know when it will work your way."

I frowned. "Has anyone ever told you that you're a terrible teacher? You couldn't start with something that makes sense? You jump right to, *You will never be able to predict anything, so don't try, because you'll always be wrong?*"

"The sooner you learn to expect the unexpected to be unexpected, the better. Trust me."

As the sun set, Myles announced, "I have a challenge for you."

"A challenge?" I echoed. "What do you mean?"

He waved his hand to the trees. "You're going to find us a safe camp for the night. You have been able to sense the portal since I pointed it out. I want you to work on strengthening your aura so next time you don't need me to say anything."

I frowned. "I don't know if I'm ready for that. If I mess up, we could get hurt."

"You're not going to mess up. All you need to do is trust your aura and find somewhere that's safe. I can sense everything within a five-mile radius; I won't let you take us somewhere dangerous."

My jaw dropped. "You can sense everything within five miles of us?"

"Everything that's letting me sense it, anyway." He shrugged. "I've had years of practice. That's why I want you to try; you need to expand your reach too."

"All right," I agreed. "I'll try."

He smiled. "You can do it."

I turned in a slow circle, trying to sense what was "good" and "bad" near us. At first, there was nothing. But as I focused, the presence of our surroundings began to feel as if they were tangible.

To our right, there seemed to be a faint bad aura, so I turned left. Before I began walking, I glanced at Myles.

He gave a slight nod, confirming I had been right about the bad feeling. I cautiously led us forward, and a presence of safety started to spread over me.

Myles stood a few yards behind, watching. When he saw my look for guidance, he wagged a finger. "Don't look at me. I'm not going to help you."

I turned back towards the feeling of safety and Myles followed from a short distance away. While my aura provided nothing more than a presence, it was as if the air around me was electrified with a world of its own. Magic. And as I focused on the magic and the guidance it carried, it was as if the puzzle pieces of the magical world slid into their assigned spots.

Myles continued to follow without offering his opinion, and it fast became apparent how much I had been relying on him. Did he feel this constant, intense focus all day, or was he so used to it that it didn't provide a strain?

As the shadows lengthened, my awareness of both good and bad didn't appear to be hampered. Instead, it provided the same steady presence as I stepped over what looked to be the corner of an old wall.

The wall was about a foot high and created a corner, full of moss and dried leaves. The sway and pull of the magical auras felt relatively neutral and I turned to Myles. "How's this?"

He stepped into the corner with a smile. "It's perfect."

My face lit up at his praise. "Really?"

"Really. You did better than I expected, actually. There weren't any strong safe pulls around, but you found one anyway. I think you're already stronger than you realize."

"I am?"

"Yeah, you're powerful. I can sense it."

"Oh." I furrowed my brow. "I hadn't thought of that. You can sense my aura, can't you?"

"That's how I found you."

I looked down at myself, envisioning what my aura must look like, or... *feel* like? My fingers tingled and I twitched them, looking back at Myles and attempting to focus on his aura instead. Strength seemed to flood over me in waves. Myles's aura was even stronger than the terrifying presence the mountain lion had brought with it. No wonder he had worked solo for so long, there likely weren't many opponents he couldn't handle.

Teleporting, shields, and lightning... He wasn't someone you would want on your bad side.

Myles watched me closely, his expression revealing that he knew I was uneasy. "You don't need to be scared of me," he promised. "Hurting you hasn't once crossed my mind."

My cheeks flushed. "No, I trust you." I hesitated. "I haven't felt your aura before, and I hadn't realized how strong you are."

He nodded. "Yeah, I knew you hadn't checked me. I could tell by the way you've been acting. You should always check; not every strong Mageye is a trustworthy person."

"I'm lucky you're here," I admitted. "You're better at this than me."

At that, he smiled. "I have years of practice on you. You'll get there."

While Myles cleared room for us to sleep, I took our waterskins to a nearby bubbling stream.

The faint auras on the opposite side filled me with a sense of security. We were safe. At least for tonight.

I stepped across the stream and when my foot touched down on the other side, the faint portal pull tugged at my gut. No longer waving me forward, it was ready to start reeling me in.

"Myles!"

Chapter 11

Lightning crackled and Myles appeared out of a purple orb. "What's wrong?" He looked around for my nonexistent attacker, lightning arcing from his fingers. "Are you okay?"

"The pull," I said, pointing in the direction it seemed to be urging me. "It's much stronger over here."

He relaxed, the purple sparks disappearing with his panic. "We're getting close."

"Then we can go now." I started to walk off, but he grabbed my arm to stop me.

"Wait, it's too far to go tonight. It is stronger because we crossed that imaginary border between the two radii I told you about."

My hopes plummeted. "What if something else uses it?"

"I doubt that will happen. And this one is so strong that even if something else does use it, it will likely stick around for a bit. I know you're excited, but we don't know where we'll pop out. It's better to go during the day when we can see."

The pull continued to tug at me, and I took a step forward.

Myles caught my arm again. "I know you want to keep going, but think of it this way. If we keep going day in and day out, we'll stand less and less of a chance. If you wear yourself to exhaustion, what help will you be when we find your family?"

"We could rest after the portal," I whispered, though I turned away from the pull. "Are you sure it won't go anywhere?"

"If I'm wrong, you can slap me," he said.

"Slap you?" I echoed. "Why would I slap you?"

His eyes flashed with purple sparks and he laughed. "You have three older brothers, are you telling me you've never slapped any of them?"

"That's different," I said, though I was fighting my own laughter now. "If the portal is gone, then you need to carry my bag and waterskin the rest of the journey."

"Deal." He wiggled his brows as he took the waterskins from me and stepped back over the stream.

I followed, and the pull faded back to the same weak tug we had felt all day. With it no longer urging me as insistently, some of my nerves faded. Nevertheless, I stared north until Myles urged me away.

"Tomorrow," he promised. "We'll find it tomorrow, Rose."

Tomorrow couldn't come soon enough.

The stars above me stubbornly refused to go away and I frowned at them. Despite the late hour, I was wide awake, anxiously awaiting the moment when Myles declared it time to pursue the portal.

The stream and the invisible border it created was tantalizingly close. If I strained my ears hard enough, I could hear the faint bubbling.

Myles's back was to me, and I couldn't tell if he was asleep or not. I lifted my head, looking towards the stream and then back at him. "Myles?" I whispered.

"Yeah?" he mumbled without moving.

I rolled onto my side to face him. "Why didn't you know how close we were until we crossed the stream? You said you could sense everything within five miles, but that was hardly twenty feet."

Leaves rustled as he rolled onto his back, bumping me a little in the tight space. "I can sense everything within a five-mile radius that lets me sense it. If the portal's pull strengthens on the opposite side of the stream, it strengthens on the opposite side of the stream. Even the strongest Mageye wouldn't be able to tell before crossing. That's the way the portal wants it to be."

I raised my brows, studying the air around him, where I imagined his aura must lay hidden from sight, but not senses. Surely, he must be one of the strongest Mageye, seeing as he had traveled solo across Alveraada for years now.

"I'm not the strongest," Myles said, staring at the stars.

"What?"

He rolled onto his side to face me, propping himself up on one elbow. "I'm not the strongest Mageye. Though I am one of the strongest *in* Mageye City. My godfather told me there are Mageye stronger than me outside of the city. I met one once and she told me she felt too powerful, and wanted a chance to feel normal in Alveraada."

My brow furrowed. "What do you mean?"

"Your question. I'm not the strongest."

"I never said anything."

"What?" He gave me a bewildered look. "I thought you were wondering if I'm... oh." His gaze locked on our legs, which were still lightly touching, and he moved his away. "We were touching."

Heat rushed to my cheeks and I inched back from him. "I'm sorry, I must have..." I stopped, my brow furrowed. "What does our bumping into each other have to do with you knowing my question?"

He grimaced and I shot upright before he could respond, declaring, "You can read minds!"

"Yeah." He sighed, sitting up. "I can read minds."

"And you read mine? That's why you knew my question even though I didn't say anything."

He grimaced, sheepishly rubbing his leg where we had touched. "Sorry. I don't like reading minds without permission, but when we touch, sometimes I can't help it. Especially since your aura is so strong. Physical touch and strong auras act as a conductor, and sometimes random thoughts pop in."

I raised my brows. Mindreading must be an incredible power, and that certainly explained why Myles's aura was so strong.

"Have you read my mind before?" I asked.

"I read your mind when we first met," he confessed. "I needed to ensure you had good intentions. As important as helping new Mageye find their way to Mageye City is, it is even more important to ensure I don't introduce anyone dangerous to the city. Auras can be misleading, and mindreading is often the only true way to confirm. But other than that, no. I try not to do it without permission."

When we first met? My eyes widened and I laughed. "When we were talking by that boulder, I was all relieved mindreading wasn't a thing. You heard that, didn't you?"

His lip twitched. "And when I told you we both knew your jackknife wasn't much against me, you were mad because only you knew you were lying about knowing how to wield it."

I pulled the knife from my pocket. "Well, I do know how to use it. I'm just not experienced."

"You know how to use it to chop," he teased. "Not to fight."

"I can stab with it in any grip," I argued, opening the blade and demonstrating a stab at the air. "See?"

He laughed and took my hand, carefully adjusting my grip. I swung again and faltered—it really was more powerful.

Myles started snickering and I glanced at him. "What?"

"Your thoughts."

"My thoughts?" I folded the jackknife and tucked it away. "Is it like a voice in your head?"

"Yes. Sometimes I think of it like reading, but that's more so when I am trying to delve further into someone's thoughts." He lay down and tucked his hands behind his head. "You know, you'd be surprised by the amount of people who get annoyed when they find out I've read their mind."

I slid the knife back in my pocket. "Why would I be annoyed? You were doing your job, and if you can't always control it, that's fine. Besides, I think that would be a fun power."

He shook his head. "Not really. It is useful, but not fun. It invades people's privacy. I wouldn't like it if people read my mind, so it doesn't seem right doing it to others outside of work."

Now he sounded like Raymond, and I smiled. "I get that."

"I used to use it for fun." He shrugged. "I guess I kind of realized how rude it was as I got older. But it has its advantages." After a beat, he added, "I'd be lying if I said I never use it for fun... but I try to be respectful."

I laughed. "Is your mindreading part of the reason why you have worked alone for so long? King Duncan probably doesn't need to worry about you getting mixed up with the wrong people."

He smiled softly. "That's exactly why. And like I said, I can also guarantee whoever I bring into Mageye City isn't a threat."

"What do you do if you find a Mageye who isn't trustworthy?"

His smile faded. "That depends."

I lay back down, careful not to bump him, and he chuckled. "I don't mind if you kick me in your sleep."

I turned my head. "So, now you are reading my mind for fun?"

"No," he said, rolling over so his back was to me again. "Maybe," he added.

"Well, don't kick me in your sleep," I whispered. "Ren used to do that in our forts. Raymond once tied his legs together to stop him."

"So, you do roughhouse with them," he mumbled.

My gaze drifted back to the stars. "Yeah, and I look forward to it again, when we save them."

Chapter 12

The first streaks of dawn lit up the sky when I opened my eyes, and I sighed in relief at the sight of the fading stars. Myles was still asleep, one arm draped over his eyes. I quietly shook stuck leaves and morning dew from my skirts, before packing our things to ensure we could leave as soon as possible.

Dawn had fully set in by the time Myles finally got up. He pulled his arm from his face and raised his brows when he saw me waiting with our stuff already packed. "Impatient much?"

I patted the bag closest to me. "The earlier we start, the better, right?"

He stood and stretched, grabbing his satchel. "You're right. Let's go."

"Right now?" I asked, surprised. "You haven't even been up for a minute."

He laughed. "I know. My dad finds it weird too, but once I'm up, I'm up. And I thought you were in a rush."

"Well yeah, but not if you aren't ready."

He waved away my concerns. "I'm ready."

We gathered the rest of our bags and the pull strengthened to an eager tug the second we stepped across the stream. "We keep following the pull?" I asked.

He nodded. "It will keep getting stronger until we reach it."

I shifted from foot to foot while Myles refilled his waterskin. The thick woods surrounding us hadn't changed much since I first entered them in Sunset Hollow, yet they *felt* different. It felt magical now, and as the pull continued to get stronger, that magical feeling increased too.

"What do portals look like?" I asked.

"They look like glowing orbs... maybe around the size of an orange until you open it," Myles said, kicking a pinecone aside. "Once it is open, it will grow tall enough to let us in."

"A glowing orb that... opens? How do we open a light?"

"Yeah," he laughed. "We open a light. You need to tell it where you want to go and it will let you inside. Sometimes people have trouble on their first try because the idea of walking into thin air throws them off. But even then, the portal will let them through. And they don't rely on confidence or knowledge to work. Technically a non-Mageye could go through one, but they would risk going into a coma. They wouldn't die, though."

"What?" I stopped walking. "Is that supposed to encourage me?"

"Well, yeah, kind of. You'll be able to go through."

"But *minor* side effects may include a coma?"

He burst out laughing. "We're Mageye, remember? No pesky side effects for us."

"Well, even if I did risk the side effects, it would be worth it to save my family." I eyed him. "Though, maybe you should go in first, since you're the expert."

By noon, the portal's pull was more like a rope tied around my waist, reeling me in like a fish on a rod. I turned to Myles questioningly, and he grinned, anticipating my question. "Feel like you're being pulled in? That's because the portal knows we need it."

"It does? How?"

"Magic has a mind of its own. It can probably sense your desperation for the portal and is responding to it. You caught its attention, and it's waiting for you."

"For me?" I asked. "But you're the one who noticed it first."

Myles shrugged. "Anyone can use a portal, and anyone can sense them. But only a powerful Mageye with the right intentions can call it."

"I *called* it?" I put a hand to my waist, where the center of the tugging seemed to be. "But I don't even know what I'm doing. How can I call something that I know hardly anything about?"

"You want the help of magic to save your family, not for anything selfish. Auras react to that, so does God."

I touched my fingers to my heart. "It's like you said about things being unexpected... I might not understand why auras are choosing me to respond to, but if it is good magic, then I think I can accept it."

He smiled. "You'll understand more as you experience more."

"I guess I will." The portal's pull continued strengthening and I paused as a tall pine tree seemed to peer through the trees. "There," I whispered, and Myles nodded.

The leaves on the bushes rustled as I pushed them aside and entered a small clearing. The pine tree towered above me, and floating about five feet into the air at its base was a small, yellowish-white glowing orb.

Myles pushed through the bushes after me and I turned to him. "Is that it?"

"Yes."

"Can you open it?" I asked.

He smiled and stepped up to the portal, gently cupping his palm underneath it. "Take us north towards The End. As close as you can take us."

The orb flickered, almost like it was blinking with understanding. Then it expanded until it was taller than both of us.

My eyes widened in awe. "Do we walk into it now?"

"Yes." He reached out his hand. "Here, I'll help you since it's your first time."

I took his hand, and together we stepped into the light. Instead of walking into the pine tree, we stepped onto the crystalline floor of a rainbow tunnel.

I gasped, sliding my hand from Myles's and admiring the interior of the portal. It was as if we stood inside the aurora borealis.

The walls of the tunnel reflected glowing images of biomes I had never dreamt of seeing. An ocean with glistening waves, a pine forest with trees as wide as houses, and a cabin in the midst of the woods surrounded by purple flowers.

I started to reach my hand towards the wall, then stopped, looking at Myles for permission.

"You can touch it, just don't go all of the way through," he said.

"Is it not solid?"

"Touch it, and you'll see."

I reached my hand out, and it went through the portal wall to my wrist. Like touching water, without getting wet. As we continued walking through the tunnel, I ran my hand along the wall. The colors danced at my touch, and more swirling images appeared.

Myles stopped at the end of the portal. Like the walls, it was made of a sparkling swirl of rainbows, reflecting the image of sand and scraggly trees.

"This is our stop," he said.

I nodded, mesmerized. "We just walk out?"

"And we will step out onto the sand."

Peace washed over me as I followed him out, like cuddling up by the fire with a book. The portal blinked a farewell before disappearing without a trace. A breeze swept past, bringing the salty smell of the ocean and the distant sound of screeching seagulls. Scraggly trees scattered about on sandy flats, and I turned slowly, taking in everything around us. "This looks nothing like where we were before... This looks nothing like anything I've ever *seen* before."

Myles looked around, nodding to himself. "I think I recognize this area. If I'm right, we just gained ourselves almost a week."

My jaw dropped. "A *week*? That means we traveled hundreds of miles in a matter of minutes."

"Magic has its advantages," Myles said with a smirk.

"At this rate, we will make it to The End in no time." I glanced at the sun and turned to the north. "I don't think we need to worry about them finding us on a northern trail anymore, do you?"

"I don't think so." Myles took another careful look around us, his aura washing over me as he searched for any danger. "Now we forge our own path north."

Chapter 13

Myles created sparks to light a fire and cook a fish he had caught for dinner. We had found a shallow cave with a front open to the sandy, boulder-strewn flats the portal had brought us to.

"Tomorrow," he began, "I want to teleport if you are comfortable with it. That will speed things up."

I hugged my knees to my chest, watching as he turned the fish in the fire. "How do you do it?"

In answer, he held up his hand and let purple sparks crackle before snapping his fingers. "You won't feel a thing. The lightning will surround us, and when it snaps, we will be in another place."

"How far can you go at a time?"

"I'll probably only take us a few miles the first time, and larger jumps once you are more used to it. Between my teleporting and any more portals we find, I think we can shave time off of this mission."

"*Only* a few miles?" I emphasized. "You say that like it isn't impressive."

He smiled. "It's second nature. My dad once threatened to handcuff me to himself if I didn't stop vanishing."

I giggled. "The sooner we get to The End, the better. I am more than comfortable with teleporting—no handcuffs needed."

He pulled the fish from the flames. "I thought you'd say that."

X

A bright light shone in my eyes and I squinted, gasping and sitting upright hurriedly. Had we overslept? Myles slept soundly beside me and I froze, turning back to the light that was not possibly from the sun, as it was *inside* the cave we slept in.

It resembled the orb of the portal, but this orb glowed orange, like fire, and carried an unnerving feeling with it.

"Myles?" I whispered, inching back from the glow and nudging his shoulder. "Myles?"

"What?" he mumbled, hiding his face in the crook of his arm.

The orb flickered and pulsed, its shape being replaced by a terrifyingly familiar X.

"Get up!" I shrieked, shaking him.

He shot upright, lightning crackling from his fingers. The X slowly faded into the night and I fumbled with my pockets, tugging out Ren's jackknife.

"What was that?" I demanded, dropping my voice. "Myles, are the Volcaniacs—"

"Shh!" He slapped his hand over my mouth and I froze, straining my ears for whatever he had heard.

A howl.

The howl seemed to carry forthcoming danger and Myles and I shared a wide-eyed look.

"The Wolvien Guard," he breathed, pulling back from me and frantically shoving our belongings back into our bags. Auras pulsed inside the small cave, but then Myles's presence seemed to disappear.

I grabbed his hand, my heart racing as another howl echoed through the night. "What do we do?"

"Run," he answered, tugging his hand from mine and shoving my satchel in its place. "Be quiet, if there is any chance that searchlight didn't fully tip off our location..."

"What if my family is nearby?" I asked, squeezing Ren's jackknife until my fingers hurt. "What if the wolves are with the trader, and—"

He slung his satchel over his shoulder, nudging me out of the cave with hurried movements. "The wolves hunt with only their pack. We need to run."

He jumped to his feet the second he was outside, silhouetted with the rising sun. Another howl seemed to electrocute my very being with fear, but while Myles flinched, I remained frozen in the mouth of the cave.

His aura still seemed to be missing, but the rest of the world was full of auras. None of which filled me with terror besides the sound of the howls. And none of them felt safe enough to be my family either.

I crawled the rest of the way out, still clutching the jackknife. "I can't sense them."

"Let's pray that means they can't sense us either," he said, grabbing my free hand and tugging me into a jog after him.

Every inch of his body appeared alert and I kept glancing over my shoulder at the fast-lightening woods with the coming dawn.

"Close the knife," Myles suddenly said.

"What?" I gasped. "But if we are being hunted..."

"Close it," he ordered, tone urgent. "We need to find a way to evade them and that way might be teleporting." He looked over his shoulder, scanning the trees nervously. "But then they'll know what I can do..."

A long-drawn-out howl made us both wince before going silent. Too silent. The click of Ren's jackknife shutting seemed to echo through the silence and I dropped it into my pocket.

Myles's fingers twitched and he turned back the way we had been going, growing stiff when the next howl was louder than any of the others.

"They found a portal," he whispered, grabbing my hand and pulling me close. "Run."

The sound of the ocean waves crashed in the distance, disrupted by the howls. Each one pumped more fear through my veins, as if the very sound was meant to serve as terror-filled poison.

Another long howl was interrupted by silence, and then pounding paws were behind us. I looked over my shoulder, and my heart practically stopped.

"*Myles?*"

Half-a-dozen members of the Wolvien Guard ran after us. Easily six-feet tall, they were covered in scars, their thick gray manes lifted with their hackles. Light reflected off of the pack leaders' bared fangs, drawing attention to its face and the X-shaped scar that lay where its left eye should have been.

"Keep running!" Myles shouted, tugging my hand.

His strides lengthened and my legs burned as I struggled to keep up and not be dragged. Ahead, the last of the scraggly trees disappeared, and what looked like open air greeted us.

"Trick them!" Myles wheezed, now practically dragging me towards the cliff. The wolves growled and snarled behind us and we skid to a halt near the edge. Huge waves crashed over the ragged boulders, dizzyingly below us.

My chest heaved and my throat burned too sharp to scream. The wolves had already covered half the distance between us, their howls deafening. "No..."

Myles tore his gaze from them. "You need to trust me."

"What?"

He pulled me to the very edge of the cliff. "When I say jump, jump."

"Jump? We'll die!"

He didn't respond, lightning flickering violently in his irises as he watched the wolves. They were now only fifteen yards away, the ground shaking beneath their pounding paws.

Ten yards.

"Myles? What are we going to do?"

Seven yards. I attempted to twist my hand from his grip, but he only tightened it until I nearly winced.

Five yards left; the wolves' eyes glowed like burning embers, alit with malice that sent a burning chill down my spine.

With three yards left, the pack leader launched itself into the air, and Myles whipped back towards the cliff.

"Jump!"

Chapter 14

For one still moment, we hung. Then we plummeted. My stomach dropped, and my skirts and hair with it.

A bloodcurdling scream escaped me as the bottom of the cliff neared. The water was too shallow, and I flailed my arms. We'd be crushed on the jagged rocks.

The wolves let out one more ferocious howl as the air crackled around us. Instead of landing at the bottom of the cliff, we were encased within a purple orb of lightning. The orb burst with an electric snap, and I crashed to the ground, tumbling head over heels onto grass.

I rolled onto my back, gasping. An oak tree towered above me, and grass tickled my neck. My chest heaved and I strained my neck up, blinking rapidly as the rest of the world returned to focus. The wolves, the cliff, the ocean waves and jagged rocks... gone. Birds now flitted past, and a squirrel climbed up a nearby tree, stopping to eat the nut it held.

"What happened?" I whispered, wincing at my own voice. It didn't seem right to be existing in these woods when moments before I had been about to die. Unless, maybe I *had* died, and this was Heaven.

Someone groaned, and Myles sat up slowly, holding a hand to his head as he grimaced.

"Myles!" I nearly fell over myself in my rush to get to him. The only part of the world that made sense, aura and all. He didn't appear nearly as panicked as I was, just tired. "Where are we?" I asked. "The wolves... did..." I leaned back, trembling. "Did we die?"

"No, we didn't die." Myles caught my shoulders. "I told you to trust me, remember? I got us out. We're alive and we're safe."

"But—"

"I teleported. Normally I'm a lot smoother, but that last howl threw me off. And I wanted to wait until the last second to try and trick them into thinking we died."

I sucked in my breath. "You mean we're safe?"

"For now. I moved us fifty miles away."

My racing heart began to slow and I looked around again. One second we were about to be crushed by rocks and the next second we were safely nestled in the grasp of a sprawling forest... fifty miles away.

No more howls. No more glowing X's. No more Wolvien Guard.

I peered closer at Myles. He was pale, and his grip on my shoulders slackened, breath growing shallow as if he were about to faint.

"Lay down." I put my hand on his chest and gently pushed. "Are you okay?"

He panted. "Yeah... Yeah, sorry. I need a minute." He shut his eyes and took a deep, shuddering breath. "That took a lot out of me."

I took his wrist and frowned; his pulse seemed weak, slowly gaining a little strength as he continued taking breaths to steady himself. Myles had told me before that overusing your power was dangerous, and his current state appeared to be evidence of that.

Our bags had made it with us, though our waterskins had burst open. I grabbed them. "I'm going to find some water for you. I'll be right back."

He covered his face in the crook of his elbow. "Stay close."

"I will." No more fear-inducing howls deterred me and to my relief, we had appeared close to a small pond, with clear water flowing into it through a rocky stream. I approached and eyed the bank of the stream nervously. No tracks, no howls, no bad auras. But there were blueberry bushes. With no basket, I stuffed my pockets with them, glad I had worn my apron on this journey. The sugar from the blueberries might help Myles recover from cool-down.

If that was indeed what was happening to him. I glanced around myself as I screwed the topper into the first waterskin. Since the Wolvien Guard belonged to the Volcaniacs, had we just witnessed a taste of the fear my family must currently be surrounded with? Fiery orange lights, fear-inducing howls, and no Myles to save them.

When I returned to the spot we had reappeared in, Myles sat with his back against a tall tree. Some of the color had returned to his face and he smiled weakly as I handed him a waterskin.

"Thanks." He drank as if water had been withheld from him. "That's much better."

While he had been drinking, I had found a kerchief to empty the blueberries onto and I motioned to them. "I got some blueberries."

He took some with a trembling hand. "Thank you."

I only nodded, and neither of us spoke for a few minutes. Myles ate a few handfuls of blueberries and leaned his head against the trunk of the tree. Most of the color had returned to his face and his ragged breathing had evened out.

"Are you all right?" I asked.

"Yes. I hit my cool-down hard, but I'll be fine once I've rested."

"So, you *are* in cool-down?"

"Yeah," he huffed.

I wrung my hands together. "Take your time."

He shut his eyes. "Thanks."

A bird sang happily from the tree we sat under, and I fidgeted with the hem of my dress. When I closed my eyes, it was as if I could see the glowing X again, and if I strained my ears, the breeze sounded like faint howls.

Myles nudged me with his boot. "What's bothering you?"

I looked up, surprised to see he had lifted his head. More color had returned to his tanned skin, and his chest rose and fell evenly.

My lower lip trembled. "Scared," I answered.

His expression softened. "Me too."

"If you hadn't teleported..."

"No, if you hadn't woken me," he corrected.

"What?"

He met my gaze. "The searchlight woke you up; all of that happened in less than an hour. If you hadn't woken me up the second you saw it, we might not have been able to react in time."

My breath caught and a pit seemed to form in my stomach. "I didn't," I whispered. "It was an orange orb first, and I got nervous. I started waking you, but I didn't really get you up until it looked like an X, and..."

He put his hand over my mouth, gentler than he had when he first heard the wolves. "That light was a searchlight; it is essentially a window into a different location. Kind of like the images on the sides of portals." He pulled his hand away. "That is likely how the wolves found us, but we evaded them. And the reason I had us jump off of the cliff was to hopefully trick them into thinking we died."

"But... then, who sent it?" I asked. "The trader?"

"The searchlight?" Concern etched across his expression and he shook his head. "I have a lot of questions about the trader and the Volcaniacs, and how they have handled this whole thing." His voice dropped. "It doesn't make sense that he didn't just follow you to the strawberry patch, but whatever his reason... Your family wouldn't be able to save you from the Volcaniacs, but *you* can save *them*."

I pulled out Ren's jackknife, tracing the *R* with a finger. "Will the wolves go back to The End now, you think? What if... what if they take out their frustration on my family?"

Myles's expression made me still my fidgeting. "What's wrong?" I asked.

He shook his head. "If the wolves have any doubts about us dying, they will continue the hunt."

I froze. "You mean... it could happen again? More searchlights? More all of it?"

"I'd like to think that the attention the two of us seem to be getting means they care more about you than your family." He met my gaze. "Whatever reason the trader had for letting you walk after him, he did make one correct assumption."

"What assumption?"

He followed the sun with his eyes, turning towards The End. "That holding your family hostage will ensure your arrival at The End. But what he clearly *didn't* consider was you coming of your own free will. He assumed you would follow the X's until you landed into whatever trap he set, but you didn't. They're sending the wolves because they're starting to realize they underestimated you."

"So, my family will be safe until we get there, because they know I'll stop at nothing to get them back?"

"That's my hope."

While it was clear his words were meant as encouragement, a seed of worry seemed to sprout in my gut. The last time anyone saw my family alive was before they were kidnapped, and while it appeared on the surface that the trader and the Volcaniacs had made some mistakes—kidnapping a girl by kidnapping someone completely different seemed backwards, after all—maybe it was because he was actually steps ahead of us.

Maybe the bait my family had become was the kind that didn't have beating hearts. The Volcaniacs clearly wanted me alive, so the wolves would have likely dragged me screaming to The End... to be greeted by family that was no longer with us.

Myles nudged me with his boot again, though he now looked much sleepier. "Give me a couple hours and then we will be hot on the trader's tail again, I promise."

I forced a smile. "You deserve the rest."

Chapter 15

Myles napped for several hours, but braced himself to stand when he awoke. Once he finished stretching, he turned to me. "I think I'm ready to go."

"Are you sure? We can wait longer if you need to."

He shook his head. "We've already waited longer than we should have. We have no way to verify the wolves fell for my trick, and I don't want to give them a chance to catch up."

I grimaced at the reminder. "It's like you said... they are occupied with us."

He forced a smile. "Let's keep them busy, then. The Wolvien Guard may contain the best hunters in Alveraada, but they have no way to track my jumps. From now on, let's try to give them trails that continually vanish."

"But maybe not today," I fretted, studying how his eyes seemed to droop with his fatigue. "The fifty miles you gave us is more than enough."

"I'm inclined to agree." He slung his satchel back over his shoulder and turned north. "But I can walk."

I slung my own satchel over my shoulder and followed. A bird flitted past, bringing an innocent aura with it. It was a gorgeous pure white, with golden flecks speckling its breast feathers. "That bird felt..." I stopped, searching for a word before settling on the only one that truly made sense. "Magic."

He smiled. "That's a Golden Dove. The gold flecks on its

stomach are made of real gold. Many people keep them as pets for their golden feathers, but others hunt them. I've always thought of them as magical friends."

"They're hunted for their beauty?"

"You could say that," he agreed, tapping his fingers to his thigh. "But Golden Doves have an extra layer of innocence about them, killing them taints your aura."

"Oh." The bird flit past again. "Does their gold do anything magical?"

Myles grinned. "If you get the gold while maintaining your innocence, it contains healing powers. It's rare to get healing gold from them, though. Even those who keep them as pets do it partially out of greed. You must be as innocent as the bird to gain from it."

I admired the glittering feathers as they caught the sunlight. With the help of a Golden Dove, could I extend my powers? I lifted my palm and studied my fingers, before curling them slowly into a fist. Maybe healing others was something I could look forward to one day, after I had my family back.

The dove cooed softly, vanishing into the trees, but a new aura took its place. An aura that I recognized. "A portal."

Myles nodded. "It's not as strong as the last one, but I'll take anything to put more distance between us and the Wolvien Guard."

"Me too," I agreed, taking the lead as we followed the faint pull. The gentle orb floated above a fallen tree which was partially suspended by its uppermost branches. It wasn't as bright as the portal we had taken the day before, but it looked just as welcoming.

Myles used the broken branches as handholds, and once he was stable, he reached down to help me up. We inched around the rest of the branches on the upper end of the tree, until we were under the portal.

Even slightly raised on his tiptoes, Myles's fingers barely

brushed the portal. I caught ahold of his arm to keep him steady as he directed it to take us north.

The portal blinked with understanding and grew. This time, the entrance floated in front of us and I frowned; we would have to step into open air.

"Won't we fall?" I asked.

"The portal will catch us," Myles assured me.

I eyed the bottom of the portal before nodding, and we stepped in together. Instead of falling to the ground, my foot touched down onto the portal's crystal floor.

The inside of this portal was just as beautiful as the previous one. I turned and admired the fallen log we had stood on, through the swirling colors of the portal's walls. Unlike the last portal, when I looked down the path, the end was already in sight.

"It's really short."

"Stronger portals are longer," Myles agreed. He waved his hand through the image we had walked through, and it swirled together before revealing a trickling river in its place. "No wolves."

"No wolves," I echoed in relief, following him to the portal exit. Peace flooded through me as I passed through the magical wall, and out into the middle of an open field with no end in sight. The prairie grass stood about a foot tall and swayed in the light breeze that swept through the open grasslands.

Myles flexed his fingers as he scanned the open field.

"What's wrong?" I asked.

"I don't like being in the open; there's nowhere to hide." He looked behind us, shaking his head. "We'll make a camp once we find cover."

Everywhere we looked were more flat grasses, not a single tree or bush in sight. This was exactly the kind of field my brothers used to race across, and a wolf could certainly run faster than they ever could.

After several miles of nothing but grass, a few trees started appearing, but not enough to settle under.

"We should be nearing the end of the field," Myles mumbled. "It can't go on forever."

"I hope so," I said, putting a hand to my eyes and peering ahead of us. The flat fields appeared endless, but surely they would end eventually.

We ate while we walked, finishing the leftover fish Myles had carefully packed last night, and some hazelnuts we had loaded my satchel with the other morning.

Night fell, and the air was soon full of flickering fireflies. They lit up the grasses in gentle flashes, almost seeming to encourage us to forge onwards, and finally, the dark outline of trees appeared in the distance.

It looked like we had another mile to go, but it was hard to estimate through the dark. My feet dragged by the time we reached their cover. Myles, however, seemed to be stumbling over his feet, half-asleep even while he stood.

"Myles." I caught his arm. "You need to rest. Wait here, and I'll find us a spot to make a camp."

He shook his head. "No, we're too close to the edge of the forest."

His words slurred with his fatigue and I crossed my arms. "No," I decided. "You're going to wait here, and I'll come get you when I find a good spot."

"I'm fine, really," he insisted, but then he swayed, disproving any argument he may have.

"No. You're not fine. Now sit," I said, pointing at the nearest tree.

He stared at the tree and his shoulders slumped with defeat. "I don't want you wandering in the dark without me."

"Wandering is aimless, searching for a camp with the help of my aura isn't."

"All right," he agreed, lowering himself. "Fine."

I waited for him to get settled, ensuring he wasn't going to get up as soon as I turned my back.

The forest itself seemed relatively neutral, yet I couldn't shake a feeling of faint unease. After a few minutes of careful searching with my aura, I paused by a fallen tree, running my hand along its rough bark. This would offer us some protection and the bushes surrounding it would keep us hidden.

When I returned to where I had left Myles, he was asleep. I stood above him and hesitated. The teleporting had obviously taken more out of him than he had been letting on.

I looked back towards the log I had found before sitting by him. There was a faint presence of mild danger coming from the field, but that didn't mean he couldn't rest. I could stay up as a guard until the bad aura left and it was safe enough to sleep.

Crickets chirped, and branches would occasionally crack, or leaves would rustle as some small animal skittered past. As I sat watch, my mind inevitably wandered to my family.

Were they okay? The question that was impossible for me to have a clue about the answer of.

Raymond was probably acting strong, if they were together. Soon before Dad died, he had told Raymond he would be the man of the house when he was gone, and that he needed to protect us. Raymond had never hesitated to take on that role in addition to being our older brother.

I was grateful to him for it, but he showed signs of being more stressed than he often pretended to be.

Ren and Ryder refused to let Raymond protect them, and instead they also hovered over me. Ryder with his gentle nature and calming presence, and Ren with his ability to make even scary situations seem as if they would work out. Once, the three of us had gotten lost while exploring. I had started crying, thinking we were lost forever, but Ren had taken my hand and told me I was most definitely wrong and he was going to prove it. Ryder had agreed, and together, they had gotten us out of the woods.

And Mom, a firm believer that your attitude could change everything, for better or for worse. She was everyone's mother;

little kids would run up to her at the market, whether they knew her or not, and she always found time to talk to them. But above all else, she was *my* mom, Raymond's mom, Ren and Ryder's mom. Regardless of her own terror at whatever situation they were currently facing, she would force a smile, if only to grant my brothers the illusion they were safe.

My eyes filled with tears, and I let out a choking sob. They *weren't* safe. For all I knew, they weren't even alive anymore and this whole journey would prove fruitless. A cruel trap set by the trader to kidnap me for my aura and rid the world of my *family*.

After the first sob came another, and soon I had lost control. I buried my face in my knees, the sobs taking over.

What would I do if they weren't alive? There was no way I could return to Sunset Hollow without them. I had run away, after all, and how could I possibly face General Jacobs empty-handed? I could go back to Mageye City with Myles, but then what? I would be all alone. I had no one there either.

Or, maybe my family *was* alive, but they had been kidnapped by a man who wielded magic that could turn our house to ash at a speed that should have been impossible. Regardless of anything else, they most definitely weren't safe, and the chances of them being quote "okay" diminished more the longer this trip to The End dragged on.

A gentle hand touched my back, and I flinched, looking up in surprise. Myles was awake. Lightning flickered in his eyes, showing his worry.

"We'll figure it out," he said softly. "We'll save them, I promise. We're going to save them."

I took a shaky breath, wiping my eyes with the back of my hand, in an attempt to hide the obvious fact that I had been crying. "I'm fine."

"No, you're not," he corrected gently. "Your pain woke me up." He stared ahead, respecting my shyness. "You're allowed to be scared, you know. You've been so brave this whole time, but you can't always be like that."

I sniffed. "How do you know they'll be okay?"

"Because I'm not going to accept anything other than that. I'll just say no thanks and take the outcome I want."

I smiled a little through my tears. "I like that idea."

He smiled back. "I know."

I shoved him gently. "You read my mind, didn't you?"

"How else would I have known what you needed to hear to cheer you up?"

"I thought you said you never read minds without permission," I countered.

"No, I said I only read them when I have to."

My breath caught and I nodded, whispering, "Thank you."

He touched my arm. "Every second that passes is a second closer to us saving them. Don't let the fear eat away at you." He leaned closer. "If your mom and brothers are known for faking it till they make it, I will be sorely disappointed to learn you are the only one in the family without that skill."

Myles must have heard more of my thoughts than I realized, yet his words stuck to my heart. "They'd be disappointed too," I whispered. "I'm not going to let that happen."

He smiled and sat back, waiting for me to calm down. I wiped away the last of my tears and pulled out Ren's jackknife, tracing the *R* with my finger.

God, please help them stay strong... Please help us save them...

Myles finally broke the silence, sounding confused. "We're still in the same spot?"

"I found a better spot over there," I said, pointing towards it. "But when I got back, you were already asleep, and I felt bad waking you. Since we didn't want to make our camp so close to the prairie, I decided to wait up."

His eyes widened. "You mean you haven't slept? How long has it been?"

I fidgeted with the jackknife. "A few hours, I think."

"You let me sleep for hours while you stayed up, even though you were exhausted too?"

"You needed the sleep more than I did."

"You didn't need to do that." Even in the dark, I could see the flush in his cheeks. "You should have woken me."

I shook my head. "No, it's okay. You over-pushed yourself, didn't you?"

He sighed. "Yeah, I did. Normally my max is about fifty miles, but that's when I'm by myself. With two people, it's harder."

"So, you used double your max?"

"Not quite. Taking a second person with me isn't as much work as you'd think. But I feel better now, really." He stood. "Let's find a safer spot for the rest of the night."

Chapter 16

The next three days passed without any hint of bad auras. Myles had returned to his full strength the morning after we escaped from the Wolvien Guard, and he hadn't needed to use his powers defensively since. Though, we had intermixed our walking with teleporting a few times a day to ensure no trail was left for the Wolvien Guard. And besides a thunderstorm in which we had huddled together under the best cover we had found, we hadn't run into any issues magic or otherwise.

The portal we stood in front of now was duller than the other two, but I would take any form of magical help we could get.

"Take us north," Myles directed it.

Like the second one we had gone through, this one was short, but it was as beautiful as the first. I trailed my hand through the walls and Myles waited for me at the end. I started to pull my hand out, but paused, staring at a barren and rocky land. Surrounded by gray stone, the flame-like pattern on the canvas top of the cart riding down it almost seemed to have a magnified glow. "That's the trader that took my family," I said, my tone emotionless.

"What?" Myles asked.

"That's the trader..." I trailed off, staring at the cart as it rolled over the rocky terrain. "He kidnapped my family!" I ripped Ren's jackknife from my pocket, practically hurling myself at the portal wall. "We can force him to tell us what he did to them and help us break into The End."

Myles caught me before my head could pass through, tugging me back into the portal. "Wait!"

"What are you doing? Let go," I demanded, kicking my legs. "That is *the* trader. We need to intercept him. This is our chance."

"No." He watched the cart in concern, his gaze darting over the details of the reflection.

"Let go of me, Myles!" I shouted, tears blurring my vision. "What if he still has them? What if The End was a lie this whole time—"

"He's heading south," Myles said.

I stilled, my chest heaving. "South?"

"Yes..." He loosened his grip, stepping closer to the reflection but being careful not to pass through the wall. "And there isn't room for doubt that he took them to The End. Between the X's, the mountain lion, the Wolvien Guard..."

"But..." I shook my head. "But what if he has information?" I stepped forward again. "Even if he doesn't have them anymore, we can still question him!"

He caught my arm again and I attempted to pry him off, watching as the cart rolled away from us. "Let go of me. We need to at least *try*."

"*Rose.*" He stepped between me and the portal image. "He burnt your house to the ground. He left the trail of X's. A mountain lion tried to kill us, and now the Wolvien Guard is *hunting* us. Your family *has* to be at The End, and trying to talk to that trader is too dangerous. The teleportation crystal is alarming enough, and we don't know what other magical weapons he has."

"But..."

"I'm sorry." He released my arm, and we watched as the cart drove out of sight.

"Why is his having a teleportation crystal such a big deal?" I demanded. "I know they are rare, but why is that so upsetting to you?"

"Because normal people can't find teleportation crystals."

We let him get away because he wasn't supposed to have found a rock? I leaned over to peer at the empty plain in vain. "What do you mean?"

Myles took a deep breath. "Non-Mageye can have their eyes 'opened' to the magical world. Once they are introduced, they can see, interact with, and use magical objects. But teleportation crystals? Only a Mageye can find and collect them. No normal human, eyes open or not, can *find* them, only be given one. And to make things even more complex, even the most powerful Mageye could spend years searching for teleportation crystals without finding one. I think the Volcaniacs may be even more powerful than we feared." He ran a hand through his hair. "We've suspected it, how else can we explain the auras radiating from The End and the Wolvien Guard? But it has yet to be confirmed formally."

He stared at the rocky landscape through the side of the portal. "We aren't moving fast enough."

My blood chilled. "But we're already going as fast as we can."

"No, we're not." He turned to the portal exit. "We can go faster."

Chapter 17

Myles led the way out of the portal, and for the first time, the sense of peace washing over me provided no comfort.

The portal winked goodbye and left us alone in a sprawling forest. Birds chirped in the trees, but despite the surrounding auras being peaceful, every fiber of my being screamed with desperation.

"How can we go faster?" I asked, pacing.

"We teleport." He turned his gaze north. "As far as I can take us."

I stopped, turning back to him. "What? No, you'll get hurt."

He squared his jaw, shaking his head. "We have no choice."

No choice? His eyes seemed to spark, multiplying both his fearful look and my terror.

"You know more than you're telling me," I accused nervously.

"No, I don't. But I was raised to fear them and now I think those fears weren't strong enough." His expression darkened. "I remember when the Elite Guard first confirmed the location of The End." He paused, adding, "General Cornstone said he thinks they're the rebels who branched off..."

"Branched off of what?" I asked, watching a turkey strut through the trees across from us.

He shook his head. "If the rumors are correct, the Volcaniacs have been building themselves since before we were both born. For them to go from being detectable a few years ago, to unleashing the Wolvien Guard, to now kidnapping Mageye, they are much stronger than anyone has theorized."

"But, if they're stronger than we think..." I stopped, following the sun with my gaze. "You said that everything has an aura, right? Some stronger than others?"

"Yes," he confirmed, tapping his fingers against his leg. "Part of the reason you and Ren felt uneasy when you first met the trader was likely because of his aura."

"Is my family in more danger being held by Mageye than they would be by non-Mageye?" I whispered, blinking back fresh tears.

He looked pained. "A lot more."

I sucked in my breath, my voice trembling. "So, you're right. We need to go faster; we need to teleport. But what if you get sick?"

"I won't. Being scared of my teleporting would be like if you panicked every time you scraped your knee. Our powers are meant to be used."

"But..."

"We've been teleporting the last few days, haven't we? I'm only suggesting we teleport more often with farther distances. This is the best and quickest way for us to save your family." He reached out his hand and I hesitated.

"Are you sure?"

He nodded and I took a deep breath, wiped away my tears, and grabbed his hand. The air around us crackled and a purple orb formed, causing us to disappear with an electric snap.

We reappeared standing on a rocky cliff, and I studied his face for any sign of fatigue. "Are you all right?"

A breeze blew some of his hair around his eyes and he nodded. "You got a very rocky introduction to my power. Usually, teleporting doesn't take any energy out of me." He outstretched his hand again. "Let's do another."

"Already?"

"It's second nature. Think of it like running, you don't get overly exhausted until you've run for a few miles. After this jump, we will walk before the next."

I took his hand and we disappeared again. This time, we appeared in the midst of dozens of fallen trees. Myles stepped over the first one and I followed, my gaze hardly leaving the northern horizon.

"I'm coming," I whispered under my breath. "I'm coming... just hold on for a little longer."

"Rose, get up," Myles's voice pitched with his urgency as he shook me awake.

I bolted upright. "What? What's wrong?" It was pitch black out, and I could hardly see him leaning over me. The moon was nowhere to be seen, cloaking us in darkness.

We had teleported five more times this afternoon and stopped for the day after nightfall.

Myles scrambled through our makeshift camp, grabbing my satchel and shoving it at me. "Take this."

I snatched it from him, moving to my knees. "What's wrong?"

My response was a distant howl that seemed to electrify my spine with fear. I grabbed Myles's arm, trembling. "The Wolvien Guard?" I asked, my voice pitched.

He snagged his satchel and pulled me closer. A purple orb formed around us and we teleported.

We pulled apart when we reappeared in the middle of a dark forest. "Stay calm," he soothed, touching my arm before standing. His aura pulsed with his anxiety but he nodded to himself, whispering under his breath. "That put some distance..."

"Myles, if they were in howling distance before you teleported, then they probably sensed us, didn't they?" I asked. "How far is their reach?"

His eyes seemed to glow with lightning and he looked back, presumably the way we had come. "I don't know, and I don't want to find out. I moved us about three miles ahead, but we should keep moving. If we hear them again, we'll know they're actively following us. But they shouldn't be able to track my jumps, so they won't know where we went."

"I'm going to stay close to you," I decided, peering nervously into the dark woods. "So, you can grab me if we need to teleport."

"If it's any comfort," he said as we hurried through the dark woods. "I can teleport without holding onto you. But I'd prefer if you stayed close."

I stumbled, grabbing his arm for balance. He caught me and pulled me closer without a word.

"Thanks," I whispered, and he nodded, glancing around us as we walked.

Neither of us spoke as we continued through the woods, straining to listen for even the faintest howl.

An owl hooted and I jumped, looking at the branches above us. It hooted again and I relaxed; a hoot was better than a howl.

"I want to teleport us to the northwest," Myles said. "That will make my jumps even more unpredictable."

I held a hand out. "I like that idea."

He took my hand and a soft crackling filled the night as he formed a purple orb and snapped it.

We now stood in a pine forest so dark we seemed to be lost in an inky blackness. Myles cautiously pulled his hand away, his aura already searching for any sign of the wolves.

"Are you all right?" he asked. "I'd like to keep going for a bit longer."

I strained my ears for any sign of a howl and nodded. "I'm okay."

"Good." He turned back to the north and led the way onward, with me directly behind him, using his outline as a guide. Unseen roots and stones kept tripping us, but lighting a branch to use as a torch was too risky.

Myles reached back and pulled me closer, his touch a

comfort. "They once appeared nearby when I was alone. It's better having someone with you... though you probably don't enjoy being the person I'm with."

I took his hand. "I wouldn't pick anyone else... and not just because you can teleport."

He laughed softly. "We can be friends outside of our powers."

Friends... "Yes," I agreed, my heart rate finally starting to slow. "I agree."

After another hour without hearing the wolves, we found a safe spot by a stream. Myles dropped his satchel down. "Get some sleep. I'll keep watch."

I slung my satchel off my shoulder. "But you need sleep, too. And you teleported a lot today."

"Well, I owe you from when you kept watch the other night."

"You don't owe me for that," I argued, adding, "but thank you."

"You're welcome. I'll wake you if I hear anything else."

I shuddered, using my satchel as a lumpy pillow. "Two times in one night would be unfair."

He laughed, sitting by me. "Agreed." He waved his hand towards the sky. "God, I know I can't exactly make the rules... but it would be appreciated if we don't see the wolves again."

"Much appreciated," I echoed. "Amen."

"Amen," he murmured.

Chapter 18

When I awoke, Myles sat on a boulder, his back to me. "Good morning," I greeted as I walked up behind him.

He jumped, relaxing when he saw me. "Good morning."

I rested my hand on the boulder he sat on. "Thanks for keeping watch."

He nodded and stood, showing me a pile of mushrooms that lay beside him. "Ever tried these?"

I wrinkled my nose. "My mom always told us not to eat mushrooms."

"Probably because half of them are poisonous." He picked one up and passed it to me. "These ones aren't. I think we should try and stock up on more food today. Preferably something besides mushrooms and berries... but we might have to make due as we get closer to The End. Less time to spend in one spot hunting."

"I could go for a chocolate cake," I said. "What are our chances of finding one out here?"

He laughed, picking up the rest of the mushrooms. "I'd love a nice steak. And a baked potato, loaded with butter."

"How do you usually get food on missions?" I asked. "The same as we are doing?"

"Between towns. I actually bought rolls stuffed with smoked meat in Sunset Hollow. But they were in my stomach before we met up."

"We will get a good meal as a reward once we have my family back. Though, I could eat grass and twigs all my life if that was the trade needed to have them be safe."

He smiled. "I'd do that for my dad, too."

As we continued through the pine forest, birds chirped and squirrels chattered as we passed. But after a while, the birdsong quieted, then seemed to shut off entirely.

"Myles?" I asked cautiously. "Why is it so quiet?"

He stopped walking and frowned. "I was wondering the same thing."

I couldn't sense a bad aura; it was more of a still one. An empty one. Then it started fading until there was nothing left, leaving us standing in a world that seemed devoid of... everything?

The colors began to fade next; the deep green of the pine needles fading to a dark gray, and the sun shone in a muted gray sky.

I blinked a few times, rubbing my eyes before looking at the muted trees in disbelief. It was as if we stood in a photograph, a photograph that moved and reeked of danger despite the very air now feeling... silent?

Lightning sparked from Myles's fingers. "I don't like this." He reached out his hand, and I took it. The air started to crackle with purple lightning, but it abruptly flickered out as Myles slumped to the ground with a groan.

"Myles!" I stepped forward, but froze when a deep voice spoke behind me.

"Don't touch him."

I whipped around, reaching into my pocket and clutching my jackknife as I faced a man covered in shadows. He was tall and broad-shouldered; a dark collar rose from his coat and hid his face, and from a distance, it looked like everything about him was gray, including his skin.

My heart pounded in my chest as we stared at each other.

My hand still clutched the knife hidden in my pocket, and I looked back at Myles. He was perfectly limp, and even his aura had faded away. The only assurance he was alive was his breathing.

The man stepped closer, his dark cloak billowing around him. "You are much farther north than you should be." With each step he took, the gray landscape grew paler.

I stared, trembling as I took a small step closer to Myles. "We're just passing through—"

"Just passing through?" he interrupted in that same monotone voice. "Do you think I'm thick? You and your friend are traveling north, to a location you have no business walking into freely."

His dull eyes seemed to stare through my soul as he approached, and a chill went up my spine. I had been right when I first noticed his skin was gray. Even his eyes were a lifeless color, and he lacked pupils. It was as if he was missing what made him human.

A soul.

As he continued towards me, I began pulling the knife from my pocket, but his gaze caught the movement and my fingers suddenly went too numb to move. "You bring human weapons to a battle of powers?" he asked flatly as he brushed past me.

My breath caught; he must have sensed our auras and realized that we were Mageye.

He kicked Myles with the toe of his boot. "He's strong. Feeding off of him is pleasurable. I'd sap some of your strength too, but I can't carry you both." The numbness in my arm suddenly faded but I resisted the urge to grab the knife quite yet. "You will walk."

He was *feeding* on Myles? My gaze darted around the gray forest, terror shooting through me as the man picked Myles up, easily throwing him over his shoulder. Even Myles's clothes and skin were now gray, and so was I.

"Follow me," the man directed. "If you try anything, I will

hurt your friend."

I looked at Myles's limp body and then back at the gray Mageye. As long as he had a hold of Myles, I could do nothing. I slowly pulled my hand from my pocket, showing him that I held no weapon.

He was right that I had only standard weapons against his power to... to what? Make people pass out? Turn things gray?

Myles's power had several aspects to it, but they all seemed to center around his purple lightning. What power centered around the hold this man had on the forest, Myles's consciousness, and the color and numbness of my skin?

He turned to go, but my feet remained planted in place. If I could distract him...

"You're a Mageye," I stated.

He stared at me blankly. "It shouldn't matter to you whether or not I am a Mageye."

"Um... What do you do? You caused him to faint?"

The first expression I got from him was a smile, and I fast wished he had remained expressionless. "He didn't faint; I took his consciousness from him. I can take away color, emotion, life."

"*Life?*" I put my hand to my heart, counting its racing beats.

"Follow me," he said, ignoring my question.

With no other choice, I followed him through the woods. Myles's arms hung limply down the man's back and I resisted the urge to grab his hand.

The forest grew dimmer the longer we walked, and the already gray trees got darker, duller, more lifeless.

"What are you going to do with us?" I asked nervously.

"Help someone achieve their goal." His gaze cut to me. "You walked right into it."

I bit my lip hard to stop from whimpering. What was I supposed to do? Attacking this man when he had the ability to rip me of my consciousness seemed unwise, yet, would he not just take away my consciousness when we arrived to wherever he was taking us?

"Please, sir, let us go. We aren't here to cause you any harm."

"On the contrary, your arrival will earn me a significant reward."

"No..." I looked around again. Talking wasn't working; I needed another way to distract him.

Not a single bird sang in the dull trees, leaving the forest eerily quiet. And with everything merging into gray, it made it difficult to search for any form of help. No matter how far I strained my eyes, everything was... muted.

The sky, the grass, the trees, our skin... everything. The Mageye marched forward, his cloak billowing out around Myles's limp form, but a slow hope kindled in my chest.

This Mageye must be using a lot of energy if he was drawing out all color and auras from our surroundings at once. Maybe instead of distracting him, I could force him into cool-down? If I did that, he would lose whatever hold he had on Myles and we could teleport to safety.

Yet, Myles said both we and our powers knew our limits. The man was draining color from everything he saw and he had referenced that "feeding" on Myles felt good, so I had to find a way to force him beyond what he considered a pleasant feeling.

The trees dispersed around us and we stepped onto a rocky cliff. The man threw Myles's limp body down with a thud and turned to me.

"Who are you working for?"

I took a small step back. "We... we aren't working for anyone, sir."

His expression didn't change. "You are a clueless Mageye who has somehow managed to wander nearly to The End with a singular companion. That should have been impossible."

I looked north, my heart racing. Nearly to The End? "We really aren't working for anyone. We're working on our own. But maybe you can help us?" Remembering the money that I had taken from Pastor Wilson's house, I pulled it out. "We have money."

"Help you?" He laughed. It was husky, as if he didn't use it often. "No, I don't care how much money you have; it makes no difference. The reward I have set aside is far greater."

I bit my lip. The way he was talking, it sounded like there were other people... other Mageye around. And this clearing offered nothing to urge him into cool-down. I needed more time.

"Why is everything gray?"

He glared. "I don't like color. Your dress, for example, an eyesore really."

I looked at my blue dress, freezing when a glimpse of something besides gray poked out from deep within my pocket. Ren's jackknife. And the blood inside my veins wouldn't be gray either. With my ability to heal, I could lose a lot of blood, maybe even enough to force him into cool-down to maintain his love of gray. He had made my arm go numb before, but if I was quick enough... I plunged my hand into my pocket and yanked the knife out.

Before I could flick open the blade, he grabbed Myles and put a dagger to his throat, causing me to freeze. Ren's jackknife faded to gray and the man met my gaze. "One false move, and you'll watch your friend bleed to death. Not in color, of course, but it will be just as grisly in gray."

I dropped the knife to the ground; Myles would bleed to death much more quickly than I would. Yet, my theory he would have to turn the blood gray was correct, so how was I meant to get myself to bleed enough to force him into cool-down?

He let Myles drop back down and motioned for me to come to the cliff. "I've had enough of this. The sooner I send you, the better."

My throat felt suddenly very dry. "Please don't do this. We'll leave you alone."

He shook his head. "You ruined my peace the minute your disobedience sent me to this blasted hut."

"Ple—" My voice cut off as if it had been stolen. My hands went to my throat, and I tried again to speak, but no sound came out.

"I've had enough of your questions and enough of this wretched place. Come here."

I walked on trembling legs towards him, but paused beside Myles. He was completely limp, past the normal stage of sleep. His consciousness was simply gone.

Tears flooded my eyes as I knelt and slid my hand under his shirt. Upon feeling his warm skin, I squeezed his shoulder as hard as I could. The Mageye had taken my voice, not my thoughts.

Myles, I thought. *Myles, wake up. I need you. Myles, help. Help. Help. Help.*

The man interrupted me. "Get up." I slowly stood, my fingers slipping from Myles's bare skin.

He watched silently as I approached, still gripping the dagger he had threatened Myles with. Maybe he wasn't going to push me.

When I got within arm's reach, he grabbed me, and my head swam with dizziness as he held me over the drop, the heels of my boots barely on the rocky edge. He *was* going to push me.

The steep cliff went down for several hundred yards. Even the bottom of the cliff was gray, except for one part directly below us that almost appeared to be glowing, kind of like a portal. Maybe he was pushing his power to its limit?

But even if he was, what could I do about that?

Myles! Help me! I tried to send my aura out to him, but it was no use. I couldn't sense his aura, which meant that even if he was conscious, he probably couldn't sense me either.

I twisted to face the man, shaking when his dagger caught my eye. He still held it towards me but made no move to use it, his pupilless gray gaze sending shivers down my spine.

If he wasn't going to stab me with his free will, then maybe I could stab myself.

As his grip loosened from my arm, I planted my feet on the edge of the cliff. Breaking free from his grip, I let myself fall; but away from the drop. In his surprise, he moved the dagger, and it hit me square in the gut. The blade sank in deeply, and he yanked it back, cursing as my legs gave out from under me. I crumpled to my knees, trying to scream, but no sound came out.

Pain shot through my body, and my hands clutched against the wound. Warm blood gushed from between my fingers, and it quickly turned gray.

"Stupid girl," he snapped.

The pain was unlike any pain I had ever experienced, and as the blood continued to gush out, my heart sank. Why wasn't I healing?

While the entire world had been muted of sound and color, not one ounce of my pain dulled and I silently gasped for breath, pushing against the wound. Had I, in my effort to force this man into cool-down, forced myself into it instead?

"I can still send you injured," he decided.

I whimpered as he finally granted me my voice back. Or maybe he was starting to lose his grip. Maybe he was nearing cool-down. But that didn't matter. There was nothing I could do to stop him anymore.

I only had one chance left. *Myles*, I thought weakly as I screwed my eyes tightly shut, hot tears squeezing out as I helplessly awaited the stomach-dropping feeling of freefall.

"Stop!"

I slowly turned my head. Myles attempted to pull himself up, but his legs remained limp behind him. His gray face contorted with pure hatred as he stared at the Mageye who, for the first time, appeared mildly amused. Myles reached out with one of his hands, and it started to shake as he fought to send out a bolt of lightning.

"Come. On." Myles groaned through gritted teeth. His fingers curled and shook with the effort. Finally, a blast of gray lightning shot from his hand.

It hit the man square in the chest, and he blasted backward, shouting as he disappeared over the side of the cliff.

Chapter 19

"Rose!" Myles staggered to his feet and stumbled to my side, his purple eyes filled with horror.

My grip on my wound faltered as my gaze locked on the purple in his irises. The gray was gone. The trees around us were a lively green, and the blue sky behind Myles's brown hair was as bright as ever.

He appeared fully awake, the exhaustion he had been fighting off only moments before, completely gone. The sound of leaves rustling and birdsong had returned to the cliffside.

The Mageye's hold must have broken when he fell off of the cliff... when he died.

But not one ounce of my pain had gone away. When Myles saw the deep red wound, he gasped and pressed his hands on my stomach, causing me to scream.

"It's not healing? Why isn't it healing?" He trembled, and when he adjusted his hands, they were stained crimson.

My panicked gasps slowed and my muscles slowly slackened. The world began to lose color again, but this time it had nothing to do with the man's powers.

"Rose, no!" Myles shouted, leaning over my stomach to apply more pressure to the wound. "Don't close your eyes. Please... don't die on me. You need to heal! Heal!"

His lips continued to move, begging me not to close my eyes, but his voice came to me muted, as if he stood at the far-away entrance to a cave.

"Rose," he pleaded, fumbling with my skirts to try and get a better look at the wound.

I could only watch as he stripped his vest off and pushed it against my stomach. The dull colors of the world seemed to slowly regain their vibrance and I took a deeper breath. The blood on Myles's hands started to disappear, and he faltered, staring at his clean, trembling hands. "Is your power taking over?"

His voice shook and I sobbed, weakly twitching my fingers. He took my hand, stroking it gently with his thumb as his tear-filled eyes watched my wound heal.

I weakly squeezed his hand to distract myself from the pain, and he squeezed back, his lightning-filled gaze meeting mine.

"You're going to be okay," he whispered. "I'm right here. You're safe now."

Another couple of minutes passed, and the last of the wound finally sealed up.

I took a shaky breath of relief, weakly pushing my skirts down. Myles helped me with trembling hands, sparks of lightning flickering in his purple irises.

"Are you okay?" he asked.

"I-I think so. I thought I was going to die." I glanced at where the cliff dropped into open air and nearly burst into tears. "Myles!"

He helped me sit up. "Shh, he's gone, and you're healed. We're safe."

I leaned into his chest, the steady beating of his heart helping to calm my panicked one. "Safe," I whispered.

He awkwardly pulled me closer, stroking my hair gently. "Safe," he agreed.

I wrapped my arms around him, hiding my face in his shoulder. "I didn't know what to do. You... you fainted, and... and he threatened you, and had a dagger to your throat, and I... I couldn't let you *die!*"

"I'm not dead," he whispered. "And I have no plans to do so

anytime soon."

His heart indeed beat in his chest and I sniffed. "G-good." A few final tears slipped down my cheeks and I sat up. His cheeks were flushed and heat rose in my own face—I had just soaked Myles with my tears and had him cradle me in his arms. "S-sorry."

"For needing a hug after what just happened?" He didn't look upset or embarrassed, and I relaxed. The flush in his face wasn't because of the hug. Instead, his gaze flicked to the tear in my dress. "You're fully healed, right?"

I looked at the tear and adjusted my apron to cover it. There was no way for me to sew it back together out here.

"Yes," I confirmed, experimentally pressing my fingers above where the wound had been. Next, I leaned over and took his wrist, feeling his pulse. "What about you? Are you okay?"

"I think so." His brow furrowed. "When I woke up, I couldn't move..." He looked around the cliffside. "What happened? The last thing I remember was everything turning gray, then I was suddenly here, and that man was..." His eyes began sparking fiercely with lightning, and he didn't finish his sentence.

"You collapsed," I explained again, calmer now and less discombobulated. "And that man was a Mageye. He said that he could suck the life out of everything, and he took away your consciousness."

"So that's why everything went gray, and why I felt so messed up when I woke up? What was he doing? Why did he stab you?"

"He didn't stab me," I whispered, smoothing my skirts. "I ran into the blade. He said he was going to push me off the cliff and kill you too. I had to do something to stop him."

Myles blanched. "Did he know we are Mageye?"

I nodded. "That's why he took away your consciousness. He could sense you were stronger and didn't want to fight you. And he... he said taking your power felt good."

His expression darkened. "Not every Mageye is kind, but those who are truly willing to use their powers to cause harm...

We can do more damage than your average person. There is a big difference between someone only having their fists as a weapon and someone who can suck the life out of you with a single thought. Was he connected to the Volcaniacs, do you think?"

"I don't know," I whispered, looking at the open air beyond the cliff. "He made it seem like he was kind of working with other people, but he never said what that implied."

"The Volcaniacs seem to want you alive," Myles mused. "I don't sense any other Mageye around, though."

I only nodded and inched closer to him. The Volcaniacs might not have been involved with what had just happened, but if there was one stray Mageye around, could there be more?

Myles's satchel had been dropped a few feet from us and he leaned over and rifled through it, sitting cross-legged. "Here," he said, pulling out what looked to be peppermint candies. "Suck on one of these. They help reduce stress."

"Peppermint?" I questioned.

He shrugged and popped one into his mouth. "Special kind of peppermint that grows magically. I was gifted these by another member of the Elite Guard. She said my stress over an exam was stressing her out and she'd go into cool-down if she tried to stimulate positive emotions with her power alone."

I put the peppermint on my tongue and sucked on it. "She can stimulate positive emotions?"

He rolled his candy on his tongue and nodded. "You'd like her. All of the Ansleys, actually. Avery, Sadie, and Savannah."

"They're from Mageye City?"

He nodded again and I turned to the north. I had promised Myles that in return for helping me save my family, I would go to Mageye City with him. That meant I would meet some of his friends... but I needed my family back first.

"The Mageye who tricked us referenced The End," I said. "He said it is the only place up this far north, but that we shouldn't have been able to get this close alone."

"He said we're close to The End?" Myles perked up, turning his gaze north. "King Duncan doesn't want his citizens near The End alone, so yes, we shouldn't be here... but if that Mageye thinks our proximity is relevant to that rule." He looked back at me. "We're close."

"How close?" I asked, holding my breath.

"Close enough that I think we have reached the end of safety."

"Safety?" I echoed, my heart picking up speed. "You call *this* safety?"

He looked grim. "Compared to where we are headed."

I took a shaky breath and nodded, chewing on the rest of the peppermint. The end of safety meant we were close enough to my family that we could call this the final stretch. Finally. "That Mageye mentioned having a hut. Maybe we can find something we can use... unless you think that's too risky?"

Myles shut his eyes, nodding to himself. "I don't... and it seems odd for other rebel Mageye to be near The End if they aren't Volcaniacs..." He opened his eyes. "But the Volcaniacs want you alive, not... dead."

"He also referenced a reward," I fretted. "For what he was doing to us."

Myles stood, offering me a hand. "Let's see if there is anything at his hut, and then take our leave."

I let him pull me up and adjusted my apron a final time, before following Myles back to the woods. He paused, bending to pick up Ren's jackknife and handing it to me.

Thankfully, there were no scuffs on it, and I gently wiped the dust off the handle, tracing the outline of the *R* with a finger before putting it back in my apron.

We soon found a worn path and followed it. It led us between a wall of tall boulders and into a small clearing, nestled in the back of which was a hut.

Everything about the clearing looked... gray. Even the reeds growing outside of the hut looked as if they were missing the joy of life. This was exactly the kind of place I could envision the power-sucking Mageye living in.

We cautiously approached the hut and the door creaked open as Myles entered, one hand outstretched to fend against an ambush. He relaxed once it was obvious we were alone. Everything inside the hut was old and various shades of dusty brown and gray. A dead cactus sat on the windowsill, shriveled and dry.

A small, four-poster bed sat in the corner with a worn quilt on top, and a bare shelf stood next to it with nothing but a few sacks of dried foods and nuts.

We searched through the entire hut. I emptied the drawers on a small desk while Myles pulled the mattress off the bed.

Besides a few changes of clothes, including what looked like old dresses, long-since forgotten, it seemed like the man had kept only the bare minimum.

Myles shook his head and frowned. "It doesn't look like he has anything we can use."

My shoulders slumped and I took a final look around the ransacked hut, pausing at the sight of a paper poking out from underneath the shelf. It was yellowed with age, yet when I tugged it out, it felt sturdy, and not fragile.

The backside was marked with nothing but a small inscription. M-V-CJ. The script was so small, I could cover it with one finger, but when I flipped the paper, I stared in disbelief.

A map.

Chapter 20

"No way." Myles knelt beside me. "This is impossible. How did he...?"

We stared in awed shock at the map. Translucent features rose from the yellowed paper—trees, and cliffs, and the hut we sat in.

I touched the highest-reaching part of the map and my eyes widened as the translucent image continued to reflect the walls of the volcano around my hand. Small ticks along the side measured distance, and it appeared that the volcano was surrounded by a nearly fifty-mile radius of barren land, full of burnt rocks and trees. Etched throughout the charred land were intricately marked trails, guard entries, and even a few secret entrances leading into the volcano.

I pulled my hand from the map and the tall volcano flickered before standing tall again, a plume of smoke frozen above the image. Only one hundred miles separated this hut and the start of the charred land.

The End.

"We can use this," Myles breathed, tracing his finger across one of the trails. "We can follow this trail, or even one of the more secretive ones, and break into the heart of the volcano." He picked up the map, hands shaking with his excitement. "We're holding the key to *everything*. If we get the Elite Guard and the army together, we can get in and overthrow them—"

"The Elite Guard?" I interrupted. "What about my family?"

He lowered the map. "You're right, we don't have time to get the army together before we break in, but once we get your family out, they will likely change their system. We only have one strike."

I resisted the urge to snatch the map away. Myles couldn't be thinking about leaving *now*, could he? Not when we were so close. If he left to gather Mageye City's army and they returned before my family was freed, that could risk their lives. And with nothing but a jackknife and healing powers, I stood very little chance of breaking into the volcano on my own.

I needed Myles to stay or else my family may be doomed.

He hadn't noticed my bitter change in mood, and mouthed ideas to himself as he continued studying the map.

"Myles," I said.

He looked up and his excitement seemed to fade when he saw my expression. "What?" he asked.

I motioned to the map, fighting to keep my voice steady. "We can use this to get in and save my family."

His purple gaze darted between my face and the map before shaking his head. "This could save the Mageye as a *whole*. When I joined the Elite Guard, I swore to put the citizens of Mageye City above all else, even my own life. If King Duncan found out I had the answers to overthrowing the Volcaniacs and passed them up..."

I stood, wiping my eyes angrily to stop my tears from falling. "I know you said you were only helping because it was the right thing to do at the time. That's fine. You can go."

"Well, wait," he began. "Don't get upset yet. I am not abandoning you. We just need to consider this new option. Going back to Mageye City first might be the wisest decision."

I left the hut before he could continue his pathetic excuse to abandon me and my family. Sure, his *Mageye City* was important, but those people weren't being held hostage. My family was.

I ignored his calls to come back and stormed out of the hidden clearing. Hot tears threatened to spill and I blinked rapidly. Myles may have said he was willing to discuss our options, but his true intentions were clear the moment he laid eyes on the magical map.

Mageye City held all of his loyalties, not me, and not my family. And though we had just almost died together, that clearly had no sway on what he valued the most.

I sat on a boulder and buried my face in my hands. I never should have pulled that map from under the shelf. We didn't truly need it to break in with just us two, but to break in with an entire army, that map meant life or death.

Lightning crackled, announcing Myles's presence. "I don't want to talk right now, Myles," I said without looking at him. "I might not be a mind reader, but it's obvious you're..." I choked up. "Leaving."

"Maybe I am." He sat beside me. "But passing up something as valuable as that map could ultimately doom all of the Mageye. Even Alveraada is at risk as long as the Volcaniacs are around. So, sometimes we need to make sacrifices..."

"Sacrifices?" I echoed, glaring at him. "Like leaving my family to die? Is that what you're suggesting I do?"

"Of course, not! Rose, please listen to me, if your family is alive, they are most likely going to stay that way. If we go to Mageye City, we can build up a stronger force to overthrow the Volcaniacs and save your family in the process. We won't leave them there when we go. I will even explain to King Duncan that you found the map and a condition to our utilizing it for Mageye City is that we prioritize saving your family."

I shook my head, mouth agape. "That's not good enough. I'm not going to abandon them on a *most likely* they'll still be alive. I told you that I will go with you to Mageye City after we save my family, not before. If you leave, you will go alone, and you will be abandoning me."

Pain-filled lightning flickered in his eyes. "I'm not

abandoning you or them. I won't force you to come, but they're four people. We're talking about an entire nation of others. I'm not saying they don't matter, but we can stop this from happening again. This is a few versus the whole, and so maybe they need to wait a little longer so that we can save them *and* Mageye City."

"What if it was your mom that was there? And your family? Would you leave them?" I challenged.

"My mom is dead," he answered carefully. "Both my birth parents are."

Of course, they were. Myles was so willing to abandon my family because he had already lost his. "Good! I think if your parents were still alive, they'd be disappointed, because you're no help at all," I snapped.

Mom, Raymond, Ryder, and Ren couldn't afford for me to sit and argue a useless battle against Myles. I stood angrily. "Goodbye, Myles."

Lightning crackled again, and he stepped out of an orb in front of me, his expression lit with anger. "What was *that*? You expect me to risk my life for your family, whom I have never met, yet you are telling me it is good my family is gone?"

"I thought you were going back to Mageye City," I said bitterly, side-stepping around him.

He put his hand out to stop me. "I have gone out of my way to help you. I almost *died* for you, and now you say I haven't done anything? I didn't need to do anything, and maybe I shouldn't have. You can say and think what you want about me, but leave my family out of this." His chest heaved, and his eyes sparked with anger and hurt.

His aura flooded over me, and I gulped, taking a step back. "Fine," I admitted, shaking my head. "I shouldn't have said that about your family, and you have made sacrifices. But the second a better option came up, you tossed me aside. I have a right to be angry."

"Maybe, if I had been the one to propose this near-suicide

mission. But you vowed to do this on your own first; I only offered my aid because I couldn't in good conscience let you walk into this trap all alone."

"That's exactly what you're doing now," I shouted, attempting to walk past.

He blocked me again. "Wait. Just... wait." He took a deep breath. "You're a strong Mageye, Rose, but you are nothing compared to the Volcaniacs. Letting you go alone..." His expression hardened. "We are going back to Mageye City, and that is my final decision."

"*We?*" I asked incredulously. "I don't think so."

He shook his head. "I will use force if I have to. I am asking you not to make me do that."

I faltered, but grit my teeth and walked past him. He caught my arm and I whirled back, attempting to yank it from his grip. "I am going to save my family," I snapped. "You cannot stop me."

"We are about to have a miserable trip back to Mageye City," he muttered as he began marching me back to the hut.

I stumbled and attempted to pry his fingers off of my arm. "What are you doing?" I demanded. "Let go."

He shook his head and I looked around wildly for some form of help. The woods were full of color, yet nothing offered an easy escape. My jackknife was in my pocket, but there was no way I could muster that kind of courage.

"Good to know you won't stab me," he said, staring straight ahead as he dragged me back through the boulders and to the hut.

"Traitor," I hissed. "What will your king think of you when you come back dragging a girl against her will? I thought you gave me a speech all about how you don't force Mageye to come."

"This is for your own good, Rose. I'm sorry."

I planted my feet. "So, leaving my family to end up dead like yours is for my own good? Thanks for that. I love the thought of being orphaned."

He stopped walking and sparks began flickering off of him. "That's enough."

"If my family is dead when you finally bring your army to the volcano, it will be *your* fault!"

His grip on my arm tightened and sparks jumped from his hand. I shrieked, blisters bubbling up on my arm and tears rushing to my eyes.

Myles pulled his hand away. "I'm sorry." He took a step towards me and I stumbled back. "I'm sorry, Rose, that was an accident."

I stared at him, then looked at my blistered arm, open-mouthed. "You... you shocked..."

"I'm sorry," he repeated.

"No..." I tucked my arm closer to myself. He hesitated and hot tears spilt from my eyes, somehow representing grief and anger and frustration and guilt and... and *betrayal.* "Go away," I choked out. "Go away, Myles."

"Away?" He shook his head, taking another step forward, hands trembling as he reached out. "I didn't mean to do that. I know you were saying those things out of fear, and..."

"Go away!" I sobbed, falling to my knees, still cradling my arm even as the blisters healed. "You threatened to drag me against my will to a city I have never been to and then you shocked me! Go. Away."

"I lost control, and it won't happen again. I..."

I hugged my arms to myself. "Go home and find your army, Myles. I don't want your help anymore."

He stilled, his shoulders slumping. "I'm sorry." He took a step back, then another, then he turned and left the clearing altogether. A faint electric crackle marked his final departure and I doubled over, alone and without the only person who stood a chance at helping me save my family.

Chapter 21

It took me a long time to calm down, but my tears finally slowed and I wiped my eyes. Crying wasn't going to change anything. It wasn't going to save my family or bring Myles back or take away the cruel things I had said that led to the betrayal.

The clearing was quiet and I examined my arm where Myles had gripped me. The blisters had faded, but the helplessness within me remained.

Myles was *gone* and now it was me against the entire army of Volcaniacs in order to save my family. The map had told us we were nearly there, and yet it now suddenly felt as if I was in Sunset Hollow again, clueless to everything I was walking toward.

But I wasn't clueless anymore, was I? I stood, dusting off my dress and sliding my hand into my pocket to clutch Ren's jackknife. With only one Mageye, that meant less of a chance of my aura being detected. And Myles's aura was even stronger than mine, so without him, any Mageye in the volcano may not notice me.

Sure, Myles was a better fighter than me, and he could shoot lightning, but I could *heal.* I could walk into any attack thrown at me and come out the other side unscathed.

If Myles wanted to return to Mageye City and try to bring an army to the volcano, that was fine, because I had been willing to do this alone before and I was willing to do it alone now.

I wasn't going to end up like Myles, losing my family. I was going to save mine. And, maybe if Myles and I ever crossed paths again, I could apologize for what I had said about his family.

However painful his betrayal was, telling him he deserved losing his family was a boundary Mom would be endlessly disappointed I had crossed. Yet what was done was done, and I had my own family to save.

I just had to make it to The End first.

The uplifted roots of a tree provided cover for me to sleep, and I lay flat on my back the next morning, fighting an immediate rush of tears. Searching for bad auras, finding my way through the woods, and simply being under this tree by myself was much harder without Myles.

I pushed my palms into my eyes. "God, please help me. Please give me strength."

A bird began a cheerful song and I slowly pulled my hands away from my face and crawled out from under the tree. "I can't keep going like this. There is no time to feel bad for myself," I said aloud. A passing squirrel cocked its head, probably wondering why I was talking to myself. "I'm saving my family," I told it, turning north.

If the map Myles and I had found was accurate, the distance between the hut and The End was about one hundred miles. While there was no real way to measure the distance I traveled yesterday, ten miles was probably a safe estimate, which meant I had ninety miles to go.

That had been because I had walked late into the night, but if I could walk fifteen miles today and keep that pace, I could get to the edge of The End in six days. Then I would have to cross the fifty miles of blackened land leading up to the volcano.

And then what? Volcanos were mountains with a hole full of lava, right? So, how was I supposed to get in? The map had made it seem like there were entrances at the bottom of the volcano, but wouldn't that lead straight to magic lava?

If Myles were here, he could teleport us inside, but Myles

wasn't here, and I didn't have the map memorized nor with me. Where were the secret entrances?

A bad aura made me grimace and I frowned at the woods to my left, veering right instead. The uncomfortably familiar, anxiety-inducing feeling faded and I nodded to myself, raising my hands to the sky. "See world, I can take care of myself. I don't need any help from stupid Myles." I took a deep breath. "And I'll get into the volcano too, no problem."

Clearly, if people *lived* in this magic volcano, there were accessible ways to get inside. With any luck, pretending to be a Volcaniac would be an easy ticket in, and if that failed, well, I had made it all the way from Sunset Hollow, hadn't I? Nothing was going to stop me from saving my family.

Not even something like the Wolvien Guard... I paused, turning slowly in the direction of the bad aura I had sensed.

A distant, blood-chilling howl echoed faintly through the woods and I shook my head, taking a few stumbling steps backwards.

No. No, no, no. Not the Wolvien Guard. Not when I was alone. Nothing but trees surrounded me, and most were pines with branches too high to reach. But a few other trees were dispersed through them, and these had lower branches.

Another howl made me wince, and I spun on my heel, running through the woods and looking frantically for somewhere to hide or a tree to climb.

But if I climbed a tree, wouldn't they circle beneath it and wait for me to come down? I would be trapped until I eventually lost my grip.

That left running, which was impossible compared to their speed, unless I found something like a portal. I sprinted through the woods, leaping over fallen logs and small ditches. Another howl echoed behind me, this one closer.

Myles and I had evaded them twice before, but we had only been able to do that because of his teleporting. A portal would help only if it shut down behind me, and hadn't Myles said they often stay for a couple uses?

I tripped over a root and sprawled to the ground, scraping my palms and knees. I stumbled back to my feet, panting as I pushed off from a tree and began sprinting again.

There was something else Myles had told me about portals. He had said I called that first portal because I wanted to use it for good. Needing one to save my life and in turn, save my family, definitely wasn't a bad thing.

Come on, portal. I need you.

The howling continued to get closer, and with each new howl, more fear flooded my veins. A stitch in my side caused me to wince with every breath, but my power quickly took over, taking the edge off the pain.

"Please!" I shouted to the trees as their thin branches whipped my skin. "Please!"

The next howl seemed to last forever and I nearly burst into tears. Nothing but empty woods surrounded me and I took the chance of changing the direction I was running; would zig-zags throw them off?

Probably not, but as long as there was a chance.

Right... go right... I turned to my right, following the sense that there was something good ahead. *A portal.* My gaze skimmed frantically around me, searching for the small orb of light, wherever it may be.

By now the howls were deafening, and I sobbed when a flickering light caught my eye. "Take me away," I shouted to the portal. "Take me away from here!"

The portal blinked, and a huge wolf erupted from it, snarling even before it hit the ground.

I screamed and skidded to a halt before stumbling backwards. The portal hadn't been preparing to let me in, it had been preparing to let the wolves *out.*

Five more wolves appeared, and they surrounded me, growling. Each towered over my head, and the leader snarled. Its one eye seemed to burn through me, and the X-shaped scar where its other eye should have been sent chills down my spine.

I pulled out Ren's jackknife, waving it towards them in vain. "Get back! Stay back, leave me alone!" My voice pitched, and only seemed to further excite them.

They threw back their heads and howled. My legs gave out from under me, and I crumpled to the ground, sobbing. It was over. They were done playing.

The pack leader prowled closer, its breath hot against my face even from the three-foot distance. I screwed my eyes tightly shut as crackling filled the air. I whimpered, hugging my arms around my head, but then the wolves howled in pain. My eyes snapped open to see the pack leader slam against a tree and slump to the ground, purple sparks jumping from its fur.

My arms shook as I turned and attempted to drag myself away, clutching Ren's jackknife tightly in my hand.

Unfortunately, whatever force had flung the wolves aside didn't deter them for long. The ground shook under the pack leader's paws and I screamed as it flung itself into the air to finish me off. A figure suddenly darted from the woods, grabbing my arm and twisting us away from the huge wolf.

"Need some help?" Myles asked as the air crackled and a purple orb formed around us, this one with two layers. The top layer blasted out towards the wolves, toppling them once more. And before they regained their balance, we disappeared into the other with an electric snap.

Chapter 22

We reappeared next to a bubbling brook. My hands trembled as I folded my jackknife, though I clutched it tightly, turning to Myles.

He took a few steps back, holding his hands up so I could see that no sparks were coming from him. "They didn't hurt you, did they?"

I shook my head and took a half-step away from him, my gaze darting between his wide eyes and his hands. "What are you doing here? I thought you went back to Mageye City."

"I couldn't do it." He lowered his hands. "After what happened and when you started crying... I'm sorry, Rose. I shouldn't have grabbed you." He curled his hands into fists. "And when I started sparking, I should have let go."

I took a few shaky breaths, unsure of how to respond. Was he here solely to save me from the Wolvien Guard, or was he planning to drag me back to Mageye City? I adjusted my grip on my jackknife, still gripping it tight. Myles's gaze lingered on it, and his expression fell.

"You didn't answer my question," I said shakily. "Why are you here?"

He looked up. "I tried going back to Mageye City. I thought if I traveled fast enough, I could get help from the Elite Guard and use teleportation crystals to intercept you." He shook his head. "But then I started worrying, and the wolves beat me to you."

I glanced around us, at the quiet woods, devoid of howls. "Thank you for that, but... but if you are here to convince me to come with you, my answer is the same as yesterday. I'm not going to leave my family to die."

"Me either," he agreed.

I slowly relaxed my hand. "What do you mean?"

"I am here to help you save your family." He took a few steps forward. "Your emotions are washing over me and I know you are scared, and I know you feel betrayed. So I'm not asking you to forgive me, but I made a promise and I want to keep that promise."

"How do I know that I can trust you? How do I know you won't get angry and try to drag me to Mageye City again?" My voice lowered. "How do I know you can forgive *me?*"

Pain flickered in his purple eyes. "I can't take any fear I caused back, but I can stop it from happening again. Please, Rose, let me help you. Don't turn me away."

I could say yes. I could accept his promise of help, help I sorely needed. But the feeling of his aura washing over me in anger, the feeling of his sparks, even accidental, burning my skin...

"No, I-I can't. Not without proof. I don't think I can trust you again, Myles..." I choked up, blinking rapidly to stop my tears. "You have all the reasons to hate me now and after being shocked, I can't..."

If only I could say yes. If only I could undo the cruel things I had said that had gotten him angry. If only we hadn't found that map.

In the short time we had known each other, Myles had fast become one of my most trusted confidants, but it was over. He was now a liability in regards to saving my family, and unlike him, I couldn't read minds. I could never know for sure if he was truly dedicated to the mission, or only waiting for an opportunity to sweep me away to Mageye City.

"I can prove it," Myles said. "Please, let me prove it. I can do it right now."

I studied him distrustfully. Purple lightning flickered in his irises, and he slowly unslung his satchel from his shoulder, dropping it down and removing his dagger too, lightly tossing it out of reach. He met my gaze before looking down at himself and fumbling with his vest, opening it to reveal he had other weapons hidden.

My breath caught as he dropped the vest on the pile, turning back with his palms raised towards me. "I can prove it," he promised. "But you need to let me come over to do it."

I hugged my jackknife to myself, shaking my head. "How? You saved me from the wolves, and I'm grateful, but—"

"I'm not talking about that. I can actually show you my intentions. Please, let me prove it to you." His brow creased with his earnest, and I hesitated.

What would Mom want me to do? What would Raymond want? Ren and Ryder? I glanced to the north, to the volcano they were trapped in, to The End. They would want me to forgive him and in turn ask for forgiveness. "How can you show me?"

He took a step closer. "I need to be close." His gaze darted to the jackknife I clutched to my chest. "You can open the jackknife and hold it to me; I won't be offended. But I can't prove my intentions from here. I need to come closer."

I clutched the jackknife even tighter but didn't open it, blinking back fresh tears as I hesitantly nodded. Myles stepped around the items he had dropped, approaching me slowly and holding out a hand.

"I won't hurt you," he whispered.

Tears glazed my eyes as I met his electric purple gaze. His expression held only sincerity and I slowly took his hand.

Ask me a question, he said, but his lips didn't move. I jerked back, and his voice faded from inside of me.

"What?" I flexed my fingers. "Your voice sounded like it was..."

"Inside your head?" He rubbed his neck sheepishly, nodding.

151

"When we hold hands, I can let you hear my thoughts, and I'll be able to hear you, too. Thoughts can't lie, because you have to think of a lie before you say it."

"So... I can ask you questions? This is how you can prove I can trust you?"

He offered his hand again. "Yes."

I grasped his hand and shut my eyes, taking a deep breath before thinking, *Can I trust you?*

Yes, he answered in my head.

Why?

Because I meant it when I told you that I won't take no for an answer if something happens to your family.

I opened my eyes and looked at him. His eyes were tightly shut and his head bowed. *Will you leave again?* I asked.

No. Not unless you send me away.

I half-loosened my grip, then paused. Like Myles had said, his thoughts came at me quickly, leaving no time for a lie to form between his words.

Why are you helping me and not returning to Mageye City?

Because you and your family aren't a part of the few I'm willing to sacrifice for the whole.

I stepped back and he opened his eyes, watching as I hugged both hands to my chest. "Do you forgive me, too?" I whispered, tears blurring my vision.

His lips parted and he nodded. "Yes," he breathed. "I know you didn't mean it."

"And... you promise not to drag me back to Mageye City?"

"Never." He put a hand to his heart. "I swear it. I am here to help you save your family."

Tears welled in my eyes and I ran forward, wrapping my arms around him. "Thank you."

Chapter 23

Myles hugged me tightly. "We're going to save your family. I promise."

I sobbed. "Thank you for coming back... and I'm sorry about what I said about you being horrible, and how I was happy your family is gone. I didn't mean it, but that doesn't make it okay. I... I was really cruel."

He shook his head, staring towards the north. "I'm not upset. It's okay."

I wiped my eyes. "Well, I still want to tell you this. They wouldn't be disappointed in you. I think they'd be proud of you. You've devoted your life to helping people. There's nothing to be disappointed about."

His eyes widened, and he turned back, blinking back tears of his own. "Thank you."

My lower lip trembled and I wrapped my arms around him again. "You're one of my closest friends, Myles. I don't want to lose you."

He stiffened, but slowly relaxed, hugging me tight. "I'm not going anywhere, Rose. You're stuck with me."

I sniffed, offering a watery smile as I stepped back from the hug. "Good."

"Good," he agreed, wiping his eyes. "Let me pick up my things and then we can pick up where we left off."

I watched quietly, giving Ren's jackknife a final squeeze before dropping it into my apron pocket. Myles was back. *Thank*

God.

"That was too close with the wolves," I said when he finished hiding his weapons. "Do you think you could maybe... teleport again?"

"I was going to suggest the same thing." Myles grimaced. "I think they're getting desperate. We have evaded them three times now, and they've never lost a hunt before."

"What do you mean they've never lost a hunt?" My eyes widened. "Without your teleporting..."

"They would have caught us at that cliff," Myles finished. "But thankfully, my teleporting seems to be exactly what we need to evade them."

"But they keep finding us anyway," I pointed out with a frown.

"I know. They won't stop hunting until they catch us, which means we need to keep staying one step ahead."

He held out his hand, and I didn't hesitate to grab it this time. Lightning crackled around us and when it snapped, we reappeared in a semi-open field. Myles released my hand and stepped around a large puddle. I followed him and studied his back.

Though his voice had faded from inside of me, looking at someone after being *inside* their thoughts felt... different. Almost as if I had been given access to a secret part of Myles that none of the world had seen before. Is that what Myles experienced on a daily basis?

Ironic, seeing as he seemed so secretive. Working for a king in a hidden, magical city, always having a new aspect of his power to unveil, a level of magical knowledge that suggested decades of studying rather than eighteen years. And his family. Myles had grieved for his family as deeply as I currently feared for the safety of mine.

As we ducked under some low-hanging branches, the smell of pine sap making my nose tickle, Myles glanced at me. "You can ask."

"Ask what?" I rubbed my nose to rid it of the tickles.

He sighed softly. "My family. You want to know what happened?"

My cheeks flushed. "That's private. You don't need to tell me."

"I was five," he responded. "I'm okay talking about it."

"Five?" I whispered in horror.

He nodded. "The Elite Guard was attempting to train Ackley Elephants to help guard the city. When they stomp their foot, the vibrating earth turns people to stone. One got loose and broke down the walls of my house. My parents tried to stop it, but turned to stone in the process. The guards arrived and were barely able to kill it before it could kill me."

I covered my mouth with my hand. "Myles, I-I'm so sorry, that must've been horrible..."

"I could have saved them..." His voice cracked, but he cleared his throat. "Even back then, I was powerful. But I didn't have full command of my powers. I didn't know how to properly shoot lightning. I didn't know how to save them."

The guilt that flooded me with his words nearly brought tears to my eyes. How could I have said such cruel things to him about his family? No wonder he had been so deeply hurt; I had accused him of something he already blamed himself for.

"I don't blame myself." He must have heard my thoughts. "I feel guilty, but I guess... over time, I came to terms with it. Besides, King Duncan can talk to ghosts. He let me say goodbye to them when I was old enough, and they told me it wasn't my fault. I wouldn't have been able to come to terms with it without King Duncan's help."

"I'm not sure I could ever come to terms with that," I whispered. "I'm so sorry, Myles."

"I've said cruel things out of fear too," he said. "Another advantage of mindreading is I know exactly when you mean something or not." Our gazes met. "You mean your apology."

Some of the guilt seemed to lighten and I wiped my eyes.

"I'm still sorry, in general, too."

He held his satchel out to show me. "I took this before I moved out of our house. It was my dad's and has a form of magical protection on it. It's all I have left. That and my old bear." He hesitated. "Kind of like your jackknife. I... I heard your thoughts. I know it's important to you."

I instinctively reached into my apron pocket and clutched the knife as Myles continued, "So, I know how you feel. Thinking you lost your family, and maybe even blaming yourself. But I won't let you go through what I went through. We'll save your family."

I moved closer to him. "Thank you." I wanted to say more about how truly grateful I was, but then again, I was talking to a mind reader. He already knew.

He smiled slyly. "I don't read minds without permission, remember?"

I laughed. "Your saying that implies that you knew what I was thinking, and I don't recall giving you permission to read my mind."

He shook his head. "It doesn't bother you; I can sense it. Most people are different, more defensive, but you let your thoughts go free. You aren't trying to hide them."

As he said that, his aura shifted and I tilted my head. "You stopped reading my mind."

He turned back sharply. "You can tell?"

I nodded. "Your aura shifted."

Lightning flickered in his irises. "No one has ever been able to tell before. King Duncan can sometimes block me, but even he can't tell when I try."

"What do you mean?"

"King Duncan's aura is strong enough that he can use it as a shield against me. I know hardly any other Mageye strong enough to do that. But he does it when he doesn't want me to read his mind, not when he can tell I'm doing it." His brow furrowed. "Was it anything besides my aura? Can you feel me read your mind?"

"Your aura merges with mine more when you read my mind. There is this slight pressure. But when you stopped, it moved back."

He nodded slowly. "I guess that makes sense."

"It does?"

"Yeah. You have the most powerful aura I have felt in a long time. Your senses must be heightened."

I lifted my hands to examine my fingers. "I don't feel strong."

"You don't need to *feel* strong. You just are. I mean, you can sense portals almost as quickly as I can."

"Isn't that normal? Being able to sense it from a distance?"

He shook his head. "Not from that far of a distance. The stronger your aura, the stronger your reach. I have friends in Mageye City who wouldn't have been able to sense that first portal until we crossed the stream."

My jaw dropped. "Are you serious?"

He nodded. "Your reach can be stretched with training, but a large part of it is simply how strong your aura is naturally. King Duncan helped me increase my reach."

"Oh." A rabbit erupted from the bushes ahead of us, causing me to jump.

Myles laughed. "You didn't sense it?" he teased.

I raised an eyebrow. I was fairly certain I had seen him jump too. "Did you?"

"Maybe not," he admitted.

I smiled. "I have another question. Outside of auras."

"Sure."

"Is King Duncan more than just a king and mentor to you? The way you talk about him... It sounds like you're describing family."

"That's because I am." He hesitated, tapping his fingers. "After my parents died, King Duncan took me in. I was raised in the palace."

"So, that's why he trained you?" I asked. "You were in the

palace, so he must have known first-hand how strong you were."

"It's more than that," he said. "King Duncan adopted me when I was eight. I call him Dad."

I gasped. "What? He *adopted* you?"

Myles grinned, taking a bow with a flourish of his hand. "General Myles Hilton Duncan at your service, ma'am."

"General?" I echoed.

He nodded. "I'm a member of the Elite Guard. The position comes with the title of general. There are twelve of us at the moment, and we make up King Duncan's top advisors."

"Really?" I tilted my head, trying to recall what Myles had told me about Mageye City's customs. "If your last name is Duncan, does King Duncan use his last name in his title, instead of his first?"

"Yeah." Myles shrugged. "I am General Duncan and he is King Duncan."

"Don't kings and queens go by their first names?" I asked, confused.

"King Duncan goes by his last name because he hates his first name."

"What's his first name?"

"He would kill me if he found out I told you. Actually," he added, "he would kill me if he found out *I* knew."

"Did you read his mind?"

He snickered. "In my defense, I was twelve."

I laughed. "I can keep a secret."

He shook his head. "I can't tell you. That would be betraying his trust. It's bad though," he added playfully.

"Come on, give me a hint. What letter does it start with?"

"No!" He laughed. "Then you'll start guessing. And I can't risk you getting it right, because then you'll know by my reaction."

"Fine." I pouted.

He laughed again. "I can tell you other secrets about the palace. Just not that one."

"What kind of secrets?"

He shrugged. "What do you want to know?"

"You tell me. I've never been in a palace before. You're the one who was raised in one. Wait." I turned towards him excitedly. "You're a king's *son*. Does that mean you are a prince as well as a general? Prince Myles?"

He shook his head. "Not exactly. To be a true heir, you need to be biologically related. However, King Duncan never married and doesn't have any biological children. Because of that, he needs to choose his successor. I am second in line."

"Second? Who's first?"

"General Cornstone. He is my dad's top advisor; always has been. King Duncan unexpectedly received the throne when he was thirteen. General Cornstone was supposed to be the next ruler, but the previous king changed his mind at the last minute. Instead of being angry, General Cornstone took my dad under his wing, and King Duncan has repaid him for it by making him first in line."

"He sounds like a good man."

"He is. And he is my godfather, too. If King Duncan isn't around, he's the one I go to." He smirked. "And between you and me, General Cornstone is the one I used to go to, to complain about King Duncan."

I laughed. "You complained about your dad and *king?*"

"Well, of course. When he was being annoying. But to be fair, I used to go to King Duncan to complain about General Cornstone a lot more than I went to General Cornstone to complain about King Duncan." He cast me a glance. "Are you telling me you have never complained to any of your brothers about the rest of your family?"

My lip twitched. "Ren and I used to fight a lot, and normally I went to Raymond about it since he was big enough to stop Ren from picking on me. Although... the fighting may or may not have started because I broke his favorite toy... purposefully..."

"May or may not?"

"Innocent until proven guilty," I said gleefully.

"Your thoughts suggest guilt."

"Hey!"

We both laughed, our conversation turning to our families. I smiled while I told Myles more about mine, but it did nothing to numb my worry.

Chapter 24

The next two days passed without mishap, but Myles's warning about the Wolvien Guard never failing a hunt continued to concern me. Would they follow us to the volcano and corner us inside? Or, would we spend the rest of our lives after freeing my family attempting to evade them?

I had confessed the latter fear to Myles yesterday and while it had disturbed him; he had assured me that King Duncan and General Cornstone would be able to figure something out.

Now, as we finished packing our camp, I had the sudden feeling I was being watched. Myles sat across from me, sharpening one of his daggers, and he lifted his head. Lightning flickered in his irises as he looked behind me, towards the north.

I also turned in that direction and a light breeze seemed to bring tendrils of faint danger with it.

"We're getting close," Myles said, going back to his dagger.

"Is that what the aura is?" I asked. "I feel like I'm being watched."

He nodded, grimacing. "We need to walk straight into it."

I shuddered; if the pull was anything like the portals, it would only get worse from here. But I straightened my back anyway. "Should we leave?"

He put his dagger in its sheath and stood. "Let's start with a jump."

"Okay." I grabbed his hand, and the air crackled around us. We disappeared with an electric snap and reappeared at the very edge of a lush green forest.

Myles's eyes widened and I gasped when I saw what lay before us. The tree line marked the start of miles of charred black land. Scorched boulders and ashy stumps, surrounded by a mild warmth that provided anything but comfort.

The entire place radiated an aura that warned of danger and death. Far in the distance, the smoking top of a black volcano loomed. With gray clouds muting the light of the sun, an orange glow was visible from within the smoke of the volcano.

Every fiber of my being screamed for me to turn and run as far away as I could, but the thought of my family kept my feet firmly in place.

Myles's expression reflected my fear. "I've never seen anything like this."

"The End?" I asked.

He blinked and nodded, taking a step away from the charred land. "Let's go back into the forest so we can make a plan."

He didn't need to suggest that twice. We hid in the bushes, and Myles pulled out the map we had found in the hut.

I hadn't expected to see it again. "You kept the map?"

He looked up from spreading it on the ground. "Yeah, why?"

"I didn't realize you still had it. I thought it was still at the hut."

"Leave the key to getting in?" He motioned to the volcano. "After seeing that, I'm not so sure we would stand a chance without this map."

He finished smoothing it out, and the translucent images rose from the pages. The hut we had found it at now seemed infinitely far away, knowing we stood at the edge of The End.

Myles studied it closely and I knelt across from him, looking at it upside down. On the northeast side of the volcano was what appeared to be a main entrance. It was marked with several guards, two of which were wolves.

"The wolves are out hunting, right?" I asked, pointing at them. "They won't be here?"

"No." Myles pointed out another area marked with wolves. "There are more than the six hunting us."

My heart sank. "Do you know how many?"

He shook his head. "I wish. Look here." He pointed to an area highlighted by the gray Mageye. "There are a few secret entrances, but this looks like the best one. It looks like he has used it before."

"It's also the closest one to us. The others are on the far side of the volcano." I frowned. "It looks like all of the entrances are along the base of the volcano."

"I noticed that, too." Myles peered at the top of the volcano and sighed. "The smoke on the map makes it impossible to see inside. But I imagine it is like an anthill, except they don't use the hole at the top."

"Do you know if the volcano has ever erupted?"

He shook his head. "I asked my dad, and he said he imagines there is a magical seal that keeps it at bay." He fell silent as he studied the trails and traced his finger along the edge of the woods, stopping at a specific spot. "This is us, and we don't seem to be too far from the highlighted trail."

"Do you think you could teleport us to the secret entrance? Well..." I reflected on the last time Myles had taken us fifty miles. It hadn't ended well. "You can take us partway, right?"

He shook his head. "If I teleport that distance, I won't be able to fight when we get there. Besides, they might sense me using my power. Once we are in their territory, I think we should walk."

I frowned. "Walking across will take several days. It would be hard enough to stay undetected during the day, but what about at night?"

"What do you mean? We will find a spot to hide and take turns sleeping. Besides, we can use the darkness as a cover."

I shook my head. "That's not what I meant. I don't think we should be out there in the dark. The wolves would see us before we see them. And if that happens, it's over."

"I hadn't thought of that." Myles frowned at the map. "I don't see how we can avoid staying out at night. We can't possibly walk fifty miles in one day."

The tally marks on the edge of the map only confirmed the impossible distance and I sighed. Despite the risks, there really was no way to avoid staying out there at night. Magic or otherwise. "We'll need to pray they don't see us." I frowned. "Since they have a bad aura to us, will we have a bad aura to them?"

He nodded. "We will, and we're both powerful, so they might sense us from a distance. That's why I'm going to have us mask our auras."

Mask our auras?

Myles answered my question without me saying it aloud. "Remember when I told you that I can sense everything within five miles that *lets* me? Strong Mageye can mask or even completely hide their auras."

I frowned, judging my aura. "How do you hide something invisible? Even sensing things with my aura... it's like controlling the oxygen we breathe, it just... happens."

"I'll teach you," he assured me. "The problem is that it takes energy, and we can't afford to take a break from masking while we cross. Even if we only slip up for a few seconds, it could blow our cover."

My heart sank. "I don't think I'll be able to mask properly."

"If you say you can't, you won't. But, I know you can do it, because you're stronger than you realize. It's tricky but doable. Trust me."

Regardless of how naturally strong my aura was, this was a lot different from finding us a safe campsite. Myles waited for me to respond and I took a shaky breath. "How do I do it?"

He smiled. "Think about trying to stifle a sneeze. That is kind of what we're doing. Then imagine pulling your aura in and folding it like a blanket inside of you."

I stared. "All at once?"

"All at once."

"That's not just tricky," I started, but he shook his head.

"Try it," he urged. "I know you feel rushed, but we are safe right now. Take your time and mask."

I glanced towards the charred land, hidden by the trees. "How will we know I did it?"

"Once you're masked, your aura will fade and I won't be able to feel you anymore."

"All right." I shut my eyes. Pull my aura in... Since Myles said our eyes reflected our auras, I imagined a pale green haze spread around me, being reeled in and stuffed inside of myself. It didn't fit very well and I opened my eyes. "Did it work?"

Myles shook his head. "You need to relax more; you're letting your nerves stop you." He grabbed my shoulders and pushed them down. "Loosen up."

I relaxed, ordering my tense muscles to calm down, which only seemed to make me more tense.

Myles hummed. "Don't overthink it. Here, can I touch your face?"

"What?"

"It's a trick my dad used to do." When I nodded, he leaned over and put his hand under my chin, pushing up so I looked at the sky. "When I let go, look down and relax your shoulders at the same time."

He pulled away and I relaxed my shoulders as I looked back down at him. He nodded in approval and I took a slow breath before shutting my eyes again. This time, instead of yanking, I pictured myself pulling gently, opening up an imaginary cupboard, and placing my aura inside.

As I slid the imaginary drawer shut, a chill went through me. It started at my fingertips and traveled up my arms and seemingly into my heart.

Even before I opened my eyes, I knew I had done it.

Myles grinned. "I told you that you were strong enough."

"Are you sure?" I looked at my arms. "You can't feel it at all?"

"It's even more hidden than I could have hoped for you to be able to do on your first try."

"Are you *completely* sure?" I pressed. "I don't want to mess this up."

He nodded. "I'm sure. I can barely sense it, and I am sitting right next to you. Don't start doubting yourself now that you've done the hard part. All that's left is to hold onto your aura."

I exhaled slowly. "Thank you."

Myles's aura suddenly faded as he masked himself. So that must have been how he knew I masked mine. Now, it was like before I was a Mageye again, he was here simply by being here and with no aura accompanying him.

We turned back to the map and studied the trail Myles had picked.

"Are you sure we can trust this map?" I asked. "He couldn't have been a Volcaniac if he was living on his own, but it's odd for him to have this with no connection. Especially since some of the entrances are marked. And he did mention *others*, even though we didn't see any."

"I honestly don't know. Maybe he was affiliated with the Volcaniacs at one point? Or they crossed through his land and he decided to spy?"

"I guess we don't have a choice," I admitted. "We'll have to hope he was right about it being a secret entrance."

"Exactly. We hope." Myles frowned. "This doesn't mark anything inside, but we can assume they have a dungeon or somewhere else to hold prisoners. We can loosen our holds on our auras enough to feel for them once we are inside. If we're lucky, we won't be detected."

"And how will we get back out?"

"We'll teleport. I can get us part of the way back across, then we run."

"Can you teleport five other people at once? Plus, my brothers will be heavier. Are you sure you can do that?"

"Do you have a better idea?" Myles asked seriously.

I sighed. "No. Just don't push too hard."

"I won't. Besides, I doubt any of the Mageye here are as strong as I am. They can chase us, but we can fight them off. And if we find weapons, your family can help."

"So, we get my family and teleport as far as you can without getting sick, then fight the rest of the way out? It is fifty miles back to the woods from the volcano, but even then, the wolves will come."

"We will need to pray for a portal."

"And if we can't find one?"

Myles looked down, and that was all the answer I needed.

Chapter 25

Myles lifted the map. "Are you ready?"

I stood beside him, clutching Ren's jackknife in my pocket. "I'm ready."

He led us back to the edge of the charred land and turned left. "Walking and keeping your aura masked isn't too difficult?" he asked.

"It's like carrying a heavy box," I said and he nodded.

"That's a good way to describe it."

Myles followed the map to the start of the highlighted trail. "It looks like it is pretty much a straight shot from here."

I stared across the charred land before us. *You only need to wait a little longer.*

"I agree," I told him, nodding at the map.

He folded it and stuck it in his pocket. After a final look to ensure no one was near, we stepped out of the woods.

The moment I stepped onto the charred land, the presence of forthcoming danger filled my lungs. Myles's breath caught and he put a hand on my shoulder. "I guess the start of this blackened land is both a physical and magical border."

"It's like that first portal, isn't it?" I asked, eyeing the rocks at my feet.

"Exactly like that," he agreed. He pointed to a nearby boulder. "Let's hide there until we are a little more used to the auras."

The fear in my veins didn't fade, but as we knelt behind the boulder, my racing heart steadied.

Myles put a hand to his head, whispering under his breath, before glancing at me. "We're feeling the auras of the volcano. False fear to deter us."

I dared to peer around the boulder. "It's not deterring me. Not when my family needs me."

"It's not deterring me either," Myles agreed, pointing at another large boulder. As we trekked farther into The End, we attempted to stay low to the ground and darted from any cover we could find to the next. The sun eventually burned through the clouds directly above us, yet the volcano looked no closer than it had when we first stepped into The End.

"Look at the woods," Myles said.

My brow furrowed and I glanced at the dark mass that was the trees we had left behind. "What about them?"

"Miles away."

"You read my mind, didn't you?" I accused and his lip twitched.

"Sorry."

I looked back at the volcano. "Every step is one step closer."

"Every breath, every second," Myles murmured. He lifted his gaze to the sun. "We have at least six or seven hours until sunset, and that will mark another day closer."

"Thanks, Myles," I whispered.

The charred land appeared empty of life, and the only sound were our footsteps, which I started counting. With our constant ducking and pausing behind cover, I never got much higher than fifty steps. But, if I multiplied all of those fifties by the amount of times I reached the number, that equaled a much bigger, and closer, number.

The land dimmed as the sun sank below the horizon, and Myles pointed to a hollowed-out divot in the ground. "That looks like a good spot to spend the night. We don't know when we will find a better one."

I nodded wearily. Being out in the sun all day and holding

my aura in was taking its toll. My head pounded and I panted in an effort to ward off the accompanying lightheadedness.

The divot was about a foot deep, which meant we could lie down and be hidden from sight.

I slipped in first, and Myles followed. The bottom was covered with sharp stones, but I didn't mind. All I cared about was being off my sore feet and letting my powers heal them.

"How far do you think we walked today?" I asked.

Myles shut his eyes. "I'd say about fifteen miles, maybe more. If we can cover that same distance tomorrow, we can get through all the guard towers the next day. We should try to do those all at once. Setting up a camp between them is too dangerous."

A few stars faintly twinkled and I sighed. "And then we'll get inside."

"And then we'll get inside," Myles echoed.

He pulled himself into a partially seated position, careful not to let his head rise above the divot. "You should get some sleep. I'll keep watch."

"Well, wait." I started sitting up, but he put a hand on my shoulder.

"I'll wake you when I need to sleep."

I shook my head. "What if we unmask our auras in our sleep, or something else happens?"

He sighed. "If we wake up to an ambush, I'll teleport. And we shouldn't lose our grip on our auras. General Cornstone told me he thinks of sleeping with a masked aura like being tucked under the covers by God."

"Meaning we won't accidentally reveal our location in our sleep?"

"Exactly that. Now, you can sleep and I'll wake you in a few hours."

I tilted my chin. "Really? Because the last time I sat up on watch, you were horrified."

Myles pouted, a guilty expression on his face. "That was

different."

"How?"

"It just was."

I rolled my eyes. "Wake me up in a few hours. Then I'll finish the night."

He sighed. "Since we stopped early, I'll wake you in about five hours. Then I'll rest until we start again. Is that fair?"

"As long as you don't *accidentally* forget."

"I won't. I promise."

Myles shook me awake. "Time to switch," he mumbled, his words slurring together with fatigue.

I yawned and pulled myself up, blinking the sleep from my eyes. "I'll wake you when it's time to go."

He slid down onto his back. "The wolves have been howling occasionally, but it's not directed at us."

I stiffened, but nodded anyway. "Thanks for the warning."

The next words out of his mouth were nothing more than an incoherent mumble that trailed off as he drifted into sleep.

He was sacrificing so much for me, yet he never complained. Not even when he probably felt faint and sick from fatigue.

"Thank you, God, for sending Myles," I whispered, watching him sleep. I reached out and gently brushed some of his hair. "And thank you for coming back," I whispered to him. "I don't want to ever say goodbye... much less like that."

An hour passed before the wolves howled, and I clutched Ren's jackknife to my chest.

The howls were faint, likely coming from the wolves in the guard towers or even from inside the volcano itself.

As another howl sounded, I slowly turned to peer over the edge of the ditch.

Nothing moved in the darkened land, and I shut my eyes, resting my forehead on the edge of the ditch. The wolves didn't know we were here. We were safe for tonight.

No one was hunting us.

Yet.

When the first streaks of dawn finally touched the sky, I gently shook Myles awake. We ate a small breakfast from what was in his satchel and each took a few sips of water.

"Before we start," Myles said, "we need to plan something. If we can cover the same distance we did yesterday, then we should be in sight of the first barrier of guard towers tonight."

He sounded concerned, and I frowned. "That's good, right?"

"Well, yes, in theory. The problem is the time. I know we talked about the wolves having better night vision than us, but we don't know what the barriers are like. If we need to climb over something, I'd rather do that at night."

I eyed the rising sun. "Do you want to not stop tonight, and go straight through?"

"No, I think we should stop early this afternoon. Then, after dark, we will keep going until we are about a mile away from the first ring of towers. We will stay put tomorrow, and break in tomorrow night."

So. *Close.* "I don't like wasting a whole day," I said, but my shoulders slumped. During the day, we were at risk of Mageye guards and wolves spotting us; at night, only the wolves would have an advantage. "But, that will leave us well-rested for tomorrow night... and scaling a fence in broad daylight is asking to get caught."

Myles nodded grimly. "Exactly."

Chapter 26

I insisted on taking the first watch during our day break. There was no howling this time, and when Myles took over, I hardly shut my eyes before he shook me awake.

His purple eyes flickered softly with lightning in the dark. "We'll set up our next camp when we see the guard towers."

The wolves howled in the distance and I shuddered. "I wish they didn't do that."

"Same here," Myles agreed.

We crouched behind what appeared to be a charred bush and waited until the howling stopped. The air seemed to be growing hotter, as if we were walking into a hot spring.

"Why is it getting hot?" I asked. "We shouldn't feel the heat yet."

"I think it is a part of the volcano's magic. This land had to burn somehow."

"How do they control it?"

"I don't know. Because the wolves have flames in their irises, they probably have something to do with it. But they made their first appearance after we discovered The End."

I eyed the dark mass of the volcano. "I guess it doesn't affect our plan, whether it is wolves, or Mageye, or something else."

He only nodded and neither of us spoke as we continued through the dark. I strained my ears for any sign of nearby Volcaniacs. Besides the distant howls, there were none.

The rising sun revealed the first ring of guard towers, and we stopped. Dark steeples seemed to rise above the charred land, spaced evenly apart until they eventually faded into the distance. No barrier seemed to connect them, though they looked impenetrable at a glance all the same.

Through those towers, and the next, and the next, then inside the volcano... my family. They were so close now; it was as if their presence had settled inside my racing heart.

Myles interrupted my spiraling thoughts. "What do you think about not having a guard today?"

"You mean, we both sleep at the same time? Isn't that too risky?"

"It is risky, but I'm concerned about our auras. Holding them in for days will take its toll even though neither of us have been using our powers."

I wiggled my toes in my boots. "I've been healing my feet," I confessed. "I can't stop myself from doing it."

He raised his brows. "Sore muscles... That gives even more of a reason for you to rest."

"Without proper rest, are we risking hitting cool-down faster?"

"Yes, our magic needs rest, too. Besides, I doubt they have patrols this close to the towers. And even if they do, it is likely only at night." Myles lay down slowly, careful not to lean out from behind our cover and I frowned at the bags under his eyes and the flushed sunburn on his cheeks. Pains I didn't have, thanks to my power.

I carefully lay beside him with a sigh. If we were going to need to fight our way out, we would need to be as well-rested as possible.

"I don't think we have a choice," I conceded. "We can't risk hitting cool-down once we are inside. Especially you, you might be our only way out."

"Let's hope it doesn't come to that."

The setting sun lit up the land with an eerie orange, slowly fading to black. Myles was already up, and appeared better rested than he had since we entered The End.

"Are you ready?" he asked.

I nodded, and we snuck out from our hiding place. The first ring of towers stood about a mile from us, hulking shadows in the darkness.

Each stood on four legs, and the rooms had pointed steeples resembling volcanos. No shadows moved on their outside balconies, and nothing connected them together.

Following the same pattern of ducking from cover to cover, we snuck through the ring. The land appeared the same within the first ring of towers, but the strong auras heightened, as did the heat.

Despite everything suggesting added danger, I took this as a good sign. It was as if we were peeling an onion. Each layer made your eyes sting more, but eventually we would reach its heart. Though the heart of the Volcaniacs was the volcano, not nearly as sweet as an onion.

By the time we could see the next ring of towers, I was sweating. Myles pulled a kerchief from his pocket and wiped his face. "This one has a fence."

"And they are closer to each other," I murmured, my gaze traveling across the unending ring.

He nodded, and we snuck up to the fence, using a large boulder to block the nearest tower's view of us. Like with the first ring, the towers resembled volcanos, and there appeared to be no movement inside.

The fence was tightly twisted together out of steel wire. "The towers are too close," Myles breathed. "They'll see us if we climb."

"There has to be a gate somewhere?" I suggested doubtfully as I eyed the fence. I paused when I noticed the ground underneath the wire was uneven, but the bottom of the fence was flat, leaving gaps. "We can crawl under," I said instead. "Look at the space between the ground and the fence."

Myles scanned the perimeter of the fence and pointed to one of the gaps. "How about there?"

A boulder seemed to be wedged under the wire, creating a hole large enough to crawl through.

Myles knelt by it. "I'll go first." He stuck his legs through the gap and laid back, grabbing the fence with both hands and wiggling under.

He grimaced when he arrived on the other side. "The aura is much stronger over here. Don't come through until you're ready."

I took several steadying breaths and shut my eyes, imagining a lock in front of the cupboard I had shoved my aura into. With the key safely tucked into my imaginary pocket, I copied what Myles had done by grabbing the bottom of the fence and wiggling through.

As my head passed under, a tremendous weight of fear seemed to press onto my chest and I put my hand to my heart, breathing heavily. The volcano seemed to tower above us and my heart raced under my hand.

Myles helped me to my feet, and I squeezed his hand tightly as the increased heat seemed to smother me, alongside the auras.

He didn't flinch from my tight grip. "Remember, it's a magical warning, not actual danger."

"It will turn into actual danger soon," I whispered.

"Lucky for you, you are with someone who can teleport," he reminded me. "Try to take a few deep breaths and exhale slowly. A lot of what you feel is adrenaline."

"My family is in there," I whispered. "The amount of danger doesn't matter. With or without teleporting."

"Are you ready to keep going, then?" he asked.

"Yes." I released his hand, but didn't move my gaze from the volcano.

We're coming.

Chapter 27

The final barrier of guard towers loomed over us, connected with steel fences. Unlike the last set, the twisted steel went into the ground. No gaps and no chance of making one by digging under.

"I don't think we can scale it," I whispered. "We would be spotted."

We hid behind a large boulder, panting from the heat. Not only had the last set of barriers created a more intense feeling of danger, but it had also brought on a continual increase in temperature.

The towers were spaced out within easy shouting distance of each other. Even if we somehow managed to climb fifteen feet of barbed steel, it would be impossible not to be seen.

A guard's outline was visible in the tower to our right, staring across the burnt land. Apparently, he wasn't worried about anyone being near the fence.

Myles tapped his fingers against his thigh. "We could really use Soph right now."

"Who's Soph?"

"Sophie. She can turn invisible. She could cut a hole in the fence without being seen."

"Well," I began, resting my hand against the fence. "We can do it without her, right?"

"Done harder things before," he whispered. "I think I can cut the fence. But they might notice..."

"If you cut it, would you create sparks?"

"Yes, I would focus my lightning and burn through. It would light up purple."

"Is there any way for you to form something that isn't purple?"

Wolves howled distantly and Myles waited for them to stop before asking, "What do you mean?"

"You can read minds through an invisible electric conductor. Can you control that conductor and cut the fence with it?"

"Maybe." He held out his hand. Faint purple sparks jumped between them and I moved closer, hiding the sparks.

"Careful," I whispered.

"Invisible conductor," he breathed. "I need the presence of electricity without the sparks, like when you walk on a rug barefooted and touch someone. You feel the shock without seeing the spark."

He flexed his fingers and then curled them slowly. The little light the moon provided revealed what looked like a hazy cloud of electricity stretching between his fingers. Similar to how the air had been moving with the continually rising heat.

"Invisible lightning." Myles grinned. "This will come in handy."

We crept closer to the fence, and Myles reached his hand toward it. The hazy line jumping from his fingers crackled faintly, and I watched anxiously as the fence glowed orange where the steel was melting.

"Go quickly, they might notice the fence glowing," I whispered as I shifted to block the glow from the guard in the tower to our right.

"I know." His fingers trembled and as he made the final cut, the square fell away from us. "Shoot!" He frantically reached for the metal piece and barely snagged the cooled center before it clanged to the ground.

He held it, frozen, and neither of us made a sound as we

waited for some reaction from the Volcaniacs. When none came, he gently placed it next to the fence on the other side.

"That was close," he said with a nervous chuckle.

I nodded shakily. "Good catch, though."

Myles nodded and we wordlessly crawled through. Instead of the evil aura and unbearable heat increasing on this side of the fence, the heat dissipated. I took a deep, refreshing breath and Myles did the same.

"The heat must be a deterrent," he whispered as he grabbed the broken piece of the fence and propped it against the opening. "Hopefully they don't notice this."

"Can you smelt it back on?"

"Technically, but that will take too long. Besides, we can't block the light from this side of the fence. As long as we're out before sunrise, we should be safe."

"All right. Let's keep going, then."

Our footsteps were the only sound, and the volcano rose higher and higher above us. Myles whispered an estimated countdown of miles, and with three left, I stopped walking. From this distance, it looked as if the side of the volcano was moving. "Look," I said, pointing.

"Wolves," Myles whispered. A pack of wolves climbed the volcano, their outlines making the volcano's side come to life, rippling like deadly water.

We watched in fear-filled silence as they let out a chorus of howls, and a glowing orb appeared in front of the pack leader. One-by-one, they disappeared into the portal.

"Did they... call that portal?" I squeaked.

Myles frowned, his brow creasing. "I think so. I didn't know they could call them whenever they wanted."

"That must be how they hunt so well," I whispered. "And why there is such a long howl before they suddenly appear behind us."

"I guess we're not the only ones who can teleport," he agreed grimly.

Standing at the foot of the volcano made me feel dwarfed by its towering presence. A curl of smoke rose from the top, blocking the stars, and an evil aura seeped out, sending fear through my veins.

Myles pulled out the map and pointed to the highlighted area. "This is the secret entrance we are looking for."

"Then what?" I asked. "How will we find my family? We don't know what the inside looks like."

He folded the map. "We will need to send out our auras, but lightly. The aim will be to mingle with theirs without letting our masks slip."

I fidgeted with Ren's jackknife. "So, we sneak in through the secret entrance and start searching with our auras once we are inside?"

"Exactly, and not before. I want to avoid teleporting inside the volcano if possible. If we can get your family out undetected, we can follow this trail again."

"So, you don't want to teleport at all? Not even after we are back out?"

He shook his head. "I can't guarantee the Volcaniacs' auras won't taint the jump. And when I jump, my aura flashes, which could blow our cover. Remember that we still need to travel back to Mageye City from here. The more space we can put between us and the Volcaniacs before they notice that your family is missing, the better. We want a head start, and *then* I will teleport."

I looked back the way we had come. The final barrier of guard towers cast eerie shadows in the distance. We would need to pray for a portal once we escaped, but it was probably a safe bet to say there wouldn't be any in the fifty-mile radius surrounding the volcano. Which meant that we had to travel fifty-plus miles with six people, four of which might be weak from neglect... without getting detected.

Myles also looked back the way we had come. "If I have to teleport at any point, I will. And if the two of us keep our auras masked, even if my aura flashes, we should be able to hide again."

"We will stick close together, then, in case we need to teleport at the last second." I turned back. "But what if they are hurt and can't walk?"

"If they can't walk, we will help them walk." He met my gaze. "Rose, I hate to say this, but you need to know we are doing this on a whim. They might not be—"

"Don't say it!" I interrupted. "You said you won't take failure as an option, so don't even mention it."

His sparking eyes reflected his sorrow. "All right. But the Volcaniacs want you. And if they try to get you, and it comes down to it—"

"I'm not leaving them."

"Let me take your place," he finished.

"What?" I stared in disbelief. Was he actually thinking about sacrificing himself?

"They want the two of us now, and we can't let them have us both. If you won't leave your family, leave me. I will fight any guards that come and give you time to escape." His breathing shallowed and he pulled a small stone from his satchel, handing it to me. It reminded me of the walls of the portals we had been in, full of rainbows. "This is a teleportation crystal. I'm not allowed to use it except as a last resort. As long as I can still teleport, I swore not to use it."

He gently folded my fingers over the crystal. "It is a very powerful piece of magic, but if I'm not with you, you can't teleport, which means this is your only option. Once you are out of the volcano, you need to throw this at the ground and tell it to take you to Mageye City."

My breathing shallowed. "What about you?"

"This is only if the worst-case scenario becomes reality." He looked away from me as his expression darkened. "I will fight until you are safe, and then I will have to end my life. I can't let them have me; I know too much.”

“No!” I argued. “I’m not going to leave you, either.”

He turned back, purple lightning making his irises glow. “Promise me. It is my job. I swore to protect the Mageye whatever the cost. If I tell you to leave me, you need to leave me.”

“And let you die?” My voice dropped to a whisper. “No, I can’t... Myles... If you die...”

“Please, don’t fight me on this.” He stepped closer, his gaze imploring me. “Just promise me.”

Determined lightning continued to flicker in his electric purple irises, and it was clear this was a battle I couldn’t win.

I threw my arms around him and he stumbled, before hugging back just as tightly. “I promise,” I whispered. “But that doesn’t give you an excuse to sacrifice yourself.” I sniffed, hiding my face in his shirt. “I can’t lose you, Myles.”

“I only... I only want you prepared for the worst,” Myles whispered, voice thick with emotion. “I’m not planning on going anywhere.” When I looked up, he met my gaze, adding, “You’re one of my closest friends too. I don’t think I ever told you when you said it.”

I sniffed and managed a small smile as I stepped back from his arms. “The sooner we go in, the sooner we can leave again. Together.”

“Together,” Myles agreed, turning to our right. “Stay close, and I’ll grab you if we need to teleport. But hopefully it doesn’t come to that.”

We followed the curving base of the volcano and slowed our pace when an orangey-red light glowed from ahead. The entrance was nothing more than a crack in the volcano’s side, yet it appeared to be solid and not at risk of caving in.

Myles peered into the entrance, the eerie glow casting strange shadows across his face. “It’s quiet,” he whispered. “Let’s head in.”

This was it, then. We would be free, or dead, by morning.

Chapter 28

The crevice walls were made of roughly cut stone and while there was no obvious source of light, it maintained an orange glow. I took shaky breaths as I searched for my family with my aura, careful not to lose my grip and unveil us.

"I don't feel anything," I whispered.

Myles's aura mingled with mine and he nodded. "Me either. But we don't know how large this volcano is, and your family is likely closer to the bottom. That's where I would hold prisoners. Right now, we are at ground level."

"But you said magic is unpredictable."

"Magic is, but we're dealing with people now."

As we followed the crevice, the faint glow grew slowly brighter. Eventually, it opened into a large tunnel with a smooth stone floor. This tunnel went up, twisting both left and right. Caves and other corridors branched off on either side, but every room we passed was empty.

I continued to search for my family with my aura, but paused at the quiet buzz of voices coming from outside the tunnel. A large cavern opened before us and we cautiously stepped onto the outer lining of the inside of the volcano.

Trails etched along the walls, leading into countless corridors. Far down, in the hollow center pit, lava bubbled, which explained the orange lighting.

Additional pools of lava filled open-topped rooms throughout the volcano, obsidian stepping stones creating pathways through them. I stepped back from the edge, my head swimming at the thought of the fall.

"It's huge," Myles breathed.

The trails easily covered miles from top to bottom. Far above us, the sky was blocked by a cloud of black smoke.

Even at night, the inside of the volcano seemed alive. Volcaniacs passed through corridors, and wolves made their way along the walls. A woman on the other side of the volcano suddenly shrunk, turning into what looked like a cat or weasel, and scurried off.

Myles grabbed my arm, distracting me from the woman. "I feel them."

I clenched my hands into tight fists. "Where?"

He pointed diagonally down to our left. Close to the bottom of the volcano, a dark corridor led into a black abyss. From deep within, four auras pulsed faintly.

They were good auras but terrified, which left only one option. And even more importantly, it meant that my family was alive.

"Let's go," I whispered, fighting the urge to run.

We began our descent, hugging the wall to the best of our ability.

Two men suddenly appeared from a corridor behind us. We flinched, and Myles tensed his fists, but they hardly gave us a second glance.

One of them wore a dark cloak that hid his scarred face in shadow. "He is recruiting younger and younger," he muttered in disapproval.

"Not the baby anymore, hmm?" his companion snarked and the first scoffed, saying something I didn't quite catch.

"They don't suspect us," I whispered. "They thought we're Volcaniacs."

Myles nodded, lips drawn in a thin line. "That gives us more freedom while we look."

Another Volcaniac passed, her dark skin seeming to be

embedded with gold. She caught my eye and hers pulsed with gold as her gaze flitted over me.

I ducked my head and stepped closer to Myles, touching his hand once she was gone. He offered a tense smile. "Quarter of the way down."

"You wanted my presence, Your Majesty?" a monotone voice said from below us.

I stopped walking, and when Myles noticed, he came back. "What's wrong?"

"That voice," I whispered, trembling. "It's the Mageye who tried to kill us."

"The gray one? But he fell off of the cliff." Myles narrowed his eyes, confusion sparking in them when he saw how serious I was. "Are you certain?"

I nodded numbly, and peered over the edge. We stood above a lava-filled chamber, and two men stood amongst the obsidian stepping stones. One of which was a man I had met before.

The gray Mageye.

Myles's eyes sparked with shock. "How is he here?" he breathed.

The man the gray Mageye spoke with wore an obsidian crown and held himself with superiority. "They're here," he said. "Which means your trip wasn't a complete waste after all, Gray. If their transition goes well, you may have the younger twin and the mother. The other two may have their own uses yet."

Mom and Ren.

My knees buckled and I leaned into Myles as the gray Mageye—Gray—bowed. "Thank you, Your Majesty."

Myles clutched my arm. "We'll save them," he whispered. "That's what we're here for."

I shook my head. "But he said he knows... is he referencing us?"

A slow look of horrified understanding filled Myles's gaze and he pulled the map from his pocket. "It was a trick. He left this to lead us here." He stepped away from the edge. "But how does he know we are inside?"

The map suddenly burst into flames, and an X burned into the air before us; a searchlight. In his surprise, Myles dropped the paper, and it fluttered into the chamber the men stood in.

"No!" I tried to grab it, but only succeeded in showering loose stones down the side of the volcano.

The man I assumed was the Volcaniacs' leader looked up, and his face twisted into a cruel smile.

He had only one eye. Where his left eye should have been was a ragged X-shaped scar, and his right eye was dark, with orange flickering through it like a smoldering ember. "Seize them!"

Chapter 29

Myles grabbed my hand and pulled me into the nearest corridor. My hold on my aura slipped and before I could catch it, I had lost my grip. The air vibrated around me, making the hairs on my arms stand on end, as my aura pulsed and unfolded into the volcano. Followed by another pulse as Myles lost his grip.

"He's stronger than any Mageye I have met," Myles huffed. "He knew we were here even before we let our auras out."

"How strong is he? Stronger than you?"

Myles didn't answer my question directly. "I hope not."

We ducked into a small room, pressing our backs to either side of the doorway and panting. The corridor was silent and I fumbled with my pockets for Ren's jackknife, clutching it tightly. "Why aren't they chasing us?" I asked. "Someone must have seen us leave the center."

"He's like the wolves," Myles whispered. "He's got us cornered; now he wants to play."

"Or maybe he will go after my family," I said, my voice eerily steady as I straightened. "We need to play our own cards."

His eyes flashed with fierce lightning and he held a hand across the open doorframe. "Mask your aura."

Masking my aura was easier this time, the peridot green wisps shutting into my imaginary cupboard without complaint. I grasped his outstretched hand and the air crackled. With an electric snap, we reappeared in a dark tunnel. Myles stepped past me, his hands spread towards the entrance of the corridor, and a large, purple blast of lightning burst from his hands. Magnified crackling seemed to float away from us, accompanied by shouts and howls.

"That should distract them," Myles said, turning back. "Your family is down this tunnel."

So close. My breathing shallowed and I turned, backpedaling when a huge mountain lion turned the corner before us. Its hackles rose and the black X seared into its shoulder appeared to glow orange like the Volcaniac leader's eye.

I jumped back as it lunged forward, paws outstretched towards my waist. Purple lightning lit up the tunnel, charring the wall behind us as the mountain lion barreled me over.

Ren's jackknife clattered across the stone floor and I screamed as my apron was torn from me. Myles's next bolt of lightning hit the mountain lion and it shrieked, leaping over his head and disappearing down the tunnel that led back into the volcano.

"Rose," Myles gasped, throwing himself beside me. "Are you hurt?"

My chest heaved and I stared at the charred mark his lightning had left on the wall. "It got away!"

He looked after it, shaking his head and helping me to my feet. "Catch your breath, let any scrapes heal, and we'll pray that we can get your family out before it comes back."

I patted my skirts. Now apron-less, the large cut in the fabric from Gray's knife was unveiled, but even worse... "The teleportation crystal," I said.

Myles froze in picking up the jackknife, turning back to me and taking in my apron-less dress. "It was in your apron pocket, wasn't it?"

"Yes." I looked both ways, one side of the tunnel leading to my family and the other side leading back into the volcano. I turned back to the volcano. "That is our way out, and now the lion will be able to lead Volcaniacs back to us. We need to stop it."

"No," Myles said. "It isn't our way out. It served as an option, and now we will find a new option. If we leave this tunnel to chase the mountain lion, more Volcaniacs will have a chance to come back here before we find your family."

I held my hand out for Ren's jackknife and he pressed it into my palm. "You shocked the mountain lion," I said. "If it's badly hurt, that might buy us more time."

"Then let's not waste a second."

His boots clicked against the stone floor in time with his hurried pace and I followed. Though the auras of my family were invisible, it almost seemed that a soft glow, not unlike that of a portal, grew brighter as we followed the corridor deep below the surface.

The corridor ended in a domed room, the front and back half separated by obsidian bars. Bars that now remained as the only separation between me and my family.

Mom. Ren. Ryder. Raymond. They were *alive*.

Raymond lay on a cot in the back of the cell, and Ryder sat on the floor by him, legs stretched out. Mom sat in the opposing corner, stroking Ren's hair as he rested his head in her lap.

"Mom," I choked out, glued in place.

She looked up and Ren lifted his head, their eyes growing wide when they saw me.

"Rose?" Mom shouted as she rushed to the bars of the cells, reaching for me. Ryder scrambled to his feet, nearly falling onto Raymond's cot, and their movement seemed to unglue me.

I ran past Myles and threw myself into her arms. "I'm here," I sobbed.

Ren and Ryder came on either side of her, eyes wide with their shock. "What are you doing here?" Ren asked, his voice quavering.

I pulled back enough to look at them. "Saving you."

Their faces were gaunt, and Ren's eyes appeared almost hollow, no longer lit with the life and mischief I had grown up seeing. Mom tugged me back, pressing herself against the obsidian bars. "Are you all right? How... how did you get here?"

"I'm alive," I answered, disentangling myself and wiping my eyes as I looked at Myles. "This is Myles, and he... he is here to help me save you."

Myles stepped forward, frowning as he ran his hand down the obsidian bars. "We are going to get you all out," he promised.

Ryder stared at him. "How? We..." He looked back at Raymond, who sat up on the cot, wide-eyed, then back at us. "We haven't been able to figure out where we are. All we know is this place is ridden with black magic."

"We're in a place called The End," Myles said. "And the people holding you here call themselves Volcaniacs. I don't see a key or gate anywhere along these bars. How were you locked in?"

"One of the men here can make the obsidian grow," Mom said, peering at the corridor behind us worriedly.

"Can you cut through the bars?" I asked Myles.

"Not through obsidian," he said. "But I can teleport. The Volcaniacs already know we are here, and I don't see a better option."

"Then do that," I said, stepping back to watch.

A purple orb formed around him, and with a crackle of electricity, he reappeared on the other side of the bars.

Ren flinched and nearly fell. "What?"

"I'm what's called a Mageye," Myles said, holding his hands up. "It means I was born with a magic power, not black magic, but God-gifted magic." He looked between everyone. "Magic that is going to help me get you out. I need you to hold onto me, and we'll reappear outside the bars."

Ryder put a hand on Ren's shoulder. "Anything to get out, right?"

Mom stared at Myles before straightening her shoulders. "I have questions for you, but they can wait for us to be safe." She went to Raymond, who still sat on the cot. "I'll help you."

My heart skipped a beat when Raymond slowly swung his legs

to the floor. His left leg bent at an odd angle and he held it off the ground tenderly as Mom helped him up.

"Your leg!" I gasped, riffling through my satchel for any medical supplies. "What happened?"

"I'm fine, Rose. I'll just need help walking."

Myles walked to Raymond and grabbed his arm. "Here, lean into me. I'll make sure you don't get jostled when we teleport."

Raymond nodded and accepted the additional help as Ryder led Ren over. A purple orb formed around my entire family, and they reappeared in front of me with an electric snap.

Mom grabbed me and I dropped my hands from my satchel, hugging her with all my strength. "You're alive." I sobbed. "I was so scared..."

My brothers joined us, and for one still moment, we were safe in each other's arms, like no time had passed at all.

When we pulled apart, I turned to Myles, hurriedly introducing my family. His purple gaze studied them each in turn and he nodded. "Besides Raymond's leg, is anyone hurt badly?"

Ryder put a hand on Ren's shoulder and shook his head. "We're okay."

"Good," I whispered. "The Volcaniacs are... well, even the air in this volcano feels dangerous."

Myles murmured his agreement while Raymond shook his head. "These people are more than dangerous, Rose."

"I know." I met his gaze. "But I had to save you."

He leaned against the obsidian bars, his expression softening. "Thank you."

Myles had his back to us and the air around him seemed almost electric as he felt out the auras surrounding us. "I want to try and make it as far as possible before I teleport again. At least with these tunnels, we have a better cover. Once we are outside, it's open air. Then I can teleport us a farther distance when we are out of the volcano."

"With Raymond's leg?" I fretted, opening my satchel again. The bandages I had would provide little support for a sprained ankle, much less a broken leg.

"We can help him," Ren said, taking Raymond's arm. "Like how he always helps us."

Ryder took Raymond's other arm, slinging it over his shoulders. "Whatever um… the Mageye thinks is best."

"You lead, we'll follow," Mom said, gently tucking a strand of hair behind my ear. "As long as no one spots us, we will be okay."

I exchanged a look with Myles. "Not with Mageye around," I said.

"We'll just have to be as unexpected as magic," Myles said. "This corridor is only one way, so let's get back out."

With the mountain lion gone, the corridor was empty of auras—besides the general fear-inducing presence of the volcano itself—and we crept back down the way we had come.

Raymond leaned most of his weight into the twins, and I clutched Ren's jackknife tightly, walking alongside Mom.

Myles stopped at the entrance, the orange glow of the lava half-lighting his face. "This leads out into the hollow center. We'll be spotted if we go up the trails."

"Can we find another corridor that goes inside the walls?" I asked.

He hesitated. "I really hate being in these tunnels. It is like a maze to us." His expression darkened. "But they are our best bet."

A voice shouted something that echoed across the volcano, followed by a couple shouts. Mom put her arm out as if to block Raymond, Ren, and Ryder, while Myles cautiously stepped out of the corridor we stood in. "Raymond, can you make it up this slanted path to get to the next tunnel?" he asked.

Raymond grimaced. "It doesn't look like I have much of a choice."

Ryder shook his head. "We'll get you out."

"All right," Myles said, tilting his head back to the smokey roof miles above us. The center no longer teemed with life as it had been when we first broke in. Instead, voices continued to echo from inside the walls. "We need to hurry, and we can take a breather once we are inside the next tunnel."

I held my breath as we stepped out, our footsteps scuffing along the stone pathway. Myles paused outside the next tunnel, glancing continually between the interior and the open cavern we stood in. "I don't sense anyone inside," he breathed.

I stepped closer to the tunnel, holding Ren's knife forward. "Me either."

Mom looked over her shoulder and frantically ushered us inside. "Guards."

We hid inside and waited as a group of Volcaniacs ran past. They rushed down the tunnel we had just left, and Ryder's eyes widened. "They'll realize we're gone."

"Wait here," Myles said, darting back out of the tunnel.

"Myles!" I gasped, but Mom caught my arm.

"He'll come back," she whispered, before turning her attention to Raymond. "Are you all right?"

He panted, leaning heavily against the wall of the tunnel. "Sure," he wheezed.

Myles ran back to us, chest heaving. "I put a forcefield over the entrance. Blocks those Volcaniacs in, and with any luck, anyone else will assume the forcefield is sealing us in with them."

"Give us a chance to get away," Ren whispered, stepping aside to give Ryder room to get Raymond upright.

Unlike the corridor my family had been kept in, this one had many smaller corridors branching from it. Each time we passed one, Myles stopped to ensure no Volcaniacs were hiding inside.

The shouting we had heard outside grew fainter, but the same orangey glow lit up even the darkest corners. "Why is it all lit up like this? It isn't some sort of tracker, is it?" I asked.

"No, it's not a tracker," Myles assured me. "It is some form of magic, though. My guess is the lead Mageye's power lets him light things up."

"His eye looked like smoldering coals from a fire," I

whispered, and Ren shuddered, stepping closer to Mom.

Myles's expression darkened. "I know. I think we finally have our answer on who is controlling the volcano."

"By himself?" I asked in disbelief. "Won't he eventually hit cool-down?"

"I don't think so. Our powers can use fuel. His fuel could be the lava, so he can suppress it as well as use some of it to increase his power. Now if he were to fall into the volcano, that might overwhelm his aura and end his life."

"So, if we push him..." I trailed off, shaking my head at the impossible solution. "Forget it, but we can use elements of our powers to increase them?"

"Yes."

"We need to increase your power, then," I declared.

He shook his head. "I would need lightning. And we won't get that in here."

"Oh."

"It would be best if we don't fight at all," Mom said, looking between us. "Is that what you're discussing? Using lightning to... fight?"

Myles lifted his hand and purple sparks jumped between his fingers before he clenched his fist. "I agree with you, Mrs. Crawford, I would rather keep fighting as a last resort."

Her gaze lingered on his hand though he had quenched the sparks. "Am I correct in my assumption that your purple power is similar to some of the other things we have seen performed here?"

"A lot of the Volcaniacs are Mageye," I said. "Like us... me and Myles, I mean."

Raymond put his hand against a wall to steady himself, requesting a moment to catch his breath. Myles pursed his lips, but nodded permission, his gaze darting down either end of the glowing corridor.

Ryder tilted his head. "What do you mean you and Myles are both Mageye? What can you do?"

With all eyes on me, I froze. "Well... I can..." I huffed and flicked Ren's jackknife open. "Maybe it's better if I just show you."

"Wait," Myles said, stepping forward, but it was too late. I cut across my palm, hissing at the pain, but forcing myself to flex it and hold it forward anyway. "You'll go into..." Myles sighed. "Cool-down."

My family stared at me with equal expressions of horror. "Rose!" Mom said, grabbing my hand and examining the wound. "Why would you..."

She stopped as the pooling blood on my palm seeped back into my skin. Ren looked suddenly queasy, leaning against the wall beside Raymond, and Ryder's lips parted as he watched the wound seal itself shut.

"You can... heal yourself," Raymond rasped, dumbfounded.

I lifted my palm to display the smooth skin. "Yes. I have healing powers."

"And you just... healed yourself..." Ren said, eyes wide enough to see their whites. "That... was..."

"Her power," Myles finished, stepping forward. "It's a good thing, a blessing. She is a Mageye."

Mom traced her finger along where the cut had been, her hands trembling. "We... we will discuss this," she whispered, looking up, "later. Once we are safe. But for now, I suppose I don't need to be so worried about you getting hurt."

I forced a smile. "I only wish I could heal you all. But I haven't figured out how to do that yet."

"You can figure that out once everyone is safe," Myles said, taking my shoulder and nudging me forward. "We should keep moving. I don't want to linger anywhere for too long."

I flicked Ren's jackknife shut and cast my family a final smile, before following Myles down the corridor.

When we reached the end, Myles motioned for us to wait while he checked to see if we were alone.

Ren snuck after Myles and stood behind him. "How exactly

are we planning on getting out?" he asked. "I know we want fighting as a last resort, but..."

Myles nodded stiffly. "If that's what it comes to." His expression darkened. "How good are you at hand-to-hand combat?"

Ren clenched and unclenched his right hand, a nervous habit I hadn't seen in years. "I guess we'll have to wait and see."

"Is there a way to arm ourselves?" Raymond asked. "They have to store weapons somewhere."

"Rose and I talked about that," Myles replied. "All we have is her jackknife and what I'm carrying. But they won't be very helpful against any weapons the Volcaniacs have hidden away, not when they have magic."

I joined him and Ren, ignoring Myles's protest as I peeked out into the center of the volcano. The tunnel opened into a relatively empty part of the fortress, midway between the dungeon and the open top.

Myles pointed at a tunnel on our level, across the volcano. "I think we should take that one next. I can't sense anyone inside of it. But there is no way we will be able to get to it without being seen."

"Can you do that teleporting thing again?" Ryder asked.

"I think I'll have to." Myles sighed.

My brow creased with worry. "We already agreed to try to avoid that."

"I don't think I have a choice."

"But..." I hesitated, peering across the volcano again. "If you teleport too often, you could pass out, you could *die*, right? If you go too far into cool-down? A small jump is one thing, but across the volcano with the five of us?"

"I don't think I have a choice," he repeated. "If I don't teleport, then we have more of a chance of being caught."

I rocked back on my heels, reluctantly agreeing. "After this, we'll wait until we are outside, like you said before."

Myles nodded. "If that's possible, that will be for the best. I'll take us across and we will see if we can find a way to the secret entrance from there. I want to avoid teleporting directly to that corridor and having the Volcaniacs finding our exit."

Mom moved around Raymond and Ryder, putting a hand to Myles's forehead like she did to us when we were ill. "Are you sure teleporting won't hurt you?"

Myles started to pull back, then smiled wryly. "My dad would kill me if it does. He won't want to miss his chance to scold me for coming to The End without permission."

"I've raised four children," Mom said, stepping back. "I'll help ensure your dad gets the chance to scold you."

"We all will," I agreed.

His lip twitched, and he reached for my and Mom's hands. "Ready?"

Ren tightly gripped Ryder's free hand and nodded, so a purple orb formed around us. When it snapped, we reappeared hidden in the next empty tunnel.

The twins switched places, and Ren helped Raymond keep walking. Mom brought up the rear, refusing to let any of us out of her sight.

This tunnel was much shorter than the last, and it opened into an amphitheater. Rows of stone benches circled the theater, leading to the main floor. But where a floor had once been, a pool of lava sat. Stepping stones led to a throne of obsidian in the center, radiating darkness, fear, and *power*.

We had found the heart of the volcano.

Chapter 30

Mom took my hand and pulled me towards her. "I don't like this," she whispered, eyeing the throne sitting in the midst of lava. "It is much too open for us to cross, and that throne shouldn't be here."

"Shouldn't be here?" Ren echoed, clenching and unclenching his hand again. "What do you mean?"

"Alveraada has no king," Mom clarified. "Yet their leader wears a crown and has his followers refer to him as his majesty."

The image of the leader's one glowing iris flashed across my vision and I shifted my stance, eyeing the tunnel the way we had come. "The Volcaniacs don't follow any laws of Alveraada."

Myles's lip curled and he glared at the throne. "There is technically a king in Alveraada, within the magical layer of Mageye City." He glanced at my mom. "But his name is King Duncan, and he has nothing to do with the cruelty going on within this volcano."

She frowned. "What do you mean? Where is Mageye City?"

"My home," Myles said. "It is in Alveraada, but only people with a knowledge of magic are aware of it." His voice dropped. "The Volcaniacs are a threat to Mageye City. Once we are out, we can go there and ensure you all are safe. Then, the Elite Guard can start discussing how to stop this." He waved his hand across the amphitheater.

Mom and Raymond exchanged looks, but before either

could ask questions, I said, "I know this is a lot to take in, but you can trust Myles. He's risked his life for me already, and I think Mageye City is our best bet after this."

"Saved your life?" Raymond said, staring at me with wide eyes. He looked back at Myles. "We can... add everything with Mageye City to what we will talk about after."

"Agreed," Myles said. "There are more Volcaniacs on this side of the volcano, so we need to start moving."

Ryder took a small step into the amphitheater, his gaze flitting between the entrances spaced out along the circular wall. "How do we pick our exit?"

Mom shook her head sharply. "No, I still think this throne room is too open. If we try backtracking, maybe we can find another tunnel nearby."

"If we do that, then Myles will have wasted a teleportation," Raymond said, leaning into Ren.

"Jump," Myles corrected.

"Huh?"

"I call them jumps."

Raymond studied the empty air surrounding Myles, and nodded. "Myles would have wasted a jump then," he told Mom. "And we picked this tunnel for a reason, right?"

She put her hands on her hips. "We are incredibly blessed to have Myles here to help us with his... jumps. That has allowed us to get much farther from that horrid dungeon than they will likely anticipate, but crossing something like this," she waved a hand across the room, "puts us at risk of losing that blessing."

"I don't care how we get out, as long as we get out," Ren said, adjusting his hand to grip Raymond's side. "Rose is here and she says this Mageye City stuff is safe, so that's that."

I frowned despite his trust, studying the domed room nervously. The throne seemed to pulse, and orange and red swirled through the dark stone, eerily similar to the Volcaniac leader's one eye. Two obsidian wolves sat on either side of the throne, flames flickering in their dark irises.

Besides the throne and statues, the only other objects in the room appeared to be barrels. Each of the entrances to the room bore a staircase leading to the lava, and about halfway down, the sloping path flattened, two barrels standing on either side of the flat area.

What appeared to be staffs stuck out of them and my heart leapt. "Weapons," I breathed. "Mom, there are weapons, we have to cross this room."

"What?" She followed my gaze and slowly lowered her hands from her hips. "I see."

Myles stepped forward. "I think we should take them. They will allow you all to fight without it being hand-to-hand like if I gave you my daggers."

"I like that idea," Ren said, and even Mom nodded, so we followed Myles into the amphitheater.

The lava in the center of the room bubbled, and while a fiery haze hovered above it, none of the heat radiated towards us.

"Nine entrances," Ryder murmured, his fingers grazing my shoulder. "Can you sense any of those auras you mentioned?"

I swallowed hard. "Let's arm ourselves first."

Ren helped Raymond brace himself against the nearest seat before stepping away and pulling out one of the staffs. He frowned. "The tops are ashy; I think they are meant to be torches."

"That's better than nothing," Ryder said, pulling out a torch of his own.

"Fair enough."

Myles pulled out two torches, passing one to Mom. She weighed it in her hand. "Even if these are torches, they feel sturdy. What we need to do is pray they hold up if we need them."

"Let's pray we *don't* need them," Myles said.

"That would be even better," she agreed.

There wasn't a better prayer to be said, and I pulled out another two torches. Raymond still braced himself against a chair and I passed him one. "This can help you walk."

"Like Mr. Short. Using anything but a cane as a cane," he said, leaning his weight onto it. "You remember him, right? He used to bring us candy and he always used something new as a makeshift cane."

"I remember," I agreed with a smile, hovering my hands by him as he steadied himself, but my smile quickly faded when a shadowed figure stepped out of the entrance we had exited from.

"It looks as if you have gotten yourself trapped, now doesn't it?" the Volcaniac leader asked.

Chapter 31

Suffocating auras flooded the room, sending anxiety shooting through my veins that fast morphed into fear-filled adrenaline. Raymond nearly fell as he whirled to face the Volcaniac leader, blindly reaching behind himself to shield me. I gripped his hand, glancing at the other entrances in vain. Volcaniacs stood in each one with too many different auras to count.

Lightning sparked from Myles's fingers as he stepped past me and Raymond. "Don't come any closer," he warned.

The Volcaniac leader laughed. "I don't believe you're the one who makes the rules." His confident one-eyed gaze flitted over us. "You have nowhere to run; it will be better for all of us if you surrender yourselves."

"So, you are aware that your Volcaniacs will be injured in this fight," Myles said coldly, straightening his stance. "Good."

"To be so falsely confident," the man taunted, pulling a bright crystal from his pocket. It reflected like a rainbow from within and I gasped. He had our teleportation crystal. "Without this, you are helpless."

I tightened my grip around the staff I held. "Teleport?" I whispered to Myles.

His gaze had locked on the crystal. "We need it back."

My eyes widened and I nodded, lifting the staff. "We're not helpless," I said, though my voice trembled.

The Volcaniac leader's one-eyed gaze met mine and he

smiled, addressing the Volcaniacs calmly. "I want the Mageye alive; the rest can die."

Ren made a strangled sound as the Volcaniacs charged at us with a disciplined precision, each armed with the same staffs we carried. Even so, Ryder stepped straight forward, staff already raised. "This isn't how it ends," he spat.

"We'll see about that," a man laughed, baring fangs that dripped with green venom.

A bolt of lightning jumped from Myles's hand, sending the man crashing into two other Volcaniacs. He whirled back and caught Mom's hand, pushing her towards me and Raymond. "You three, stay together."

"What about—" I started to ask, but stopped as Raymond wrenched away the hand I still gripped.

"Behind you," he snapped, gritting his teeth as he stepped onto his broken leg, the staff I had given him to lean on now raised as a weapon.

Myles dodged the blow from a female guard and retaliated with a kick, tugging the dagger he wore from his waist at the same time.

Ren, Ryder, and Raymond now all fought, and I squeezed my staff with all my strength, lifting it as a Volcaniac ran towards me.

His eyes glowed with a hot pink undertone, and Mom swung her staff at his feet, sending him sprawling to his back.

"Mom!" I protested, but she straightened quickly, shaking her head.

"Your dad taught me how to defend myself, just like your brothers taught you. We are going to get out."

With more Volcaniacs than I could count, that seemed like awfully doubtful odds, yet God had used groups smaller than my family to defeat armies larger than this one. And if Myles could get us the teleportation crystal back, we could win this battle without finishing the fight.

The tip of a staff caught my jaw and my teeth dug into my

tongue, filling my mouth with the taste of blood. But I hardly registered the pain before I rammed the butt of my staff between the Volcaniac's eyes, dropping him to the ground as my power kicked in and the metallic taste faded.

The room echoed with the sounds of fighting, but the Volcaniac leader didn't appear to be joining in the battle. Instead, he lowered himself into his throne, having already crossed the pool of lava. He lazily waved his hand and the staffs the Volcaniacs wielded lit with flames, leaving us with cold staffs to defend against fire.

A wave of lightning lit the orange room with purple and nearly half the Volcaniacs fell. Myles's fighting technique was unlike anything I had witnessed before. While my family and I parried blows with Volcaniacs, he swiftly decapacitated one Volcaniac after another, hardly pausing for breath between strikes. He continually glanced back at the Volcaniac leader, eyeing the small island the throne was placed on in frustration as he attempted to get closer to the lava.

I tore my gaze from Myles as a woman ran at me and I copied Mom's move of striking her legs. Her torch rolled from her grip when she fell, causing a few other Volcaniacs to jump aside to avoid the flames.

As they parted, I gasped, nearly dropping my torch in horror. Raymond had been forced away from us by two Volcaniacs, backing down the stairs of the amphitheater and towards the pool of lava surrounding the Volcaniac leader.

"Raymond!" I screamed.

Ren turned and when he saw Raymond, he hurled his staff at his attacker, and began running down the stairs, but another Volcaniac caught his arm and shoved him to the ground. He disappeared behind a row of seats and I screamed again.

Two bolts of lightning shot across the room, one striking the Volcaniac attacking Ren and another striking one of the Volcaniacs corralling Raymond.

The remaining Volcaniac swung his staff at Raymond's

broken leg, and Raymond made a sound like a wounded animal, falling down the last set of stairs and stopping at the edge of the lava.

"No!" Mom screamed, practically hurling herself down the stairs, but she was much too far. We all were.

I tripped over a fallen Volcaniac, staggering to the side to avoid another attack, my gaze locked on the man towering above Raymond.

He laughed as he raised his foot, but then, like a whirlwind of fury, Ryder appeared.

His staff was raised high above his head, and he fluidly stepped over Raymond, effectively shielding him from his assailant.

Ryder's arms seemed to shake as he prepared to swing his staff down, and the sickening crunch of the man's skull echoed through the room.

He slumped to the ground, an endless, bloodcurdling scream erupting from him. The scream only stopped when Ren kicked him into the pit of lava.

They helped Raymond to his feet, and pulled him from the edge.

The Volcaniac leader stood, the two obsidian wolves standing alongside him. The obsidian encasing them folded off of their bodies, unveiling fur and teeth that glinted in the light.

Flames caught in the king's ember-like iris. "I'll finish them myself."

Immediately, most of the Volcaniacs stepped back, and it seemed as if everyone now watched the Volcaniac leader as he stepped directly into the lava. A wave seemed to rise from his feet, fast growing in height as it raced towards my brothers.

This time, no one attempted to stop me or my mom as we ran forward, and I held my hand out as if I could somehow catch the wave that no human—Mageye or otherwise—could possibly have the ability to catch with one hand.

But maybe with two.

Myles appeared out of an orb of lightning, the toes of his boots practically grazing the lava as he raised both hands above his head, arms trembling as the lava slammed into the purple forcefield he had created.

A crack slowly split the forcefield, but by the time it shattered, Myles and my brothers had already disappeared.

Chapter 32

The wave of lava rushed up the staircase and Volcaniacs dove aside to avoid it, leaving me and Mom standing alone with an orange sea of death. But two more orbs encased us, and we disappeared with identical electric snaps.

I stumbled out of the orb in a tunnel lit only with a faint orange glow. Myles caught onto me, his chest heaving but still very much alive.

Ren and Ryder were already helping Raymond sit against a wall, and Mom threw herself beside them. She tugged Raymond into her arms, trembling. "Praise God. You're alive. I really thought..." She lifted her gaze to Ren and Ryder, eyes clouded with tears. "I thought I was going to lose all three of you."

Her hair had fallen around her shoulders in a mess, and Raymond shakily reached out and tucked it behind her ears. "I'm alive. Myles saved us."

"I know." She cupped Raymond's face in her hands and gently pressed her lips to his forehead before standing and looking everyone over. "Is anyone hurt?"

I stepped closer to her and shook my head. "I'm not hurt."

"Only a little," Ren said, eyeing the large burn across his left elbow. "Maybe more than a little..."

Ryder wrapped his arm around Ren's shoulder, tugging his twin close. "Shows you're a survivor, right? I bet getting outside this volcano will make it ten times less painful immediately."

"I think so, too," I agreed, my legs still trembling. "Which way do we go? Where are we?"

Myles had doubled over, resting his hands on his knees, but he straightened now, pointing deeper into the tunnel. "That way leads out. I took us to the secret entrance we came in through."

My breath caught and I took half a step towards the secret entrance. "But I thought you said it was too risky to teleport to our exit."

"Not after what just happened," Myles said. He pressed the dagger he had fought with into Ren's good hand, before pulling a second from under his vest.

Ryder pulled away from Ren and helped Raymond to his feet. Raymond still panted, his face unnaturally pale, and he looked us all over before shrugging out of Ryder's grip. "We aren't free when we get outside, only out of their home... We'll need to run once we are out, won't we?"

"We'll help you," I said, looking at Myles. His lips were set in a firm line; he had never had the opportunity to try and steal the teleportation crystal back.

"I'm slowing you down," Raymond said.

I gasped, but Mom glared at Raymond. "Not another word if you are going to suggest we leave you. I'm not leaving my child behind."

"Mom," he tried. "There is simply no way—"

"You're stuck with us," Ren said, louder than I would have liked.

Myles winced, glancing nervously towards the center of the volcano, but the tunnel was silent besides our heavy breaths and conversation.

"The only way you're slowing us down is by trying to be heroic when you can barely stand by yourself," Ren continued, grabbing Raymond's arm with his good one. "So, shut up."

"I'm not trying to be heroic. I am stating a fact. I am slowing you down, and almost got you, Ryder, and Myles killed in the amphitheater. Besides..." He braced his free hand against the wall. "I can't keep walking much longer; you're going to have to leave me eventually."

Myles ducked between Raymond and his brace against the wall, slinging his arm over his shoulder. "Rose told me before we broke in that she won't leave unless all of you are leaving with her. So if you want Rose to get out, you need to keep pushing."

Raymond raised his brows and our gazes locked. "He's right," I said. "We'll help you."

"I'd rather stay behind and have all of you live than—"

Ryder tsked. "You're the one who has been telling us that we need to never suggest the possibility of one of us dying since we got here. Don't break your own rule."

Tears glistened in Mom's eyes and she spoke in a whisper, "They won't know when we are outside. That gives us a head start."

"And we have God with us," I said, my voice quavering. "So that means you have to come."

"All right," Raymond finally gave in. "You mentioned a secret exit?"

My heart skipped a beat and I turned back to the entrance turned exit. "Follow me."

With Ren and Myles helping Raymond, we began a slow march towards the crevice we had entered through. Raymond's good leg buckled and Ren grunted, bracing himself to not fall.

"Sorry," Raymond huffed.

I stopped and turned back, glancing behind everyone nervously. "What if someone carries you?" I suggested.

"I can," Ryder said, but Raymond shook his head.

"You can't carry me when we could get ambushed any moment."

Myles pulled Raymond's arm farther over his shoulders. "We will consider that when we are out."

"All right," I agreed nervously, watching as Raymond clenched his jaw so tight a vein seemed to pop from his skin.

"The sooner we get to the tunnel, the sooner we can get *out*."

"I still don't hear any voices," Mom said, relieved. "From what you and Myles described, we are almost there."

Almost there, indeed. When we finally found the crevice that led out, Mom turned. "Myles, can you create another one of those shields so no one can follow us?"

He hesitated, slowly stepping away from Raymond, as the tunnel was too narrow for him and Ren to both help. "I can try." He studied the tunnel silently, his expression suddenly falling as he turned back the way we had come.

"Myles?" I questioned.

"We need the teleportation crystal."

"We can't go back there," I fretted. "And... he said it himself, he doesn't think we stand a chance of getting out, so maybe we don't need it. He is underestimating us."

"And run fifty miles when the Wolvien Guard can call a portal with a single howl?" Myles asked incredulously, turning back. "With Raymond's leg and me unable to teleport that distance without going into cool-down?"

The eerie orange glow of the volcano cast shadows across his face that somehow made his concerns sound even more sinister. "How would we even get it back?" I asked.

Ren looked between us. "Are you talking about the... the rainbow rock he was bragging about?"

"A teleportation crystal," I said. "It could take us to Mageye City in seconds."

"Meaning we won't need to run..." Ryder breathed.

Mom crossed her arms, frowning back the way we had come. "You two keep talking about auras. Can we follow the false king's aura to try and steal the teleportation crystal back?"

Myles stared at her, shocked. "You mean you want to go back?"

"That's what you're suggesting, isn't it?"

Raymond slumped out of Ren's grip, leaning against the wall and panting. "We've been talking in this corridor for ages, we need to make a decision."

Auras pulsed across the volcano and I shuddered. "I'm scared to go back."

"We all are," Ren whispered, taking my hand.

"No," Myles decided, lightning flickering in his irises as he pointed at the secret tunnel. "I want you all to go ahead and wait for me outside the volcano. I am going to find the king, steal the teleportation crystal, and find you."

"What?" I asked. "No, we need to stick together."

"I have much better odds of getting the crystal alone," Myles said. "You will be safe outside, it's like your mom said. They won't expect that yet. And if I unmask my aura, they will be attracted to me."

"That makes you a target!" I said. "You want to turn yourself into bait like we have feared my family was this entire time."

"Bait is used to lure in your prey," he said. "I want the king."

"Wait," Mom interrupted. "No, I don't want to let you sacrifice yourself. If you don't come out with us, then you'll..."

Myles held her gaze. "I can't promise you will have four kids after this, if you don't let me. If we all go together now, we will be dead within the hour. There is nowhere to run."

She put a hand over her mouth, shaking her head. "Myles..."

"I've done scarier things," he said. "I have trained for this since I was eight."

"What if we come with you partway?" I started, but he shook his head.

"I'm sorry, but my decision is made and I will teleport right now if that's what it takes to get you to go ahead."

I grabbed his hand, pulling him closer and looking him in the eyes. "You made me promise to leave you if it came to it, and... and I know this isn't fully like that, but it's close enough and so now you need to promise me something. Promise me that you will be okay and come back to us. *Promise me.*"

Lightning flickered in his irises and he twisted from my grip, holding my gaze as he stepped back. "I promise. Wait for me outside, and I'll be there."

"You better," I said, clenching my fists and fighting the tears that threatened to spill.

"I don't break promises," he said, turning to run back the way we had come before anyone could reply.

I stared after him, and suddenly felt myself moving, but Ryder pulled me back. "He promised you. You need to trust that."

"God, be with him," I whispered as I ushered Ren and Raymond into the crevice. As Mom, Ryder, and I followed, I looked back, and saw a purple flash.

Chapter 33

The secret crevice was too thin for Raymond to have someone beside him, so he braced himself against the wall, stifling whimpers as I held onto him from behind myself and Mom kept him steady at his back. Ren led us, holding Myles's dagger ahead of him, and Ryder brought up the rear, whispering encouragement that he didn't hear any voices behind us.

Better than no voices, I didn't sense any auras behind us... including Myles's.

"The moon," Ren whispered. It was framed outside of the crevice, a welcome change of scenery from the inside of the volcano. He faltered, pressing himself against the side of the tunnel. "He told me I'd never see it again, but now here I am..."

"Who told you that?" I questioned. "A Volcaniac?"

He clenched his good hand tight and nodded, turning his gaze to Mom as she carefully squeezed around Raymond.

She surveyed the charred land silently, brushing a tear from her cheek as she turned to face us. "No one is out there."

"Good," I said. "Now we need to... wait." My voice cracked, and Raymond rested his hand on my shoulder.

"You saw how he can fight back there; he'll be all right."

I chewed my lip, fighting the urge to unveil my masked aura and search for Myles. "The Volcaniac leader's aura is more powerful than any other aura I've felt. And when I asked Myles if he was stronger, he didn't answer."

"If the stronger person always won," Raymond began, "then every time a cat chases a mouse, it is a promised meal."

Ryder leaned against the opposing wall of the crevice. "Remember that time when Rose beat Ren in a wrestling match and she gloated for an entire week?"

My lip twitched. "Maybe you're right."

"He's right," Ren said, draping an arm over my shoulder. "Because I agree with him, despite his example being an insult to me."

I stepped closer to him, resting my head on his side. "I really missed you all."

Mom stepped forward and took both my hands, smiling through her tears. "We missed you too. We never had any idea what happened to you, since you weren't at the house when it happened."

A lump formed in my throat and I squeezed her hands, hoarsely whispering, "I was trying to figure out what my power was and... and make it go away."

"Yes," she breathed. "Your power... You will have to tell us more, when Myles comes and we are able to use the... teleportation crystal."

"The teleportation crystal," I murmured, pulling my hands from her and stepping away from Ren. "We need to..." I hesitated, looking back the way we had come, but being greeted with an empty tunnel devoid of Myles's echoing footsteps. "We need to go outside, and when Myles comes, we will use the crystal."

"Then we will go outside," Mom said, wiping her tears. She turned and took Ren's hand, gently leading him to the exit. Raymond, Ryder, and I shuffled after, all of us huddling against the side of the volcano once we were out.

Far in the distance was the faint outline of the guard towers Myles and I had slipped under only hours ago.

Ryder stepped up to Raymond, urging him to lean into his

side, before turning to me. "Should we move a little away from that tunnel?"

I looked back at it and nodded, picking a side of the volcano to walk along. It was eerily quiet outside and we stopped under a sheer length of the volcano. A short cliff towered above us, ensuring no one could attack from above without dropping and risking injury.

While Mom helped Raymond sit on a large boulder, I turned to the volcano and pressed my palm against it. Myles had told me he could sense everything within a five-mile radius, but this volcano certainly extended more than five miles across, above, and below us.

Even so, I spoke in my mind as I had done when Myles connected our thoughts before. *We are outside... please hurry. Please be safe.*

There was no answer and I rested my forehead against the volcano, lifting my head with a stifled gasp when howls tore through the night.

Ren grabbed Ryder's arm, tugging him flat against the volcano's cliff beside him, both wearing near-identical wide-eyed expressions.

"Where are they?" Raymond whispered as a second chorus of howls sounded.

I screwed my eyes tightly shut, a tear slowly making its way down my cheek. "Above us."

"They're big," Ren whispered, gripping Ryder's hand in a bone-crushing grasp. "As tall as we are."

"The Wolvien Guard," I agreed. "Myles said they are the best hunters in all of Alveraada."

Mom knelt and picked up a large rock, pressing it into Raymond's hand and casting a nervous look back at the volcano. "Should we consider going back inside?"

"We have better odds fighting them out here than in that small crevice," I whispered, my head swimming with fear.

"Better odds..." Ren whispered in a tone that suggested he was as well aware our odds were close to negative as I was.

"Myles will come," Mom said. "Keep praying."

"Haven't stopped for a moment," Raymond said.

The howling renewed and I clenched my hand around Ren's jackknife, fighting the sob that threatened to crash from my lungs. There was no sound of pounding paws, but surely the wolves were outside—on the volcano—and looking for *us*.

The howls cut off mid-chorus and the entire world went silent, then the color faded with it. *Gray.*

I pressed my hand over my mouth to keep from screaming when he spoke from somewhere above us. "I suppose you now get to see how quickly I can remove a heartbeat from a living being."

Slowly, I tilted my head back and were it not for his power once again taking my voice, I would have screamed. Dark robes billowed in a light breeze, and he stared down at us placidly.

Raymond dragged himself to his feet, and Mom stepped out of the cover of the overhang, her gaze locked on Gray.

I stepped out with her, followed by Ren, Ryder, and Raymond. Wolves moved like dark shadows along the sides of the volcano and Gray stood still, but then he stumbled.

Myles, I screamed, my gaze darting between Gray, the wolves, and the crevice that surely provided only a brief second of safety before imminent defeat.

Gray stumbled again, and this time, so did we, and the wolves. The gray air flickered with a brief flash of color, and a few of the wolves stopped running, looking instead at the top of the volcano that now faintly glowed orange.

An electric snap made us all jump and Myles stumbled out of a gray orb, but as the last spark disappeared, it was purple. Gray was losing his hold.

Myles clutched his ribs, and tears trailed through the soot on his cheeks as he reached towards me, shoving a smooth crystal into my hand.

It was gray, but flickered as Gray stumbled again, turning his gaze back to us. Before he could remove a single heartbeat, a deafening roar from the volcano made the very air shake and lava arced high into the air above it.

The wolves' howls soon turned into screams of pain, and Gray turned, his cloak billowing as he ran back up the side of the volcano, colors flashing in and out of the area surrounding him. A brilliant purple orb suddenly encased us, and we disappeared with one final electric snap.

Chapter 34

The world seemed to erupt with light and I stumbled, tripping and falling onto Ryder's stomach.

He choked. "Are you okay?"

My arms trembled as I pushed myself up, staring at him in shock. He lay in soft grass, and the first streaks of dawn lit up what seemed to be The End transformed. The tree we sat under shuddered and life poured from it. Leaves unfurled, grass burst through the cracked ground, and a white bird flitted past, coming from the direction of the surrounding forest.

"I'm okay," I breathed, blinking at the volcano in shock. It was nothing more than a smudge in the distance, lit by the lava coursing down its sides. "What... happened?"

"Myles," Ryder huffed. "Teleported?"

"I think so..." I jumped to my feet, nearly tripping again and catching myself against the trunk of the tree. Clutched in my fist was a brilliant crystal reflecting a rainbow from within. I showed Ryder with shaking hands. "The teleportation crystal... All we need to do is throw it and shout for it to take us to Mageye City, that means... that means..." I stopped, looking around the rest of my family.

Raymond was deathly pale, his jaw clenched tightly shut as tears slipped down his cheeks. When Mom knelt beside him, he shook his head, chest heaving. Evidently, the crash-landing hadn't helped his broken leg. But he was *alive* and seemingly...

safe?

Ren had fallen near me, and he reached for Ryder's hand. "No more fire."

My lips moved as I counted heads. Mom, Raymond, Ryder, Ren... Mom, Raymond, Ryder, Ren... Mom, Raymond, Ryder, Ren...

We were short a person.

"Myles?" I called, looking around the flowering woods. Everything continued to bloom with life, leaving Myles's still form jarringly out of place.

"Myles!" I shouted, running to his side.

Purple sparks jumped and sputtered from his unconscious body. "No!" I fumbled for his wrist, pressing my fingers hard in search for his pulse, but all I got were the sting of sparks and a weak flutter.

More sparks sputtered out and hot tears blurred my vision. "You're in cool-down? Right, Myles... cool-down? That's it?"

I rose on my knees, leaning over him and grabbing his shoulders to stare him in the face. He was too pale, too clammy, too drained...

My fingers fumbled with the teleportation crystal, preparing to hurl it, but then I faltered, recalling something Myles had once said. There came a point where cool-down became more than an overuse of magic, but something that drained our physical being. And that point was something that no amount of time would allow us to recover from. Which meant Myles couldn't afford the delay of interruptions from Mageye in Mageye City. He needed me to help him now or else he would...

But *that* couldn't be Myles's fate, could it? Not after we survived everything else the Volcaniacs had thrown at us... yet, here he lay, beside a girl with healing powers... powers that healed nothing but herself.

"No," I stated, pushing against him. "Heal. Heal, Myles."

My aura felt oddly still and I sobbed, shaking my head as the final few sparks began to sputter. "God, please!" I shouted, pushing against Myles with all my strength. "Myles can't die... please..."

But, his chest rose once more, and as the last purple spark flickered out, he went still.

"No!" I threw myself on top of him. "No! Why can't I heal you?" I screamed. All the pain, and fear, and grief from the past few weeks pouring out as I lost the person who had gotten me through it all.

My family stood around me, a few sniffs, and someone gently tapping the hand I grasped Myles's shoulder with.

"No..." I tugged my hand away, but they tapped again and I looked up.

A small white bird perched on Myles's shoulder, gently tapping my hand with its beak. It straightened itself and the light from the rising sun seemed to make its breast feathers glitter.

A Golden Dove.

I scrambled upright, my chest heaving as it gently preened its feathers. Myles had said the feathers of a Golden Dove can carry healing powers if you get them with pure intentions... not out of selfishness or evil intent.

"He gave his life," I whispered, slowly reaching for the dove. "Please help me give it back."

It held perfectly still as I gently plucked feathers from its breast. It cooed as it took off, settling in the branches of the tree above us.

I gripped a feather tightly in each hand and sat up on my knees again, bracing my hands on Myles's shoulders once more. A tear slid from my face and landed on his, slipping into the grass behind his head.

"Powers can change over time," I whispered. "Wake up, Myles."

I shut my eyes and envisioned the peridot green blanket of my aura, but instead of locking it in a cupboard to mask it, I pushed it into Myles, letting it course through his veins and into his heart.

My chest grew warm, and that warmth seeped down my arms and into Myles's skin, soon returning with blooming pain in my ribs, burns across my arms, and raw agony across my wrists.

The pain kept coming and when I opened my eyes, some of the color had returned to Myles's cheeks.

"Come on, Myles," I whispered, pushing harder and squinting against pain in my cheek as a scrape faded from his skin.

Sweat dripped down my face, and I swayed, but Mom and Ren braced me, watching in awe as Myles's chest softly rose, then fell again.

A final rush of warmth seeped from my heart and I took a deep breath, this time pushing every ounce of my being into him.

Myles took another breath, then his eyelids flickered.

The last thing I saw before I passed out were his eyes. His right eye was the same electric purple I had grown so used to seeing, but his left eye was the same peridot green as my own eyes.

Chapter 35

"Shh, we have patients sleeping," a woman hushed, and I opened my eyes to find myself surrounded by cheery yellow paint and cream curtains.

A cracked window swept a refreshing breeze through the cubicle, and I sat up. "Mom?" I called nervously, tugging the blankets back when the curtains shielding me rustled and Mom came through.

"Rose, you're awake!" She hurried to my bedside. "How are you feeling?"

"I'm... okay..." I pulled back from her hug, taking her in. She wore a clean, floral dress, and her hair was neatly tied back in a bun. Besides a few clean bandages, she appeared no worse for wear, and I shakily touched my fingers to the white gauze. "Where are we?"

She smiled. "Mageye City."

"Mageye City?" I tugged my hand away, leaning over the bed to peer out the window. My view was of a sprawling courtyard where a few young guards trained. A vine shot by their feet and tripped two of them; the Mageye who tripped them laughed as he caught ahold of the green weapon. I turned back to Mom. "How?"

"Ryder said you explained the teleportation crystal to him." She gently urged me back into bed. "I know you can heal yourself now, but we were told you went into cool-down and will likely be exhausted when you wake up."

I hardly registered her concerns, as the word *we* still rang in my head. "I'm not sore, but what about you? You have bandages... and Raymond's leg? Ren's arm? Ryder? Are they—"

"Safe," she interrupted, resting her hands on my shoulders. "We are all safe. King Duncan was kind enough to lend us a room in the palace, and your brothers are there now. You are in the hospital wing for closer monitoring."

"King Duncan?" I breathed, half-leaning out of bed again, but she pushed me back. "What about Myles?" I whispered. "King Duncan is his dad, did... did Myles..."

"Gave his father the scare of his life." Mom smiled. "But hasn't shown one sign of pain since he woke up yesterday afternoon. You both were unconscious when we arrived."

Tears blurred my vision and I sank back into the cushions. "Everyone is alive?"

The mattress sank as she sat, clasping her hand over mine. "Everyone is alive."

"Thank God," I breathed, wiping my tears with my free hand. "How long was I unconscious?"

"We arrived in Mageye City yesterday morning," she explained. "So, you were asleep for a little over a day." She gently brushed hair from my face. "You seem very alert; you aren't exhausted at all, are you?"

"It's like nothing happened."

Her expression softened. "Good. I prefer my daughter alive and in one piece."

I laughed, sitting up again. She watched my every movement carefully and I examined my hands. No signs of any cuts, or scrapes, or burns. While healing Myles, my wrists had felt scalded, but my skin was now soft and pain free. "Mom," I began. "Myles opened his eyes before I passed out, and..." I stopped, reflecting on how his left iris had looked... like a magical reflection of mine.

Mom nodded as if she already knew what I meant. "Yes,

when Myles woke up, one of his eyes reflected yours." Her gaze lingered on the left side of my face. "And one of yours reflects his."

My hand flew to my left eye. "My eye is purple?"

"Yes." She stood and opened a drawer on a small nightstand, rifling through it.

The curtains rustled again and a nurse stepped in. She was young, maybe in her early twenties, and when she smiled, the overwhelming urge to hug her flooded over me. Her eyes were a warm yellow, the color of sunflower petals, and she looked as if I could melt into her soft arms. "I thought I heard voices coming from in here," she said cheerily. "It is nice to finally meet you, Rose. I'm Sadie, though you may hear me be referred to as Nurse Ansley."

"Um... hello." I glanced at Mom as she turned to Sadie.

"Do you have anything we can use as a mirror? So Rose can see her eye."

"There is a spoon in my pocket," Sadie said, laughing as she pulled it out. "Will that work?"

"I think so," Mom said, accepting it and passing it to me.

I held the spoon up, and my warped reflection stared back at me. One eye was the same peridot green I had always had, and the other eye was the deep electric purple that defined Myles's power. "Will it stay?" I asked.

Sadie hummed. "If I were you, I would hope so. My mom and sister both have lavender eyes, and I have always been jealous. But I believe King Duncan will have a better answer for you, and that is actually why I am here." She addressed Mom. "He asked us to send for him when she awakens, may he come and speak with her privately?"

Mom kissed the top of my head. "Of course. I will step outside."

I watched after her, and handed Sadie the spoon back nervously. "Thank you."

"Don't worry," she assured me. "King Duncan likes to greet

every Mageye that Myles brings home; you aren't in any trouble."

I relaxed a little. "So, it is a... greeting?"

"Something like that, and he is very kind. Not at all how you likely expect a king to be."

"Myles has only said good things."

"It is an honor to work in King Duncan's palace," she agreed. "He should be outside; I will get him for you."

She turned to walk out, but I called her back. "Can I ask what your power is?"

She laughed. "I can help stimulate calmer emotions. So can both of my sisters."

My eyes widened. Myles had told me about three sisters who could stimulate positive emotions. "I think Myles mentioned you. He said a member of the Elite Guard gave him peppermints."

"My twin." Sadie smiled. "Avery. Who would have guessed we would both wind up in the palace?"

"Your powers probably help a lot."

Her eyes sparkled. "I like to think so." She cracked the curtain and glanced back. "I'll tell King Duncan you're ready for him. But I'd love to talk more later."

"Thank you."

When she left, I swung my legs off of the bed and smoothed my skirts, looking up when a tall man with silver eyes walked in. He wore no crown, but held a regal air about him. King Duncan.

To my delight, Myles followed him into the small cubicle, and he grinned at the sight of me.

I stood slowly, turning my attention to King Duncan. "Hello," I greeted, attempting my best curtsy.

He offered his hand when I straightened. "It's nice to meet you, Rose. I'm King Duncan, as you likely already know."

"It's an honor to meet you, Your Majesty."

"Thank you." He studied my gaze. "Forgive my staring, but I've never seen anything like this."

I looked at Myles. His purple and green gaze flashed with

light as our eyes met. "I like the purple," he said.

The corner of King Duncan's mouth twitched. "Yes, I am sure your purple eye is the one you have been admiring in the mirror."

Myles's cheeks flamed and lightning sparked in his purple iris. "I was *not* admiring anything," he protested under his breath.

I bit back my smile. "Is it permanent?"

King Duncan nodded. "If my understanding is correct, Myles's heart had stopped beating when you healed him. And so, in order to save him, you gave him a part of yourself. Your auras must have intertwined, and the final result is that your eyes reflect each other's."

I glanced at Myles again, shaking my head. "But our eyes show our magic, so does that mean our auras are connected now, or even our powers?"

King Duncan opened his mouth, before looking at Myles, who was giving him a wide-eyed look. The silver in his irises seemed to swirl like mist and he chuckled. "I would like to continue this discussion, but Myles is anxious to speak with you. Perhaps you would be willing to meet with me once you are discharged?"

"Of course, Your Majesty. Thank you."

He stepped forward, his irises swirling again as he took both my hands in his. "Thank you for saving my son. Your sacrifice will be remembered."

"Y-you're welcome." I looked over his shoulder at Myles. "He sacrificed himself for me and my family. That will be remembered, too."

"I am sure it will." He released my hands and turned to go, pausing beside Myles. "Will you be staying here for a while?"

"Yes." Myles nodded. "Mrs. Crawford invited me to dinner."

"Send her my thanks for hosting you."

"Yes, sir." Myles watched his dad go, and when the curtain shut behind him, he turned back to me.

"Myles!" I gasped, running to him.

"Rose," he breathed, hugging me tightly.

When we pulled apart, tears glazed my eyes. "You're alive," I whispered, pressing my hand to his chest. His heart beat steadily and he clasped his hand over mine.

"You made me promise," he said. "But I only kept it *because* of you. Thank you."

I stepped back, meeting his purple and green gaze. "No, thank you. You sacrificed yourself, Myles. My family would have died if it weren't for you, and I never would have made it to The End on my own."

He shrugged. "Well, like I said when we first met, it was strictly a work assignment."

I put my hands on my hips. "Liar. You did it because you cared. That's why you came back."

His purple iris sparked with lightning. "I thought I was the mind reader."

Epilogue

"Rose, open the door!" Myles yelped as feet pounded down the hall.

I leaned over from my desk and opened the door to my new bedroom in Mageye City. He burst into the room, laughing as he slammed the door shut and braced himself against it.

"What are you doing?" I asked.

"Hiding from Raymond."

"I'll get you back," Raymond called through the door. "Unless Mom scolds you for shouting in the hall when half the house is still asleep."

Myles snickered, standing when Raymond's footsteps receded after a few more threats. "Beat him down the hall without needing to teleport."

"What did you do?"

He shrugged. "You said I could come over, so I teleported into the kitchen and he spilt his coffee."

"I said you could come over when you were still in the palace." I laughed. "And I didn't tell anyone else yet."

"I noticed," he agreed, still snickering as he followed me out of the room.

Raymond was in the kitchen, wiping up the spilt coffee, and he tossed the wet rag at Myles. "Nice of you to visit."

"Thanks," Myles said cheerfully, catching the rag. "Rose invited me."

"Yes, but she is the only one who can talk to you telepathically from the palace," Raymond teased.

"It has advantages," Myles decided, tilting his head at me. *Don't you think?*

I smiled as I took the wet rag from him, tossing it into the basin in the sink. The night I woke up in Mageye City, Myles's thoughts had started running into my head, and mine in his, even when we were in different rooms. Now, after a month with constant communication, it was clear that more than our eyes had changed in The End. We now had a telepathic connection that knew no boundaries. Wherever we were in Mageye City, we could talk as if we were standing side-by-side.

More than a few, I agreed.

"You owe me a coffee," Raymond decided. "One of the ones from the palace with the sparkly stuff in it."

"You mean the sugar?" Myles asked. "It tastes the same as normal sugar, it just looks special."

"It's pretty," I chimed. "We should buy some for us, I bet it would look pretty in a pie."

"Strawberry pie?" Raymond asked me, winking. "I doubt Mom will refuse."

"Me either," I agreed. "The last time we had strawberry pie was the day I found out about my power."

"Hard to believe that was over two months ago," Raymond mused.

"Yes," I agreed, sobering as I examined his leg. I had healed the break, and Ren's burn, and everyone else's scrapes the day I awoke... but sometimes I found myself expecting the wounds to appear all over again, or Myles to collapse like he had at The End.

Raymond didn't seem to notice my shift in mood, as he said, "I am going out to the stables, I am beginning to think Lucy is pregnant."

"What?" I asked, snapping out of my reverie. We had returned to Sunset Hollow to assure everyone we were safe, get our horses, and return everything I had... borrowed... from

Pastor Wilson, before making a permanent move to Mageye City. "Since when?"

"Still a suspicion," he teased, turning to go. "But you'll be the first to know when it is confirmed as fact."

"Foals," Myles hummed. "That would be fun."

"It always is," I agreed, watching Raymond's leg as he walked to the front door. "Raymond, wait. How is your leg?"

"My leg?" He kicked it to the side to demonstrate it didn't hurt. "Hasn't caused me one ache since you healed it."

I let out a breath of relief. "Good."

He smiled and left, leaving me and Myles alone in the kitchen.

Myles raised a brow. "You're not doubting your power, are you? It won't disappear or reverse itself."

"I know, but sometimes..." I shrugged. "I get worried."

He clucked his tongue. "If you keep doubting magic, I might need to teleport you off the nearest cliff—into a lake, of course."

I laughed. "You've already done that."

"It's what I do," he declared loftily. "Amongst other Mageye-related things."

"Like what?" I asked.

"Well, I snuck out of the palace before General Cornstone could catch me," he whispered, "so nothing, for today. I was thinking we could visit Soph."

"You don't need to ask me that twice," I said with a smile. "We can go now, and you can buy us pastries at the market as thanks for letting you hide in my room earlier."

"Should we start with a jump?"

I took his outstretched hand. "How else would Mageye travel around the city?"

Bonus Content

If you are the kind of reader (like me) that looks to see how many pages are left as you near the end of a book, you likely noticed that *The Mageye* has ended with a relatively thick chunk of pages left. That is because you have officially arrived at what might just be my favorite part. Bonus content.

Since you are reading the second edition of my debut novel, I wanted to make the bonus content extra special. That way, new readers and returning readers alike can enjoy the book from cover to cover. And so, I have not one, but *two* bonus short stories for you (and this trend will continue throughout *The Mageye Trilogy* second editions).

And as an extra bonus, I have a confession. The first short story you will read has been my least favorite scene to edit for *years*. Why? Well, because (as you will see) it picks up where Rose left off in the volcano. When she takes her family outside and Myles runs away to get the teleportation crystal back... Yeah... That scene... Up until this version, we had an overlap, as in, we get the same conversation in opposite POVs. That meant every time I made an edit within the actual chapter, I had to come to the bonus content and reflect it. And I found this to be endlessly annoying, that is, until the absolute literary genius, McKenna

Rowell, said, "Paris, you can just cut the overlap out and start after the switch." Mind. Blown.

I no longer find Myles's short story endlessly annoying. Now, I love it, but I think I love the short story from his dad's POV even more...

MYLES

Rose's eyes flashed with a deep green, the orange glow from the volcano lighting her face with an eerie light. *"Promise me."*

I couldn't tear my gaze from hers, but I twisted my hand from her grip, stepping back the way we had come. "I promise. Just wait for me outside, and I'll be there."

She clenched her hands into fists. Tears threatening to spill. "You better."

Of all the promises I had made and upheld in my life, this was the closest promise to impossible I had ever made. But with the warring emotions of the Crawford family flooding my thoughts, I forced the promise out again. "I don't break promises."

Before anyone could reply, I turned and ran.

Dad had started training me on how to sense with my aura soon after I moved into the palace, but my training had become much more vigorous when I was eight and told him I wanted to join his Elite Guard.

A decade of training later, identifying auras hardly took more than a thought, and right now the aura I wanted to find—the Volcaniac leader's—was above me. He had clearly left the amphitheater behind and a second aura pulsed alongside him. *The teleportation crystal.*

Purple lightning flickered around me and I disappeared with an electric snap, reappearing in another orange-lit corridor.

If auras were physical beings, it would be like a soft blanket tucking you into bed. But, if the auras radiating from before me were physical, it would be as if that blanket was weighted with scalding water, pinning you to the bedsheets and muffling your screams as you slowly suffocated from within a cocoon only you could see.

"Steal the crystal." I mouthed words to myself, careful not to make a sound. "Get information from the leader if you can... Prioritize teleporting out to save Rose."

I crept down the tunnel, mouthing more words as I went. "Steal the crystal, keep the promise you made Rose. Don't. Die. Steal the crystal..."

The tunnel led out to what almost looked like a wraparound balcony across the rim of the volcano, the open top a mere ten feet above me. A wolf growled and I quickly hid in the shadows, watching as a dreadfully-familiar member of the Wolvien Guard passed the entrance of my hiding place.

It was missing an eye, and I grit my teeth—why had the wolves hunting us returned? Had they tracked us all the way to The End?

"So, the teleporting is what led your hunt to fail," a deep voice grumbled.

I braced myself and inched forward, laying eyes on the Volcaniac leader as he gripped the wolf by its snout. It whined, tucking its tail between its legs.

"Find them," he snapped. "Bring the pack with you." He released the wolf's snout and it quickly backed away, shaking out its mane before running and leaping the ten-foot height to get outside the volcano.

Lightning crackled from my fingers and I quickly stifled it, pulling back into the tunnel. The wolf had left the volcano on the side the secret entrance was on, meaning Rose and her family would be waiting for me in its line of sight. Though they would appear far below, at the volcano's base, and even with the Wolvien Guard's shockingly fast speed, it would take several minutes for them to get down the mountain...

"You have clearly been trained," the Volcaniac leader suddenly said and I froze as he continued, "Yet here you hide."

The hair on my arms rose, but I pushed myself up from the wall and stepped out of the shadows, purple sparks flickering between my fingers. "Hiding?" I questioned. "You haven't even lifted a finger against any of us. Six of us against your entire army."

His one iris seemed to light with flames and his gaze flitted over me. "I must admit your fighting style was impressive. But I hope that doesn't fill you with false confidence, you are *nothing* compared to me."

"We'll see about that," I spat, teleporting to stand behind him, my gaze darting over his cloak in search of which pocket the teleportation crystal hid in.

He whirled to face me and his fist slammed into my gut, sending me skittering back and I gasped as my legs hit open air, over the edge of the volcano. My fingers scrambled for a hold and I dragged myself back over the ledge.

The Volcaniac leader met me, grabbing my hand and hurling me through the air. I slammed into the back wall of the volcano with a sickening crunch, my ribs screaming in protest as I slumped to the floor, panting heavily.

No one had ever reacted to my teleporting so quickly, and ignoring the pain splitting across my chest, I pushed myself to my knees, waving my hand and pushing a torrent of lightning towards him.

He didn't dodge as quickly as he had with my jump, and cursed as a bolt hit his arm. Another wave of lightning quickly followed, and another, but my wrists were suddenly caught ahold of and tugged to the ground, forcing me to kneel.

Obsidian cuffs had me chained, and I pulled against them, casting the Volcaniac leader a horrified look.

"False confidence," he growled. "I warned you."

Despite the urge to cower, I narrowed my gaze, hope surging through me when his cloak shifted and a faint rainbow glow illuminated the dark shadows in the fabric's fold.

He studied me closely, looking from me to the pocket my gaze was locked on. "It's your only escape, isn't it? You know you won't stand a chance outrunning my Wolvien Guard, even with your teleporting."

I opened my mouth to reply, but stopped, grimacing as the obsidian cuffs began to heat up, an orange trail of fire interweaving itself through the dark stone. They continued to grow hotter and tears blurred my vision as the nauseating smell of burning flesh filled the air.

"Should we give you a second chance?" the Volcaniac leader asked. "The opportunity to steal your precious crystal back?"

I met his gaze again, and forced a smile through my pain. "Please."

He raised his brows but laughed, flicking his hand, and the burning obsidian released me. I gasped, nearly falling, but caught myself against the wall, slowly dragging myself to my feet.

My knees trembled, but the Volcaniac leader looked impressed. "If I had to guess, I would say you are from Mageye City... but the girl is not, so I question where you were trained."

"I was trained by the best," I huffed, a strangled sound escaping me as I raised my hand to shock him.

He didn't look alarmed and I flexed my fingers, the bolt of electricity missing completely.

"That's a pity," he said, leisurely pulling the teleportation crystal from his pocket. "I don't plan to kill you, you know. You aren't fighting for your life..." A sinister smile twisted his lips. "You are fighting for your soul."

His words hit me like frigid ice, ice so cold it burned. "I'm fighting for a whole lot more than that," I rasped, raising my hand again.

"Don't waste your energy," he said. "You will want to conserve it for your interrogation."

Games. It was always games... I created a purple orb, this one encasing him and giving me the opportunity to approach. He stepped back, hissing in pain when he was shocked by the orb, before it disappeared and I lunged for the crystal. My fingers grazed the smooth stone, but he swept his hand away, flicking his wrist and sending the crystal flying.

"Fetch."

The crystal soared over the balcony we fought on, and dropped into the center of the volcano. When it disappeared, I shouted, running past the Volcaniac leader and leaping after the stone.

Every fiber of my being seemed to scream and tears blurred my vision, but I locked my gaze on the crystal, twisting through the air and straining for it. We plummeted together, the orange lake filling the bottom of the volcano seeming to rise to greet us.

The pain briefly faded, every molecule making up my body seeming to focus on one thing. *Too much of your power was deadly.*

If I caught the crystal and destroyed the magical barrier keeping the lava at bay, the Volcaniac leader would be burned in his own lava-palace.

Time it right... time it right...

I flipped again, straining for the crystal, and this time, my fingers clasped around the stone. A red haze hovered above the lava and as my feet grazed it, I created a purple orb around myself. My scream echoed through the volcano as I snapped it, sending sparks through the barrier and into the lava below, before I disappeared with an electric snap.

I stumbled out of a gray orb outside of the volcano and clutched my ribs, gasping as I stared at Rose's family once more.

I did it. I was outside the volcano... I was alive... But the world was gray.

Rose turned to face me and I threw myself towards her, pushing the crystal into her hands. Color flickered into the world before fading again and I took one final look at the Crawford family before encasing them in a purple orb that seemed to take the last of my strength with it.

KING DUNCAN

Myles stood with his back to me, resting his arms on the railing as he stared across the yard and into the heart of Mageye City. The speech balcony, as it was cleverly named, stood with enough room for hundreds to enter the palace grounds and listen to speeches, but Myles and I had long since been using it for occasions besides formal gatherings.

The throne room was quiet and the curtains half-shielded me while I observed him. Two weeks ago, General Cornstone had burst into my office, shouting that an unfamiliar family had arrived in dire condition alongside an unconscious Myles.

Myles and Rose had explained their story to me, and I had gladly welcomed the Crawfords to my city, but the fact that Myles had traveled to The End with only a new Mageye as company still didn't sit right with me.

I opened the door to the balcony and stepped out. Myles glanced back and his purple and green gaze caught my attention, as it had every time he looked at me since he returned.

"Spying on me?" he asked, smirking.

I rolled my eyes as I joined him by the railing. "No, I was reflecting on the days when you were too little to look over these railings without a lift."

He braced his hands on the railing and dropped to his knees. "Like this?"

"Yes." I patted his head and he scrunched his nose, rolling his eyes. "I remember you once climbed up and I came out to find you sitting on the railing. Nearly gave me a heart attack."

Lightning sparked in his purple iris and he laughed. "I think

I gave you a lot of near-heart attacks." He stood and playfully put a palm over my heart. "Don't die on me, or I'll shock you back to life."

"As someone who can speak with ghosts, I think I'd prefer to haunt you," I decided as I rested my hands on the railing and looked across our city.

Myles pulled himself up to sit, bracing his hands and leaning back in a way that one slip would send him plummeting off the balcony. "General Agar said you wanted to speak with me."

"Yes." I grabbed his arm and tugged him up so he wouldn't lean so far. "General Cornstone and I have been discussing what to do in regards to The End."

A shadowed look briefly crossed his face, and that was all the confirmation I needed. After he had awoken, he had told me much of what had happened, and while I knew the full story in regards to physical events, Myles seemed to be keeping some of the internal events from me.

"Rose said that once I pushed them out of the orb, all life came back to the charred part of the land." Myles frowned. "I kind of remember that from when she first healed me. I saw leaves, and obviously the Golden Dove wouldn't have flown into a place with such a bad aura."

"Yes, I spoke with Cecelia and she said the same. From what we know, The End is no longer a cursed place and the Volcaniacs are finished."

"From what we know," he repeated slowly. "The volcano erupted so quickly, I don't see how a single being could have survived." He grimaced, avoiding my gaze.

I put a hand on his knee. "Thank you for defending our city. You saved far more lives than were lost in that volcano."

"I know," he said, shaking his head. "I don't regret breaking the magic."

"You shouldn't," I said, relieved. "With all that said, General Cornstone and I want to confirm the healing of the land has lasted. He is going to lead a group to The End to ensure nothing is left."

Myles nodded slowly. "When?"

"They leave tomorrow."

He raised a brow. "Who is General Cornstone taking?"

I resisted the urge to sigh; he was certainly preparing his argument about why I should add him to the mission. "General Agar, General Curran, and General Silas Ansley, as well as a few lower guards."

"You should send General Laplin, too," he suggested. "The charred part had a fifty-mile radius and if it is now replaced with new trees, her ability to manipulate the shadows of leaves may help."

"I hadn't thought of that," I mused. "I will see if she is willing to go on such short notice."

He bore an unreadable expression, and I sighed. "Let me hear it. Why do you think you should go?"

He blinked. "I was actually thinking of a reason why I shouldn't go, if you asked me."

"What?" Myles had never refused a mission or opportunity to defend his city. In fact, I had spent far more time arguing with him about why he couldn't participate in everything than I had fighting him to do his chores when he was young. And that was saying something.

"I think I want a break, Dad," he confessed. "I don't want to shirk my responsibilities, but I'd like to stay in Mageye City for a little while, if that's okay with you?"

"Of course, you can," I said, gathering my thoughts and aura before he could get the chance to accidentally read my mind and realize how much his request worried me. "We have a deal, remember? On account of you being titled as general when you were twelve, you are allowed to take a step back however often you need until you are twenty."

His shoulders slumped, somehow with both relief of my acceptance as well as with the weight of whatever burdens he carried. "Just for a little while," he said. "And... you don't need to worry, I'm asking partially for selfish reasons." His lip twitched as he looked back at me. "The Crawfords are planning to take a trip back to Sunset Hollow to gather their horses, and I was going to ask if I can go?"

That request put some of my fear at ease and I nodded. "Yes, you can go." He smiled, but I held up a finger. "On the condition you tell me what's bothering you."

"What do you mean? Because I don't want to go with General Cornstone?"

"No, because I am your dad and it is my job to worry about you. You get this look in your eyes sometimes, and I can tell you are struggling with something."

"I'm eighteen," he started, but I shook my head.

"I'm your king."

"Ugh." He dramatically slid off of the railing and to the balcony floor. "Don't pull the king card on me."

I looked down at him, where he lay at my feet. "Following the 'I'm eighteen' argument with melting to the floor is not going to get you the results you are hoping for."

Myles sat up slowly, the playfulness being overshadowed by his troubled expression. "I've started getting nightmares again," he confessed. "And there is something about them that just *feels* different, but I don't know what."

"Feels different?" I echoed, concerned. Myles had periodically dealt with nightmares since he first moved to the palace when he was five. They had been the worst when he was thirteen, and for weeks, he refused to sleep. I had started having him sleep in my bedchambers and he would wake up screaming every night.

We had worked hard to help him overcome them and besides a brief reoccurrence when he was fifteen, he seemed to have beaten them. Hearing that they were back was troublesome, but I should have considered it from the beginning.

His fight against the leader of the Volcaniacs had rattled him, and his heart had stopped beating before Rose brought him back.

I joined him on the floor, adding, "Do you mean during them or when you wake up?"

"Both." He frowned at our outstretched feet. "They feel... real... like I am reflecting on memories and not viewing a nightmare."

I put a hand to his forehead and he turned his gaze to me while I examined the bags under his eyes. "Have you been able to sleep through the night at all since you returned?"

He shook his head, sighing. "Not really. The first few times, I did what you and General Cornstone taught me. I found an aura or someone's mind to read I trusted, or I tried going on walks to clear my head. And it started working, but then they started *feeling* different..."

"What you went through alongside Rose and her family at the volcano was very traumatic," I said. "Probably more traumatic than some of the other things you have gone through?"

He grimaced but nodded. "I think so."

"Well, then we will do what we have always done. I will help you and we can talk our way through it."

He leaned his head on my shoulder. "It's not so bad that I can't handle it. And, I know they will go away eventually."

"They will," I agreed. "For now, I think you need a good, *restful* night's sleep. That will probably be our best start."

"Probably," he agreed. "I don't want to bother Mrs. Ansley again, though."

Silas's wife had the ability to encourage restful sleep, and as both her husband and eldest daughter were in my Elite Guard, and another of her daughters was a nurse in the palace, it was safe to say they were life-long family friends. During some of Myles's worst periods with nightmares, she had helped soothe him when my attempts resulted in nothing but more tears.

"There are other ways to encourage restful sleep," I mused, waving my hand across the balcony. "Would a sleepover out here help?"

Myles laughed a little, lifting his head. "We haven't slept over out here in years."

"I miss our secret speech balcony sleepovers."

"Me too." He smiled, nodding. "I'll dig out BearBear."

I laughed. Myles used to carry BearBear everywhere with him, and when we slept over out here, he would have me address the stuffed bear as General BearBear.

"Go find our little general," I told him. "I need to scold him for not helping you yet, and we will meet here after dinner."

Myles laughed again, and the sound of it helped put me at some ease. He stood and disappeared into an orb of purple lightning, leaving me alone.

I stood slowly and turned to stare across my city. Perhaps sending General Cornstone to The End offered an additional benefit. It would give Myles peace of mind that his nightmarish experience with the Volcaniacs was over.

PLAYLIST

The songs that comprise my *Mageye* playlist range from "reminding me of the book" to "inspiring a scene" to "it just so happened to play while I was writing and now it is a part of the book." Here's a sneak peek of the songs from the *very long* list that remind me the most of *The Mageye*. (In no particular order. Got to keep you on your toes, so you don't start guessing what some of these songs may hint at to come!)

"Electric Love" by Borns— I hope this song goes without saying, but "lightning in a bottle" has reminded me of Rose and Myles from the first time I heard the song.

"Play With Fire" by Sam Tinnesz— This song was made for a villain, don't you think? And the Volcaniac leader was made for this song.

"Legend" by The Score— *This song right here.* I can practically hear it playing every time I think of the battle scene in the amphitheater. I could rant about how perfectly it fits for ages, but that might take a whole other novel!

"Roar" by Katy Perry— This song has always reminded me of Rose and her character development. She starts the novel out being nervous and unsure of herself and her abilities, but with her family's lives on the line, she steps out of that shell, and saves them.

"Wolves" by Sam Tinnesz— It seems like Sam Tinnesz knows how to write songs for villains. And "Wolves" is perfect for a certain Wolvien Guard.

"Legends Are Made" by Sam Tinnesz— This Sam Tinnesz song

isn't for any of the villains. It is for Myles, and I imagine it playing as he sneaks down the corridors to get the teleportation crystal back.

isn't for any of the villains. It is for Myles, and I imagine it playing as he sneaks down the corridors to get the teleportation crystal back.

ACKNOWLEDGMENTS

While I don't fully classify *The Mageye* as Christian fiction, I have always included my values and references to God in my books. One regret I had with the original trilogy is that Rose really only prays a handful of times. We start seeing more talk of God in the sequel trilogy, but I want Him in the heart of *The Mageye* too. I certainly hope the new editions and references shine through, and regardless, I want to thank Him first in my acknowledgements. He is the one who placed this story in my heart more than a decade ago, and nudged me to revamp it in order for me to fall in love with the world all over again.

To Mom and McKenna: As always, you both were the first to know my plans to revamp, and while I know you had your concerns (for my sanity) you stayed by my side every step of the way. Thank you for listening to my ideas, my rants, and my everything else Mageye related. I love you.

To my beta readers: Lea, Dana, and Aaralynn, I was nervous about finding anyone willing to beta read the entire trilogy, but you erased those fears within fifteen minutes of me putting out a call for betas. Not only that, but there wasn't a single suggestion any of you left that felt off. Thank you for being honest, thank you for making me laugh, and thank you for your support.

To Michaela: On top of thanking you for your support, enthusiasm, and help with editing, I feel I must also apologize. Sorry for making the editing hard by making you cry... but also, I might have laughed when I saw that comment.

To Fritz: No is not in your vocabulary, meaning the world is exactly as it should be. My favorite Distinguished Gentleman, thanks for the kitty cuddles.

To Belle & Fiona: You both are my biggest supporters. Why? Because you are the only two who I have ever seen wearing bows to match my books.

To my readers, both new and returning. Thank you for your support as I republish my debut trilogy. You are the reason I am able to do what I do. God bless!

COMING SOON

The Mageye:
Illusion of Fear
February, 2026

The Mageye:
Beldestine
April, 2026

Paris Kaufman is a college student with a love for creative fiction. With her writing, she hopes to spark the same passion for reading she acquired as a young teen. When not writing, you can find Paris cooking, painting, or tending to her many animal friends.

Instagram: @parisandherbooks

YouTube: @parisandherbooks

Email: parisandherbooks@gmail.com

Website:
https://parisandherbooks.wixsite.com/parisandherbooks

www.ingramcontent.com/pod-product-compliance
Lightning Source LLC
Chambersburg PA
CBHW031025310726
48969CB00007B/1870